Deadly Instinct

By
Brian Reeve

 **New Generation Publishing**

Chapter 1

John Conran placed his hands on the desk and stared at Paul Bale, the man sitting opposite him. It was eight in the evening and there were few in the building. In the distance the imposing silhouette of Table Mountain – Devil's Peak and Lion's Head on the left and right extremities – could be seen through the windows against the dark-blue sky. It formed the northern end of the mountain range that comprised the spine of the Cape Peninsula and separated the city from the vastness of the Atlantic Ocean.

'What exactly are you suggesting?' he asked. 'I suspect there are corrupt cabinet ministers but we need two things before we can replace them, evidence and conviction in the courts. There is no other way, unless I've completely missed the point. You of all people should know that.'

Bale remained perfectly still and then allowed himself the hint of a smile. 'I'm well aware of the legal process,' he said, 'but our crime agencies are not perfect and an alternative course of action is required to administer justice.'

Bale was the NDPP, the national director of public prosecutions, head office of the National Prosecuting Authority. The NPA had the Directorate: Special Operations, the DSO or Scorpions, as an independent agency under its umbrella.

'What is it?' asked Conran. 'I'm interested.'

'Replace them without using the courts,' said the man, seeing by the change of expression on Conran's face that he had his attention. 'That's what I want to talk to you about.'

3

'I knew it was important,' said Conran, 'but that's stretching things a bit, don't you think?'

'No,' said Bale. He was white, mid-forties and handsome, a small scar on his left cheek, his black hair combed back, the application of Brylcreem obvious. He was born in Cape Town, went to state school and read law at Stellenbosch University. After serving articles and practising as an attorney at an established law firm in Cape Town he had entered politics full-time at the age of thirty-five, first as a member of parliament for the Democratic Alliance and then for the African National Congress. His political career had been meteoric and he had resigned as an MP when he accepted his present position as NDPP. He was married with three children and lived in the city. He looked at Conran. 'It can be done quite simply with little effort.'

'I'm not sure I like it,' said Conran.

'It will be clean. You will have seen a lot worse, being a senior agent in the Scorpions. Now, shall I go on?'

'Please do,' said Conran.

There are thirty-five cabinet ministers in the National Executive run by the President. We are reasonably sure that of these there are four who are up to their necks in corruption but we don't have the evidence to convict them. They appear to concentrate on financial crime, money laundering, organized crime and, the most insidious of all, hard drugs.'

'Why?' asked Conran. 'If they are so deeply involved there must be something of weight you can pin on them. Are they working separately or do their activities involve one another?'

'From what we can determine each has his own thing going. The simple answer to your first question is that they cover their tracks extremely well and know powerful people they can use, without telling them anything. Recently there was a case in England in which a man

4

known as the king of cocaine was convicted and sentenced to thirty years. Specialist crime units in Britain and elsewhere had been after him for a long time. He was finally caught when they tapped his phone. A single call was his end. Up until then they had nothing that would have stood up in court. They were just very determined to get him for what they believed he was doing.'

'So you at least suspect that these men are heavily tied to crime,' said Conran. 'That's something and I'm sure it will come in useful, if you are thinking of doing what I think you are. But I want to hear how you're planning to get rid of them and what follows. Tell me why you are so keen to replace them? What about the others in our society in positions of influence who are corrupt?'

'The four men are government ministers and they have political power. Any of them could have been President. I don't necessarily think that they were corrupt before they assumed their present positions but, as we've seen frequently in African states, political power courts the desire to have wealth. Corruption can provide incredible wealth, more than almost any other endeavour. The danger comes when the guilty are so corrupt they need to protect themselves from exposure and if the heat is too great they eliminate those who pose a threat. That's one reason you get dictatorships, contract killings and governments being overthrown by force. I don't want to see South Africa go that way, but it so easily can.' Bale picked up a glass of water and drank slowly, his hooded eyes those of a hawk, never leaving Conran.

'Before you go on, who are these men?'

Bale extracted a folded A4 sheet of paper from the inside pocket of his jacket and slid it across the desk. 'You will recognize the names,' he said.

Conran unfolded the paper and ran his eyes down the short list. He folded the sheet, returned it and reclined in his large, leather-bound chair, lifting the fingers of his hands to

5

form a steeple in front of him. 'You were right,' he said, dispassionately. 'Each one could now be President if they'd played the right tune and the dice had favoured them. Those four effectively run this country. They're all white. I'm sure there are corrupt ministers but they're black.'

Bale looked at him, unfalteringly. 'The whites are the ones singled out by my friends,' he said, emphatically.

Conran went further. 'What about the President?'

Bale laughed briefly. 'We don't have anything on him,' he said. 'For that reason he can stay. The charges against him of accepting bribes on a foreign arms deal were nullified. He was the choice of the disenchanted masses, including the ANC alliance partners, the Confederation of Trade Unions, COSATU, and the Communist Party. His predecessor was perceived as an autocratic capitalist who supported an evil dictator on the northern border, empowered his cronies, suppressed allegations of corruption against them, had no connection with the people, disputed the link between HIV and AIDS and refused to introduce antiretroviral drugs when a third of the population is infected with the virus. In his words this was because it plays to the Western view that Africans are natural born, promiscuous carriers of germs and doomed to an inevitable mortal end because of an unconquerable devotion to the sins of lust.'

Bale drank some water and continued. 'At the moment we have one aim and that is the replacement of the corrupt ministers.'

'And the desire of some cabinet ministers to place the Scorpions under the authority of the police commissioner?' said Conran. 'They had the nerve to accuse the Scorpions of pursuing a political agenda against the ANC in league with the press. They feared the Scorpions were getting too close to their corrupt cronies in power. The President condones this crap by conveniently keeping quiet.'

'The Scorpions will continue as a part of the NPA,' said Bale defensively.

'We digress,' said Conran, not pusuing the matter. He dropped his hands. 'You say we. Who else is involved in this?'

'Highly influential men I've known for a long time and trust explicitly. They want the Republic to set an exemplary standard in the way it conducts its political, social and economic affairs. That means that there is no place in the corridors of power for people who are corrupt and exploit others.'

'By having these ministers replaced, these influential men are in reality assuming the power vested in the President,' said Conran. 'He alone has the power to choose any number of cabinet ministers from the elected National Assembly of 400 and can choose at most two others from outside. That's a lot of power and your friends might as well be the government. Theoretically, they could go on doing this until all cabinet ministers are appointed by them.'

'Steady on,' said Bale, 'you are letting your imagination run riot. They only want these four men replaced. The interesting thing is that if you have the power and money you can with relative ease achieve this sort of thing. Now, I'll tell you what I have in mind for you.'

'So I come into it,' said Conran. 'I knew there was a reason for this visit.'

'Yes,' said the man. 'I said earlier that these men would have to be replaced. That means removal first. We would appreciate it if you could arrange for that to be done.'

'Sometimes you are so transparent,' said Conran.

'When I choose to be,' said Bale.

'How do you suggest I remove them?' asked Conran.

'By killing them successively until we achieve our objective. After the first, we'd want two to four days between the remaining three to give the President a chance to name the replacements.'

'What are you doing in the meantime?' said Conran. 'The President will have to replace them. How do you get him to replace them with the men you want?'

'After the first one we will send an anonymous letter to the President saying we have compiled allegations of serious crime, corruption and money laundering against the deceased and three other cabinet ministers. Their names would be listed. If revealed, this would finally destroy him politically. He'll be told that investigation by him is a waste of time and that he must replace the men with those named. If he does not comply the three ministers will be killed successively until we get what we want. To increase the pressure, a report will appear in a leading newspaper the day after the letter is received citing corruption as a possible reason for the killing.'

'Why don't you and your friends tell him to remove the men before anyone is killed?' asked Conran.

'There would be no reason for him to do as required,' said Bale, confidently. 'By killing members of his cabinet he will know we are serious and, we think, start to fear for his own life. He will know that no man can avoid being killed if someone wants to kill him, however well he is protected.'

'Who are the replacements or those named in the list?' asked Conran. 'I assume your friends know them.'

'They are honest, experienced politicians without blemish,' said Bale.

'What do you get out of all this?' said Conran. 'Your motives can't only be altruistic, to help your friends. What do I get if I play along, appoint the assassin and keep quiet? I certainly don't intend to do it myself.'

'The men know I'm approaching you. For that they are paying you 750 000 pounds sterling. I'll be rewarded but that is my business. They and I are aware that after a bit of work I could find a contract killer to do what I'm asking of you but unlike you I wouldn't really know what I'm getting. You have excellent credentials and I trust you.'

'If I take the job I won't be doing the killing,' said Conran. 'That means I'll have to find a killer and, correct me if I'm mistaken, be accountable for him or her.'

'We thought you would pass it on to a professional and that's why you'll be paid so handsomely,' said Bale, 'but you will get paid the same if you do it yourself. You will be responsible for the work of anyone else you bring in and there must be no reference to me or my friends. If it's any comfort we will all be taking risks.'

'What happens if the person I select screws it up?' said Conran.

'I can't answer that. It's up to you to see that they don't.' said Bale, getting to his feet. 'I would like an answer from you first thing the day after tomorrow. That should be enough for you to make a decision. Ring me at home. I just want a yes or no. You don't have to tell me the name of your assassin. If you accept, I'll give you the details of the men and the broad timescale to which we are working. We want that adhered to after we've made final decisions.'

Conran walked round his desk. 'I'll call you then. Let me show you out.'

Conran was born and brought up in England, in his early forties and in excellent physical condition. After graduating in politics at Cambridge, he had joined MI6 in London. He was with the agency for five years before seeing an advertisement in an English newspaper for a position in the Republic's newly-formed Directorate: Special Operations. He applied, got the job and was now in his tenth year with them. He was highly intelligent, cunning, instinctive, the required qualities of a leader in the agency. Most of the work covered capital crime, murder, extortion and drug trafficking, and although his operations were usually in the Cape he had national jurisdiction. He was divorced and had no difficulty getting the women he wanted for casual relationships, mostly with sex the dominant compulsion.

After the man had left, Conran poured a large Scotch and sank into his chair. There was a lot to think about, not least who would do the killing. He knew that the qualities and powers of a successful assassin were frequently overstated and some were regarded as being supernatural because they had managed to make difficult high-profile hits. But to Conran there were only a few qualities they needed. These could be learned by anyone with intelligence and determination, and they were precise planning, patience, calm deliberation, clinical execution and the ability to perform dispassionately. Some of the men he knew in the DSO were in that category. He wanted someone with real discipline and they had it in abundance. But were they too close to home? He knew of two or three men and a woman abroad but they would want payment of at least half the sum he had been offered for a job of this type. It was not everyday that more than one target, each prominent, was wanted dead.

Conran was pouring his second Scotch when he stopped. For a while he was still, deep in thought, and then, leaving his drink, stuck some papers into his briefcase and left the office for his home. He lived in Constantia, the prime residential suburb ofCape Town, several kilometres from the city centre where the DSO had its office. Constantia was one of the six main wine regions of the Western Cape Province, theothers being Stellenbosch, Franschhoek, Paarl, Robertson and Wellington, all to thenorth east, forty to sixty kilometres along the N1 freeway from Cape Town.

Chapter 2

Durban, Republic of South Africa

Peter Smith of the Directorate: Special Operations spun his chair in a half-circle and lifted the phone impatiently. He was still at work and his thoughts had been on a case that was causing local problems.

'Smith.'

'Peter, David Hilton. How are you?'

'Surviving,' said Smith. 'Where are you? I never know.'

'It's the job,' said Hilton. 'I'm in my hotel in Pretoria. I leave in the morning for Cape Town but I'd like to come through Durban. I want to see you about something.'

Smith pressed the receiver closer to his ear. 'I'll be here. Give me the time.'

'Good,' said Hilton. 'I will change my flight. That means arrival in Durban at around ten. I'd rather not come to your office. What about the Oyster Box Hotel at Umhlanga Rocks an hour later?'

'That's the other side of the city,' said Smith, a little surprised. 'I'll be there.'

'I'll see you then,' said Hilton. 'It won't be a waste of your time.'

Smith stared at the phone for a while after Hilton had gone and then slowly got to his feet. The man was a close friend of his and they'd met when they were students at Witwatersrand University in Johannesburg. They and two others had shared a house together. While he had gone into the DSO, Hilton had become a professional politician. When the whites lost power in 1994, he'd joined the African National Congress and was now one of five whites in the Cabinet. He was Minister of Justice and Constitutional Development and very popular with blacks and whites.

Chapter 3

Tuesday, 4 August
Cape Town

Early in the morning, John Conran rang Paul Bale at home.

'Yes?' said Bale, his suave voice easily recognizable.

'Conran. I've decided to become involved. I've also found someone to do it.'

'Excellent,' said Bale. 'I was sure I could rely on you. I'll send the details to you by courier. It'll cover all four, where they live, their points of contact, and an outline of their movements over the next two weeks. You can start with the first now. The second can follow in a couple of days, two to four days to the third and the same to the last. We want a time period between them so that the President has a chance to name the replacements. How you do it is your business.'

'Thanks,' said Conran. 'What then? Do you want me to tell you or leave it to the press?'

'Ring me on this number. I'll be here for your call. I hope for your friend's sake that it's good news. We don't want to mess around with a novice.'

'He's not,' said Conran. 'He has the qualities and reputation I need.'

'Good,' said Bale.

Conran was at home and after the call he went to the window that offered a wide vista of magnificent grounds. Gardening was not for him but he appreciated what he had, and he had three gardeners who kept the abundant vegetation in superb shape. His thoughts went to what he had got himself into and he satisfied his conscience by telling himself that it was acceptable in today's world, when criminals were at large and the justice system was powerless to act. He had known Bale for a few years and seen him rise to a position of power, not in business or politics but alongside the most powerful. He was ruthless, dismissive of those without his intellect and ambitious. They were qualities he accredited to himself but perhaps for that reason he didn't particularly like him.

After a few minutes at the window, he left for work in his recent acquisition, an Aston Martin Vanquish S, to him one of the finest cars in production. Tuesday was frequently a quiet day for him and when he arrived he started the arduous job of going through correspondence, reports on current and closed cases. He worked through lunch, his mind never diverted by the more important job. He had started to lay the plans shortly after arriving at the office.

Chapter 4

Durban

At the appointed time Smith met Hilton at the Oyster Box Hotel and they found a table on the verandah overlooking the sea. When they had ordered drinks Smith leant back in his chair.

'It's good to see you.' he said. 'What's so important to bring you through here?'

'This shouldn't take long,' said Hilton. He swallowed some of his drink. 'In politics I hear of a lot that is not public knowledge. Sometimes it's criminal and the police are usually on to it. The form varies and you've seen far more than I have.'

'You've come across something criminal that the police are not chasing,' said Smith.

'Yes,' said Hilton. 'This is a guess but when organized crime on a grand scale is uncovered there is usually one person running the show, one person responsible for orchestrating events. I have uncovered a criminal organization that is not only vast and complex but is controlled by a small group of the most powerful men in the Republic. Each of these either owns a major corporation or is in the top position, the chairman or CEO. They not only run the companies and their illegal empire but they have leading figures in government eating out of their hands. I would put them in the same class as the three eminent mafia syndicates, the Sicilian Cosa Nostra, the Calabrian Ndrangheta and Neapolitan Camorra, and to my knowledge no one in the police is after them or can get near them.'

'Bring them in,' said Smith. 'I suppose you're going to tell me you have nothing against them that would stand up in court.'

14

'Precisely,' said Hilton. 'As you can expect they are very well protected, physically and from exposure of their operations.'

'How do you know they are criminals and in bed together?' asked Smith. He had been down this road before, more often than not coming to a dead end, particularly when the stakes were high.

'From informers who mix in their circles and are trusted by them,' said Hilton. 'In most cases they approached us either because they were not getting what they wanted or they got cold feet. Some people have consciences that finally convince them they are doing wrong.'

'Why can't you use their stuff as evidence?'

'The only answer I can give is that the informers find it virtually impossible to come up with hardcopy that can be used as evidence.'

'How long have you suspected all this is going on?' asked Smith.

'It first came to my attention two years ago and I asked some people I know to investigate,' said Hilton. 'Their findings were fairly insignifiBale and I didn't follow it up. Two weeks ago I heard more, this time from two different sources. It was pretty strong stuff and enough for me to initiate my own investigation. That is why I'm here.'

'Why didn't you go to the police or the DSO in Cape Town? I'm the regional head in KwaZulu-Natal.'

'I know you personally,' said Hilton unequivocally. 'That counts for a lot. I don't know your equivalent down there and you have jurisdiction wherever you want it, as long as you inform the local guys. On this occasion I wouldn't go to the police. I think it is way out of their league and I'd like this to be between you and me.'

'I can't help but be interested,' said Smith. 'Leave it with me. I'll get some people on it. I'll need to have all the information you've got, including the names of your informers and of course the men to whom you refer. How will we keep in contact?'

'At home or my office,' said Hilton. 'Failing that try my mobile. You have the numbers. When do you think you'll get your people moving?'

'As soon as I get the information,' said Smith. 'Send it by courier.'

'You'll have it late this afternoon,' said Hilton, standing up. 'Now I must go.'

Chapter 5

Durban

When Peter Smith neared the DSO building in central Durban he bought a sandwich at a local shop before going to his office. He wasn't surprised to hear what Hilton had said and he was impatient to receive the information on which he could act.

Smith's first thoughts were that he would need a core team to go to work immediately, supplemented as required. Their investigation would start with the people Hilton had used and then move on to the informers. The thought of bringing down some of the fat cats in the country gave him a feeling of excitement he had not felt since James Steiner had walked into his office with Kirsty Krige, now using her maiden name Callard, and put the two files in front of him. The prosecutions that followed were pure nectar. He hadn't heard from Steiner for a few months, the last time from London where he was living with Kirsty. He was not surprised that Steiner, with his arrogant charm and good looks, would one day land one of the most attractive women he had ever met.

The team Smith chose was one of five, three of them men. Each was a skilled investigator in all aspects of business finance and money laundering, and if anyone could come up with anything significant and anomalous they could.

In the late afternoon, Smith received the information from Hilton. It comprised full details of the five men under suspicion and covered their private and professional lives, interests, close friends, acquaintances and summary workings of the companies which they controlled. The five men were Andrew Rohm, John Ashley, Simon Boucher, David Taylor and Bryan Jones. There was also similar information covering the informers and the people Hilton had first asked to carry out investigations.

After absorbing as much of the information as he felt necessary, Smith called in those he'd selected, described the nature of the operations to which they were being assigned, and a plan of action. The briefing went into the late evening and when he was satisfied, he let them go. He was satisfied and it was now a matter of getting results.

Chapter 6

Cape Town

In the late afternoon when Conran had cleared most of his day's work, one of his agents, Peter Mellor, entered the office.

'I'm going with David Strauss to that new bar round the corner, the Nightcap,' said Mellor. 'We thought you might like to come along. You need a break.'

Conran liked Mellor and Strauss. They also reported to him and he considered himself fortunate. Working on demanding cases with people he didn't get on with would have been a nightmare. 'When are you going?' he asked, sliding his chair away from the desk. 'As you say, I can do with a break. Some of these cases never end. I like something short and sweet. Do you mind if I bring along a new guy I don't think you've met? He's Adam Fairley, a Scorpion.'

'Bring him,' said Mellor. 'Let's make it four. I'll give you a buzz. We can meet downstairs.'

At a few minutes to six, Mellor called and after Conran had joined them in the foyer they left for the bar. Once there they ordered drinks and took seats at a round table that gave a view of the large space and other patrons. Like Conran they were all single, two divorced, in their late-thirties to early-forties, and had a continual desire for available women, married or not.

'What are you working on now?' said Strauss, looking at Conran. 'You've been pretty quiet. It must be interesting.'

'At the moment I'm evenly spread across the DSO mandate, organized crime and corruption, financial crime and drugs. I prefer some aspects but there's no choice. You have to get on with what's there.'

'I think corruption and financial crime will become the big hitters,' said Mellor. 'I'm sure we only skim the surface when it comes to the real criminals, people at the top of business corporations and in government.'

Conran looked at him. 'This is not like the rest of Africa,' he said. 'If there is any sign of corruption in those areas we're onto it.'

'I thought the DSO was supposed to be proactive,' said Adam Fairley, speaking for the first time since being introduced to the other three. 'Business and government are breeding grounds for organized crime whichever the country. We should root out anything before it starts.'

'That could come under harassment,' said Conran. 'The DSO's reputation would be seriously damaged. We have to catch them executing the crime, not thinking about it. That's the only way by which we can get hard evidence.'

'Perhaps we shouldn't be so hung up on hard evidence,' said Fairley impassively. 'There're other ways of skinning a cat.'

'The only alternative I know of is to eliminate them physically,' said Conran, smiling. 'If we started doing that we would be copying that regime to the north of us.'

'That's certainly not a solution and we're hypothesizing,' said Mellor. 'The way we operate is within the law and that's how it will remain. Let's have another drink and then I must split.'

'That goes for me as well,' said Conran. 'What are you guys having?'

Chapter 7

Near Stellenbosch

Early in the evening after seeing Peter Smith in Durban, David Hilton and his wife Hilary were relaxing on the front verandah of their house, fifty kilometres north-east of Cape Town along the N1 and close to Stellenbosch.

The couple had just finished dinner and for them there was little better than being surrounded by fine grounds adorned with trees, indigenous plants and verdant lawn. The long driveway up to the garages at the side of the house was only visible from the verandah for the last two hundred metres when it appeared from the trees.

Hilton had told Hilary about his detour through Durban to see Peter Smith but had not elaborated. She knew Smith well but had not asked her husband for details. Now, seated on the verandah, she could not contain her curiosity about the reasons for the visit.

'Why did you want to see Peter Smith?' she asked. 'You don't have direct dealings with the DSO and you haven't been in contact with him for years. You always go through Paul Bale at the NPA.'

'You're perceptive,' he said. 'I'll tell you what it was about as long as you don't repeat anything.'

'Trust me,' she said.

'Two years ago, I heard that a small group of high-powered businessmen has created an organization that operates outside the law and primarily involves serious organized crime, extortion, financial corruption, arms deals, endangered species and drugs. I decided then to ask some people I know to investigate and report to me. They did and concluded there were strong indications the organization existed and was into anything that offered a high yield. By that they meant the activities to which I referred.'

'If your people got that far why didn't you have the men prosecuted?' she asked.

'They drew their conclusion largely by speaking to informers,' said Hilton. 'They could only go so far without raising the alarm and they had to work through them. To sum up, the hard evidence is pretty thin. The guys we were after and their henchmen are not clowns and certainly know how to conceal their illegal operations.'

'So you've decided to speak to the DSO about it,' she said. 'Why didn't you go to them in the first place? They're supposed to be the best there is at that sort of investigation. It's meat to them.'

'I wanted to keep it low key,' he said. 'The DSO here in Cape Town is a well-known investigative and prosecuting body and I didn't want people to know what I was doing.'

'And that's why you went to Peter Smith in Durban.'

'Yes,' he said. 'He will keep it quiet and put a strong, experienced team onto it.'

They both saw the lights of a car appear from the trees and watched as it followed the drive up to the side of the house. It went from sight and they heard the sound of the engine die.

'Who's that?' said Hilary. 'Are you expecting anyone?'

'No,' said Hilton, standing up. 'I'll go and see who it is.'

'Wait,' she said. 'Whoever it is will soon appear. They must have seen us.'

Hilton walked the few paces to the top of the steps. He heard the door of the car close and then in the dim light saw the tall figure of a man walking slowly towards him. When he could see his face he didn't recognize him and let him get closer before he said: 'Good evening. Who are you looking for?'

The man stopped on the path, three metres from Hilton and in a quiet voice said: 'David Hilton, minister of justice?' With a sweeping movement of his right hand he pulled a silenced Beretta *90two* semi-automatic pistol from behind his belt, levelled it and fired two shots, fusing as one. The bullets penetrated the heart and Hilton was dead before his body fell to the stone. Without a glance at him, the man leapt up the steps, halted near Hilary Hilton and before she could make a sound, shot her twice in the head. She died in her chair and before her body slumped forward, the man was moving to his car. He unscrewed the silencer and stuck it and the pistol into separate pockets. The pistol was a 2006 variant of the famous Beretta 92 and was noticeable for its innovative lines and rounded contours that permitted easy carrying and rapid extraction from a belt or shoulder holster. It was chambered for the 9mmx19 Luger/Parabellum cartridge.

The man started the engine and soon disappeared down the drive through the trees.

Chapter 8

Cape Town

Two hours after the deaths of David and Hilary Hilton, Paul Bale received the call he'd been waiting for.

'The job was done early this evening,' said Conran when he heard Bale's voice. 'I believe it went smoothly. His wife also had to be sacrificed.'

'I was hoping to avoid anything like that,' said Bale. He thought for a moment. 'It might be to our advantage. It shows we're serious. It sounds as if it was at their house.'

'Yes,' said Conran. 'When do you want me to proceed? I assume you do.'

'Yes, make it the day after tomorrow, Thursday,' said Bale. 'I'll make sure the letter is received in the morning. It will be a surprise. The press report will follow.'

'What happens if the President moves quickly and replaces the ministers before we can complete the entire killing spree as dictated by your schedule?' asked Conran. 'In other words, what will happen then to the ministers who have been replaced?'

'All you need to know is that you have agreed to take on the complete job,' said Bale. 'I will instruct you if there are any changes to your scope. Do you have any problems with that?'

'No,' said Conran, keeping further thoughts to himself. 'I'll ring you at home when the next one is done.'

'Excellent.' said Bale. He replaced the phone.

Conran was still for a moment and then sat down thinking about what he'd got himself into. He had crossed the line and there was no return. He had the feeling Bale would want all the ministers killed, even if they had already been released from office. But he was now inextricably involved. If he pulled out of the deal he had with Bale, the

24

man wouldn't let him get away with it. He also knew that one death or more was all the same. No one could serve more than one life sentence consecutively. In some ways it was more exciting being on the wrong side of the law, not the raptor he'd always been, and he could understand why people did it. They were not only after financial gain. The thrill of being hunted was also worth having. He started thinking about the second killing.

Chapter 9

Wednesday, 5 August
The President's office, Cape Town

When the President of the Republic received the letter by special delivery he was still in shock. He had been told of the murders of David Hilton and his wife by the police commissioner an hour previously. He'd not done anything since, except call in his head of security, Barry Tyson, who now sat on the other side of the desk.

As he looked at the envelope he said: 'I still can't believe it. Who would want to kill him?' The envelope was marked urgent. He picked it up, opened it with his thumb and extracted the single sheet of paper. The letter was brief and said:

Hilton is the first to die. The evidence against him for direct involvement in serious crime, corruption and money laundering is indisputable. Replace him and the ministers listed below. They are equally guilty. Do not waste time carrying out your own investigation of them. If you do not act immediately, the killing will continue. The choice is yours.

The President read the words and then cast his eyes down the list of names. All three were his senior ministers and held the most powerful positions in his cabinet. Without putting down the letter he looked at Tyson.

'Hilton was the first,' he said. 'If I don't comply with the contents in this letter others will also be killed.' He slid the letter across the table and Tyson picked it up. He read it quickly, replaced it on the table and looked at the President.

'How do you want to play it?' he asked. 'You can be sure that they're organized and dangerous. They're confident and the type who never know when to stop. If it's not this it'll be something else.'

'I agree. What do you suggest?'

'You must get professional help,' said Tyson. 'They obviously don't care a shit if you get it but you need it. You can count out the police. They're not up to this. That leaves the Directorate: Special Operations. I know their regional head, Bruce Weisz.'

The President leant forward in his chair. 'Contact Weisz,' he said. 'I don't need to see him. Emphasize when you meet him that this must go no further than the people he assigns to the case. After you've seen him, let Paul Bale of the NPA know what's going on including receipt of the letter and its contents. I must also contact the man nominated as Hilton's replacement. We have to play by the rules until these people are caught. Now you can go.'

Chapter 10

Cape Town

An hour after phoning Bruce Weisz, Tyson met him in his office on the top floor of the DSO headquarters in the city centre. Weisz knew about the murders. A servant had found the bodies and told the police, who had notified the President's office.

'What do you want from me?' asked Weisz when he had read the letter. 'I've said the police are now involved. To me it sounds like a plain case of murder followed by a fancy letter. There are hundreds of cranks about.'

'The President thinks it's more than that,' said Tyson. 'I do as well. The neat, clinical way in which Hilton and his wife were executed, and the fact that he was a leading cabinet minister all point to meticulous planning and organization. Hilton was clearly the target for some specific reason and it was not to protect the Republic from a criminal who holds a position of power. He is a man of absolute integrity. We believe the others, whether removed or not, will also be killed for the same reason. They need protection as of now, even though that is never enough against determined people.' He drank from a glass of water.

'If the people who did it want them dead why don't they just do it without going through the letter business?' said Weisz.

'The letter says they want them replaced,' said Tyson. 'If they just eliminated them they wouldn't necessarily get who they want as replacements. But I still believe I'm right about there being another reason.'

'I'll contact the police and call off their investigation,' said Weisz. 'I don't want them and the DSO running around looking for the same killer. I'll get them to give each of the other ministers on the list some protection, one or two guys from today. That raises another question. Why name the replacements? Surely any honest politician would do.'

'I can only think it makes the whole thing more plausible,' said Tyson.

'Does it?' said Weisz. 'Actually I'm beginning to think more like you. There is something behind this business. It's the workings of more than one person and he or she is not stupid.'

'When will you assign some people to it?' asked Tyson.

'I'm going to give part of it to a new agent,' said Weisz. 'His name's Adam Fairley and he used to work for the Specialist Crime Directorate, New Scotland Yard, before joining the Scorpions. I want him to concentrate on the charges of corruption and financial crime. I'm going to get another agent for the job of tracking down the assassin and those behind him. I might have to bring in someone from another regional office of the DSO. At the moment we don't have many of that type in this office. Fairley will report directly to me. The other person will also report to me, wherever he's from.'

'Excellent,' said Tyson. 'Please keep me informed of his progress. Do you want us to say anything to the three ministers on the list?'

'You have to,' said Weisz, surprised. 'We can't keep them in the dark now that they'll have protection.'

'I'll also tell Paul Bale about the letter, its demands and my meeting with you.'

'Yes, I must also phone him,' said Weisz.

Chapter 11

Cape Town

After Tyson left, Bruce Weisz thought about the second agent and the DSO offices where he might find one. He or she would have to be someone who had proved themselves against dangerous criminals and delivered what was required of them. Whoever they were after would be clever, completely ruthless, with killing their second nature. Patience, planning, and clear thinking were prerequisites if they were going to be caught inside what could be a very short time.

He didn't take long to decide that the best chance was the Durban office. He knew Peter Smith the regional head reasonably well and knew that a lot of their work involved serious organized crime of which murder and contract killings played a substantial part, either for protection, the elimination of competition or racketeering. He phoned Smith.

'Peter, Bruce Weisz.' Weisz sank into his seat. 'We haven't seen one another for quite a spell.'

'No,' said Smith. 'The day's coming when I won't have time to sleep. How are you?'

'I'm fine,' said Weisz. 'I want you to do me a favour. I'm sure you have heard that the minister of justice and constitutional development, David Hilton, and his wife Hilary, were murdered last night at their home.'

'Yes,' said Smith. 'I only spoke to him the day before yesterday. He was an old university friend.' He refrained from saying he'd seen Hilton in person.

'I've been asked by the President to get the person who did it,' said Weisz. 'You probably don't know that this morning the President, after he had been advised of the deaths, received a letter saying Hilton was guilty of corruption as are others in the cabinet. The letter said that if the President does not replace the men listed by others nominated they will also be killed.'

Smith lit another cigarette. 'Hilton hasn't a corrupt bone in his body. There must be more to this.'

'That's what the President thinks,' said Weisz. 'I agree with him. I've decided to get one of my agents to look into the allegation of corruption and another agent to pursue the killers. I've already asked the police to give the other three ministers some protection.'

'You wanted a favour,' said Smith. 'That means you don't have the second agent and you want me to supply him.'

'Exactly,' said Weisz. 'You have more men than I who are used to investigating organized killing. This guy would have to be good.'

Smith thought for a moment. 'I'd like to help but the type of person you're looking for is not available now. They're out on operations. I've already got a backlog of work.'

'What about the guy you had on that case involving the group of no name?' asked Weisz. 'You never did tell me his name.'

'I told you he's not a permanent agent,' said Smith. 'He had what I was looking for at the time and I took him on.'

'Where's he now?' asked Weisz.

'The last time I heard from him he was in London,' said Smith. 'He's British.'

'I would like you to contact him for me,' said Weisz. 'He must be very good to have put one over on the people he was dealing with. They were clever and ruthless. During the trials I seem to remember hearing from someone that the man behind securing the evidence used unusual methods. He was obviously referring to your guy but didn't give a name.'

'I know nothing about unusual methods,' said Smith, getting tired of the conversation. 'If by that you mean protecting himself, he would have played by the rules. Do you ask your agents for an account of every step they take?'

'No,' said Weisz. 'Will you contact him for me? As you can imagine, this is an extremely important job, more than anything else the DSO has been involved in. The President's life might be at stake and if he were killed all hell would break loose. The venom would be directed at the DSO and we'd all sink.'

'I will see what I can do,' said Smith. 'I might not even be able to contact him. If I did, I think it unlikely he would come all the way out here and risk his life looking for a murderer who has shot dead a cabinet minister.'

'All I ask is that you try him,' said Weisz. 'I'd really appreciate it. You can get me on this number, at home or on my cell phone.'

Chapter 12

Durban

When the call from Weisz ended, Smith went over what the man had said. He was reluctant to ask James Steiner to do any more work for the DSO without formally employing him, which Steiner wouldn't accept. But, Steiner had shown the ability to understand quickly the nuances of a complex case and if anyone could find Hilton's killer he could. Of one thing he was sure, Kirsty wouldn't like him getting involved in this type of work again.

Smith knew he had to speak to Steiner and hear what he had to say. He went through his private file, found Steiner's phone number and dialled. Kirsty answered.

'Kirsty, Peter Smith.'

'James was going to ring you to see how things are going,' she said. 'Are you still with the DSO?'

'Yes,' he said. 'It's the DSO I want to speak to him about. Is he there?'

'I don't like the sound of that,' she said. 'I'll get him. He's just come in.'

Smith heard her call, and Steiner came to the phone.

'Peter, did Kirsty tell you I was going to ring you?' said Steiner. 'We are thinking of coming to South Africa in a month or two. We'll fly to Durban and then drive down to Grahamstown to see her two sons.'

'James, have you heard the South African minister of justice and constitutional development, David Hilton, and his wife were shot dead last night?' said Smith.

'Yes, it was in this morning's news,' said Steiner. 'I hope you're not going the way of other African states.'

'There's something that's not in the news,' said Smith. 'It doesn't sound good. This morning the President received a letter saying Hilton, who I saw in Durban two

33

days ago, was up to his neck in corruption and three other cabinet ministers, all listed, are equally guilty. The letter called for their immediate replacement by others listed. If they were not replaced they'd end up like Hilton, dead.'

'When someone is killed with a threat to kill others, there is no end until they are all dead,' said Steiner. 'What did Hilton want?'

Smith told him what Hilton had said and that he had agreed to investigate the matter. He then said: 'I don't think it is related because what he appeared to have uncovered was without any real substantiation and hardly of concern to an organized crime syndicate even if they were alerted to possible interference. People like that are usually well aware of how close people are getting to them. All the DSO can do is act on what they have been told and find the killer. We don't know if these people will suddenly go for the President.'

'What's all this got to do with me?' asked Steiner.

'The President has asked my opposite number in the DSO in Cape Town, Bruce Weisz, to pick up the case,' said Smith. 'He's assigned one of his agents the job of investigating the allegation of corruption and he's looking for someone to do the real work.'

'You mean get someone to find the killer,' said Steiner. 'I wish him luck. He'll still be looking when all four are dead.'

'You're better than that,' said Smith. He had been waiting for his chance to go in softly.

'Let's be clear on this,' said Steiner. 'I'm not the guy you want. The work on the group was a one-off.'

'This won't take long,' said Smith. 'But if you say no, I'll tell Weisz you're unavailable.'

'So he knows you're contacting me,' said Steiner. 'He's never even met me.'

'He's heard of you by reputation,' said Smith. 'He met some guy during the trials who said the person who got hold of the evidence used unusual methods.'

'And that's why he wants me,' said Steiner, laconically.

'I told him you always stick to the rules,' said Smith.

Steiner went quiet. He had a strange feeling he was meant to go and that in some way the stuff Smith was talking about was linked to his past.

'I'll speak to Kirsty and get back to you,' he said.

Chapter 13

Cape Town

After speaking to Peter Smith, Weisz dialled Paul Bale's number at his NPA office. He was not obliged to, but it kept things running smoothly.

'Paul, Weisz at the DSO.'

'I was going to ring you,' said Bale. 'I've spoken to Tyson and I hear you're heading up the Hilton case.'

'Yes,' said Weisz.

'How are you going to approach it?' said Bale before Weisz could continue.

'I'm assigning one agent the job of looking at the alleged corruption,' said Weisz.

'Apprehending the killer is far more important,' said Bale impatiently. 'What are you doing about that?'

'Give me a chance,' said Weisz. He wasn't an admirer of Bale. 'I need a special type of agent for that. I don't have anyone free and I've asked Peter Smith in Durban to see if he can come up with one.'

'How long will that take?' asked Bale. 'The President wants someone on it now. I find it hard to believe you can't get a guy.'

'Smith is also thin on the ground,' said Weisz. 'I asked him about the man who managed to secure the group evidence that convicted most of those prosecuted. Smith says he's in London and he doubts he'd take a job like this.'

'When will you know?' asked Bale.

'Today, early tomorrow,' said Weisz. 'It rests on making contact with the guy.'

'What's his name?' asked Bale. 'I might know of him.'

'I doubt it,' said Weisz. 'Smith pulled him out of nowhere and the work he did for the DSO was a one-off.

I'll tell you when I know. The other agent's name is Adam Fairley and I've asked the police to provide protection for the remaining ministers.'

'Good,' said Bale, disingenuously. 'Please keep me informed.'

As soon as Bale had gone, Weisz buzzed Fairley to come and see him. Fairley had been with the DSO for six months. He was English, born in London, educated at the London Oratory School and University College London where he read philosophy and politics. He was one of three boys and both his parents were barristers. After university he joined the Metropolitan Police Service at New Scotland Yard and before he came to South Africa at thirty-nine he had achieved the rank of detective chief inspector in the Serious and Organized Crime Command of the Specialist Crime Directorate or SCD. It was perfect experience for work in the DSO. He arrived and took a seat.

'Adam, you know David Hilton and his wife were murdered,' said Weisz. 'This morning, the President received a letter saying Hilton was corrupt and that if another three ministers, also corrupt, were not replaced they would also die. Earlier, I spoke to Tyson, head of the President's security, and I was told to take the case. I phoned Peter Smith of the DSO in Durban and asked him if he could give me one of his agents to track down Hilton's killer and dig deeper into what is going on.'

'Why not someone from here, like Conran?' asked Fairley.

'He's too busy and at the moment I don't have the type needed for that sort of work,' said Weisz. 'I would have chosen you and put someone else on what I've given you. I'm sure you are streetwise but you need more experience of the South African political structure. Smith knows a man who has done work for him before, the case covering the group files, and there's a chance we can get him.' He drank water from the glass on his desk. 'That brings me to you.

I've decided to assign you the task of digging into the financial dealings of the ministers listed and Hilton. I want you to start with him so we can get a feeling if the allegation against him is true. If you need any help please let me know.'

'When do I start?' asked Fairley.

'Now,' said Weisz. 'He slid a sheet of paper across the desk. 'Those are the details you'll need for Hilton.'

'Fairley picked up the sheet, read the content and with a brief nod to Weisz left the office.

When Fairley had gone, Weisz went down a flight of stairs to Conran's office. He knocked and entered. Conran was working at his desk and he looked up.

'This won't take long,' said Weisz, advancing into the room. He told Conran what he had told Fairley.

When Weisz had finished, Conran said: 'That's the job I'd like. These routine cases never end.'

'That's why I didn't ask you,' said Weisz. 'If I do get the guy from London he will be operating alone. He won't be on the DSO staff. He'll report to me.'

Chapter 14

London, England

The house James Steiner had inherited from his father was in Ennismore Garden Mews, Knightsbridge, immediately behind the Holy Trinity Brompton and the Brompton Oratory. He lived there with Kirsty Callard.

After Steiner had spoken to Smith, he went through to the sitting room. Kirsty was seated, quietly waiting for him.

'Don't tell me,' she said. 'He wants you to do another job for him. I didn't think they'd let you go.'

'He does,' said Steiner. 'You know the South African minister of justice was assassinated along with his wife. Smith wants me to help his opposite number in Cape Town to find the killer.'

'He's got a nerve,' she said. 'Why can't they find someone over there? I know the answer to that. There's no one down there in your class.'

'There's more,' he said. 'In a letter to the President, the killer gave corruption as the reason for Hilton being killed. They have threatened to kill three more cabinet ministers, allegedly guilty of corruption, if the President doesn't replace them immediately. It is serious business and apparently not as straightforward as it appears.'

She thought for moment. 'Do you want to go? I don't know what I'd do if anything happened to you.' She got up and walked over to him. 'I love you so much Steiner.' She embraced him and rested her head on his chest.

He put his arms around her and drew her closer. 'When I was speaking to Smith I had the feeling I'm meant to go; no particular reason.'

'Then you must,' she said. 'It's your intuition. I have only one condition.'

'You don't need to tell me,' he said. 'You want to come along as well.'

'Exactly,' she whispered. 'Only I can take care of you.'

'We'll sleep on it,' he said. 'I'll phone Smith in the morning and give him our decision. I'd still cross the street for you.'

'Is that all,' she said. 'What you would do if you got hold of me?'

Chapter 15

Houghton, Johannesburg

After talking to Weisz, Paul Bale picked up his brief case, left his office and caught a taxi to the airport. Two hours later he arrived in Johannesburg and took a taxi to an address in Houghton, a residential suburb exuding only wealth. He paid the taxi, walked up the winding drive and rang the front bell of the house. A servant opened the door, recognized him and led him to spacious study overlooking the side of the building. Seated in front of a large, built-in bookcase was Andrew Rohm.

Rohm was born in London and educated at University College London where he read politics and law. He was an only child and when his parents were killed in a road accident he inherited their five-million pound house in Belgravia, London. In his early forties, while retaining his business contacts and home in London, he went to South Africa and became one of the leading industrialists in the country. As well as his houses in London and Johannesburg, he owned a wine estate in the Western Cape near Paarl. He was a handsome, single, athletic man of fifty-two. Paul Bale was one of those who knew that Rohm, in addition to his reputable business interests, embraced the world of organized crime. Rohm had often said that organized crime provided financial rewards that exceeded anything else and gave him the insatiable, unique thrill of operating outside the law.

The two men exchanged greetings and sat facing one another.

'I hope you have good news,' said Rohm. 'We want all this to go smoothly.'

'I think it is,' said Bale. 'Conran's man will get rid of the second tomorrow. As expected, the President's office has pulled in the DSO and their attempt to find the killer will be led by the regional head, Bruce Weisz.'

'I've heard of him,' said Rohm. 'Have you spoken to him yet?'

'Yes,' said Bale. 'I phoned him earlier. He's assigning one agent, Adam Fairley, to look into the allegation of corruption and will bring in another to track down the killer.'

'What do you mean by bring in?' asked Rohm. 'Isn't there someone available locally?'

'Apparently not,' said Bale. 'Weisz's already spoken to Peter Smith of the DSO in Durban. He's also tight but is going to try and get someone in London who has done work for him in the past. I was told by a guy I had monitoring the ministers' moves that on the day before he was killed, Hilton had taken a detour through Durban on a return trip to Cape Town. He and Smith met up at a hotel outside the city. I know Hilton and Smith were at university together.'

'Interesting,' said Rohm. 'But it's not important now. I've met Smith. He was one of the men behind the conviction of some of my best friends and business associates at the group trials. Do you know the name of the guy in London?'

'No,' said Bale. 'Weisz will tell me when he knows.' He glanced through the window. 'Is that important to you?'

'I'll answer that in minute' said Rohm, smiling thinly. 'Is Conran still happy with his deal?'

'When I first went to him I told him the reason for killing Hilton and sending the letter,' said Bale. 'I said it was to make the President realize we were serious and to give him time to replace the ministers by honest politicians of your choice because they were involved in serious crime. After the killing of Hilton, Conran asked me what would happen to the men if they were replaced immediately. That would negate the need to kill them.'

'What did you say?' asked Rohm.

'I said that killing all four was part of his agreed scope,' said Bale, 'and that we would inform him of any changes. He accepted that.'

'Good,' said Rohm. 'There is something I haven't told you. Of course we knew Hilton was sniffing around and that he would probably have confided in three close friends. But that was not the only or the main reason for wanting him and them removed. If it was we could simply have killed them quickly without calling for specific replacements. When we became wary of Hilton we saw the opportunity to get friends of ours who are already in the national assembly into the cabinet in very senior positions. That would give us unique inside information of what takes place in government and between ministers, information which could help and protect our operations considerably. These men sometimes do work for us and their appointment to posts in the cabinet is highly desirable.'

'I thought there was more,' said Bale, smiling. 'So these men are on your payroll and the minister of justice, Hilton's replacement and my boss will be one of them.'

'He will be, but I wouldn't let that bother you,' said Rohm. 'He knows about you and looks forward to meeting you when he's appointed. These four men of ours are very astute in legal, financial and security matters and we call on them for advice when required.'

'You were going to tell me why you are interested in the identity of Smith's man,' said Bale. He looked at Rohm expectantly. He had grown to like him and he knew when he was on to a good thing.

'Yes,' said Rohm. He cleared his throat. 'The result of the group trials was that very good friends of ours were convicted of crimes for which they were innocent. These men were protecting the Afrikaner people from being slaughtered by terrorists. The DSO acquired the evidence used in court and was entirely responsible for the convictions. The DSO man in charge was Peter Smith and his field agent was British, James Steiner. He acted independently in that he was not on the DSO staff. He alone was directly responsible for getting hold of two files that contained and led to the evidence that formed the case for the prosecution. In the process he was responsible for killing six men connected to the group. He also had the nerve to run off with the wife of one of them. I was not surprised when he didn't appear at the trials. I heard that he'd returned to England.'

'It sounds as if you were involved with the group,' said Bale. 'I heard it was an anodyne political party run by men dreaming of an Afrikaner state. It ceased to exist after the trials.'

'I was involved but not in daily operations,' said Rohm. 'Let me clarify things. It was a political party but its prime aim in the near term was to punish those who had opposed the white state from the inception of separate development in 1960 until 1994 when Mandela became the president. Others who perpetuated their hatred of whites by way of violence after 1994 were also targeted. Separately, the group offered protection and a new life in South Africa, and abroad if required, for those whites who had resisted black rule and were in danger of prosecution for alleged crimes committed during the apartheid period. A file that contained information designed to protect these people was one of the two stolen by Steiner and, ironically, led to their conviction.'

'And the other file led to the conviction of the blacks listed, some of whom had become very successful,' said Bale.

'That was the only good thing about the trials,' said Rohm. 'But, back to Steiner. If he is the man Smith is trying to bring in on this case then you should tell Conran to tread carefully. I hope Conran's assassin doesn't know about you. If he's nailed, we could all be in serious trouble.'

'I told Conran not to say anything about me,' said Bale. 'I'm sure he hasn't. He is too smart to reveal the names of others when it is not necessary. That is a cardinal rule. I'll contact Conran as soon as I leave here. I'll also phone Weisz and see if he's had a reply from Smith.'

Bale waited for Rohm to speak, but he'd gone quiet. 'Is there anything else?' he asked.

Rohm faced him. 'I despise the very existence of Smith and Steiner. During the trials I used to dream of having them killed.'

'How do you know they were responsible for getting the files?'

'It was no secret that Smith was leading the case,' said Rohm. 'It was also apparent that an outsider was trying to get hold of the files. We knew it was Steiner when he admitted as much to Johan Teichmann, the head of operations in the group. After Steiner had got the files he phoned Teichmann. He told him he was going to give them to the DSO and instructed him to collect the bodies of three men, two at a farm and the other at the house where he was staying with his girlfriend, the wife of Jan Krige and one of the dead men. Teichmann was also told not to make reference to the existence of Steiner or the girl.'

'I assume Teichmann complied,' said Bale.

'He had no choice,' said Rohm. 'They were his men and he didn't want the police involved. Krige's body was the only one found by the authorities and death was reported as murder. The killer was not found. But all that's history. I want you to have Steiner killed as soon as he appears on the case. After that you can do the same to Smith. This is the opportunity for which I've craved. When they are dead, a story will appear in the press saying Peter Smith, a regional head of the DSO, had again taken on a known killer of innocent men, James Steiner, to find the person who killed Hilton. Anyone else killed by that time will also be added to the report. The DSO will be totally discredited and a public enquiry called for, just what I want. When the last of the four is dead and the DSO is no further on than now in solving the case, we'll have the icing on the cake. I'm getting quite excited.'

Bale thought for a moment. He could not refuse. 'Who do you want to do it?'

'Conran's man,' said Rohm. 'Increase Conran's fee by another 200 grand and let him choose the time and place. He'll have to wait for Steiner to appear in Cape Town but Smith can be done wherever he is, probably in Durban.'

'You make it sound so easy,' said Bale.

'Assassination is not difficult,' said Rohm. 'All you need is preparation, patience, method and knowledge of your victim's movements. We're paying Conran a lot for that.'

'I'll speak to Conran about it when I phone him,' said Bale. 'I'll keep you informed.'

Chapter 16

John Delaware, minister of finance, had been in the position for three years. Before being appointed, he was Professor of Economics at Cape Town University. Like some of the other ministers had a house in the country and an apartment in the smart city suburb of Rondebosch. He invariably drove to the house on Friday nights where his wife and two children lived and was at his desk early on Mondays. The apartment was too big for his needs but very impressive in layout, superbly furnished and fitted with high-tech utilities. His mistress thought it was great, far removed from what her previous husband had been able to offer, and she was there most nights.

Delaware had been deeply shocked when David Hilton and his wife were shot dead and he welcomed police protection, usually one officer. At nights he released the officer shortly after returning from his office. The man appeared again an hour before Delaware left for work, and took up position in the passage outside the flat. The passage was external and fed by a staircase that came up from the garden.

At two in the morning a man dressed in black, his head bare, climbed over the wrought iron fence at the front of the block of flats. He went swiftly to the stairway, climbed to the second floor, checked to see no one was around and walked to Delaware's door. He had phoned Delaware at eleven the previous evening and, when he had answered, he had apologized for a wrong number. He knew the man had a mistress but didn't know if she was there. It made no difference.

The man rang the bell. He waited patiently, saw the internal lights go on and then came Delaware's voice. 'Who's there? Don't you know the time?'

'Central security,' said the man. 'This is urgent and concerns a colleague of yours.'

Delaware, in his pyjamas, his girlfriend in bed, was alarmed. 'I'll open the door,' he said.

The door was opened a few inches but when Delaware saw the man in black he panicked. As he tried to close the door, the man moved. He blocked the door with his foot, went against it with his weight, brutally pushed Delaware aside and entered. With his eyes on him, two metres away, he shut the door, pulled a silenced Beretta *90two* from inside his belt and fired two 9mm bullets into Delaware's brain.

Delaware died and as he was falling to the floor the man started to go down the passage in search of the main bedroom. He had taken only a few steps when Delaware's mistress appeared. When she saw her lover on the floor, blood seeping from the holes in his forehead she opened her mouth to scream. Before she could make a sound, the man fired twice into her heart. As she died and sank to the carpet, the man wheeled and left the flat for his car, parked down the street. It was easy work for the money he was going to get.

Chapter 17

Cape Town

The President was getting into his chauffeur-driven car six hours after Delaware's death when he received a call on his mobile. It was Tyson and he had just heard that Delaware and his mistress had been killed.

'So soon after Hilton,' said the President, maintaining his composure. 'I thought they would have given me a chance to replace Hilton.'

'This reinforces my belief that they are after all four,' said Tyson, icily.

'I'm going to my office,' said the President. 'See me there in thirty minutes.'

When the President reached his office, two national papers were folded on his desk. Tyson had not arrived and he picked up one of the papers. Staring at him on the front page was the title: Corruption against Hilton.

He sat down heavily and slowly read the report. He couldn't believe it. People who had chosen to remain anonymous claimed Hilton had been killed because he was guilty of serious crimes, including money laundering and substantial industry bribes. The report was brief but ominously clear. It ended by calling for an investigation into the affairs of government ministers and a statement by the President.

After the President had read the report he placed the paper on his desk and waited for Tyson. He soon arrived.

'This is really serious,' said the President when Tyson had read the report. 'I don't know what these people are after. Yesterday we thought their aim was something other than the mere replacement of the four men, but now I don't know what to think. Weisz will have seen this report and even though I doubt it will change what he has already initiated, I would like you to contact him and hammer home the urgency of closing this case. He has to be on it fulltime and use all the resources necessary. I want to know who's on it.'

'I'll get on to him now,' said Tyson. He left the room.

Chapter 18

Cape Town

When the President heard about the killing of Delaware, Paul Bale received a phone call from John Conran.

'I was about to phone you,' said Bale. 'Something else has come up. First, tell me what you've got.'

'The second one has been dealt with,' said Conran. 'You can find out the details from your sources. What about the next one?'

'Skip the weekend and go for Tuesday, five days from now,' said Bale. 'There is another job I'd like you to do. It'll mean taking out two men tied to the DSO.'

'That's getting close to home,' said Conran. 'I'm not sure I like it. Who are they and what have they done? Surely your mates are digressing a bit.'

Bale hated the word mates but let it pass. 'He is Peter Smith, regional head of the DSO in Durban.'

'I know of him,' said Conran. 'Apparently he's a nice guy, well respected. What the hell has he done?' He thought for a moment. 'Weisz said he'd asked Smith for an agent, in addition to Adam Fairley, to look into the present case.'

'Yes,' said Bale. 'He's the one I'm referring to. His name's James Steiner. When I told my friend that Smith of the DSO in Durban might bring in a second agent from London for the case he thought it might be Steiner. He took a serious dislike to him and wants him put down. It appears that Steiner was the person who acquired the core evidence used in the group trials. Those who stood in his way were summarily eliminated. When the DSO continue to fail in finding the people responsible for killing the ministers, it will be revealed in the press that two of their regional heads hired a killer to do it. The report will also say that one of

51

the heads and the killer has been killed. The DSO will be humiliated and an enquiry demanded. You'll get another 200 grand if you include the two on your list.'

'Two more bodies won't make a difference,' said Conran, 'but I'll only do it if you make that 250. I might have to separate the two jobs and get someone else to do it.'

'Agreed,' said Bale. 'I'm sure you can find out if and when Smith and Steiner become involved. You can do it when you like. Public anger and despair will be intense enough when they hear about Delaware today. Smith will probably be in Durban and Steiner down here.'

'What if Smith doesn't get Steiner?' asked Conran.

'They could both be spared,' said Bale. 'But the look on my friend's face when he spoke about Steiner might mean he wants him killed anyway. That would be a nice little job for your friend. He would like London.'

Conran looked at him. 'I wouldn't be involved,' he said. 'I'm not in the contract business.'

'Everyone has a price,' said Bale. 'But I don't think it will come to that. Let me know when you hear anything.'

Chapter 19

London

'That was fantastic,' said Kirsty. It was five in the morning and she and Steiner had just made love. 'I never want you to stop. You do things to me that no one else has done.'

'You let me because you want it so much,' he said.

'From you, yes,' she said.

'I couldn't do without you in South Africa,' he said. 'He got out of bed, wrapping a towel around him. 'Are you sure you want to go. I don't know what I'll face. It might include you.'

'Phone Smith and tell him we're coming,' she said.

After they had showered and dressed they went into the living room. Steiner turned on the television and BBC news was just starting. Under breaking news it announced second South African minister shot dead. A brief report followed.

'We're not going to a party,' said Steiner when the report ended. 'There is definitely more than one person behind it, they're clever, and they have a reason for doing it. That makes them dangerous. I'll contact Smith.' He went to the phone and rang the number. Smith answered.

'Peter, James Steiner. I've seen the news.'

'Yes,' said Smith. 'He and his mistress were killed early this morning in his flat.'

'Didn't he have a guard,' asked Steiner.

'Delaware lets the guy go during the night,' said Smith. 'Perhaps it wouldn't have helped if he'd stayed. These people are not incompetent. I don't mind saying that we need you.'

'Kirsty and I are coming,' said Steiner. 'When do you suggest?'

'It's not smart to bring her,' said Smith. 'You won't be on holiday.'

53

'I think that's why she's coming,' said Steiner. 'We'll be flying to Durban first. I want to see you before we go on to Cape Town.'

'Can you fly tonight?' said Smith. 'I'll meet you at the airport. SAA and BA have evening flights.'

'I'll go for the direct BA flight,' said Steiner. 'I'll let you know if there's a change. We'll see you for breakfast.'

After the call, Steiner faced Kirsty. 'We'll go BA tonight if that suits you.'

'I'll phone them,' she said.

Chapter 20

Durban

When Steiner had gone, Smith phoned Weisz in Cape Town.

'The guy in London, James Steiner, will take the job,' said Smith when Weisz answered. 'He and his girlfriend will arrive in Durban early tomorrow. I want to see them for an hour before they go to Cape Town.'

'He's bringing a girl?' said Weisz. 'Can't he do without her? This thing will be over in days.'

'She'll be with him,' said Smith. 'If you meet her you'll understand why he's not leaving her behind. She's the most sensual woman I've met and the sound of her voice is pure silk. She's also pretty good physically.'

'He'd better not bring her into these offices,' said Weisz. 'Most of these guys fancy their chances with any woman they want. After they get rid of him she'll be up for grabs.'

'I'll phone you when they leave Durban,' said Smith.

Chapter 21

Friday, 7 August
Durban

Kirsty and Steiner caught the BA evening flight at six and after a stopover arrived in Durban at seven. Smith picked them up and they went to a hotel on the beachfront for coffee. The connecting flight to Cape Town was two hours later.

'It would be nice if this was the start of the break you're planning,' said Smith when they were seated at a table on the verandah overlooking the north beach.

'We might bring that forward,' said Kirsty. 'It depends on how long this takes.'

'Why did you decide to come?' said Smith. 'I didn't think you would.'

'I'm not sure,' said Steiner. 'Just accept that we're here. Can you tell me what I don't know?'

'I have no more,' said Smith. 'I'm sure Weisz will fill you in on anything new. I don't think you will have a lot to go on. The group case gave us a starting point and this doesn't. I also think whoever is doing this is intent on killing all four, and the reason is not to protect the country from corrupt ministers.' He picked up the newspaper he had been carrying and opened out the top half of the front page. He slid the paper across to Steiner. 'That's a report about Delaware, similar to the one written on Hilton, asserting he was involved in corruption.'

Steiner skimmed the report and passed the paper back to Smith. 'There is only one line of action I can take,' he said. 'Speak to close political friends of the dead men, particularly the two remaining ministers, and try and get an idea who's behind it. Of course I'd like them to tell me the name of the assassin, who he's going after next and when. I assume the DSO has not decided to stick the last two in a safe house. If that happened, it would mean keeping them hidden until the gang are caught. That could take forever and I would not be part of it.'

'I don't blame you,' said Smith. 'When you reach Cape Town you might find the DSO has already locked the two up and want you only to carry on and find the killer.'

'That's when we might change our plans,' said Steiner. 'I can only see what Weisz says when I meet him.' He looked at Kirsty. 'What do you think?'

'I'll tell you later,' she said, looking at Smith.

Smith watched the rolling waves cascading on to the beach. He had never asked Steiner what he'd done to get the group files and whether Kirsty was involved. For him, he didn't need to know, even though others in the DSO had asked. He knew Jan Krige had been killed and wondered what Kirsty had told the two boys. He then looked at her and said: 'I'm sure you're good at looking after him. I'm never quite sure if he needs it.'

She laughed. 'Let's just say I know what he needs.'

Steiner took her hand and turned to Smith. 'We must go. I'll ring after I've spoken to Bruce Weisz. This time I'll tell you what I'm doing.'

Chapter 22

Cape Town

Bruce Weisz met Steiner and Kirsty at Cape Town airport at three in the afternoon and took them to his office at the DSO.

'I'm sure you want to hear what I know about this business and what I hope you can give us,' he said. 'It is very serious and the two killings could be a prelude to the assassination of the President. We are in the dark.'

'Smith has told me everything he knows,' said Steiner. 'That includes Kirsty, even though she's not directly involved.'

'He phoned me when you left Durban,' said Weisz. 'As well as telling me your flight times, he asked if we were going to or had put the last two men in safe houses. We haven't and don't intend to. We consulted the President's office about it and they said no because it would be a sign of weakness or paranoia on our part if we did. I agree with them and the security stays the same.'

'One guard on each man and off during the night, as in Delaware's case?' said Steiner. 'The assassin probably knew that and just ambled in.'

'That was unfortunate and a screw-up,' said Weisz. 'We believed that someone would be on duty day and night. Apparently Delaware made a different arrangement.'

'Why not put a couple of guys under cover and close by?' said Steiner.

'Again, the President wants there to be no sign of panic,' said Weisz. 'He believes it important to show cooperation with these people, even if it doesn't help. It's a risk he chooses to take.'

'What do you want from me?' asked Steiner.

Weisz laughed, brittle. 'Bring in the killer and those behind him,' said Weisz. 'Without the brains we achieve nothing because they'll keep going until they achieve their objective. It's not difficult to find an assassin. South Africa is full of guys who'd ditch their wives for the job.'

'Does that mean they want it?' said Steiner. 'Did Smith tell you where I think I should start?'

'Yes,' said Weisz. 'The two ministers are expecting to see you in their offices later this afternoon. They are Colin Dredge and Anthony Hamilton, Ministers of Defence and Education respectively.' He got out of his seat. 'All those working for us carry a Beretta *90two* 9mmx19 Luger/Parabellum semi-automatic pistol as standard issue. It's the best around. I can arrange for that now.'

'No,' said Steiner. 'I don't want to carry one. It might get me killed.'

'Please yourself,' said Weisz. 'I'm sure you have a good reason. We are not a gadget organization but you might like this.' He opened his drawer, took out something and held it up. It looked like a black pen but with an LCD display and a series of three tiny buttons on the top half of the shaft. 'This is a digital voice recorder and contains a highly-sensitive microchip with a high-gain microphone for long-range pickup. Its features include a PC interface, digital playback, a recording time of eight hours, an external connection cable and earpiece. In today's high-tech world where voice-recognition is admissible as evidence in court, something like this can be extremely useful in securing a conviction. It is commercially available for 3900 rand or 300 pounds sterling but is yours free. It can be carried anywhere on you. I'm sure some people would love to have it with them at dinner parties to record local infidelities.' He placed it on the desk in front of Steiner.

Steiner picked it up, knowing from past experience how valuable something like it could have been. 'Thank you,' he said. 'Before you offer I already have a cellphone with a camera. I can think of a couple of times when it would've been useful.'

Weisz liked Steiner. 'You're right. I was going to come up with that. Before you go, I'd like to introduce you to three of my agents. Adam Fairley is investigating the allegations of corruption to see if there's any truth in them and the other two, John Conran and David Strauss are two of my senior agents. He picked up the phone and made calls to the men.

'They're coming,' he said. 'Where are you staying?'

'Brown's Hotel just outside town,' said Kirsty.

'I know the place,' said Weisz. He looked at Steiner. 'A driver will pick you up at four-thirty. He'll always be available unless you hire your own car.'

'There'll be a car at the hotel tomorrow,' said Steiner. 'We'd like to use your guy today.' He got up. 'I'll ring you tonight.'

'I'll be at home,' said Weisz.

There was a sharp knock on the door and Fairley, Conran and Strauss entered. Weisz introduced them. 'If you can't get hold of me ring Conran and Fairley,' he said. 'They know as much as I do about this case. Strauss is for an emergency. Even though he's not involved in the case try him if we're not available.'

'Thank you,' said Steiner.

'You'll have to be pretty good to find the guy behind this,' said Fairley. 'There's less than nothing to go on.'

'I'll find something,' said Steiner. 'I'm sure we'll meet again.'

'I look forward to it,' said Conran. He had difficulty taking his eyes off Kirsty. She was in the top class and had a natural, unassuming manner that could take any man to his knees. He was sure he would never forget her.

Chapter 23

Cape Town

Paul Bale was at his office when he received a call from Weisz.

'The second agent has just arrived from London,' said Weisz when he heard Bale's voice. 'He's the man Smith used in the group case, James Steiner. I believe he has a girl with him, Kirsty Callard.'

'Excellent,' said Bale. 'Are they fixed up with a hotel?'

'Yes, Brown's Hotel, just outside town on the road to Table Mountain,' said Weisz. 'I've arranged for Steiner to see the last two ministers this afternoon. There's a chance they might give him the lead he badly needs. We have nothing and that includes what we got from forensics.'

'Thank you for keeping me informed,' said Bale.

Bale phoned Andrew Rohm at home. He had been the first to tell him the previous day that Delaware and his mistress had been killed.

'James Steiner and his woman have arrived,' said Bale. 'I've just heard from Weisz at the DSO.'

'Do you know the girl's name?' said Rohm.

'Kirsty Callard.'

'That's the one,' said Rohm. 'She's changed her name. She obviously doesn't want any link with her dead husband. Conran can deal with Steiner and his girlfriend when he likes. When's he going for Dredge? Hilton was the important one but I'd like to conclude what we've started.'

'I've suggested Tuesday,' said Bale. 'That gives the President a bit more time to act and to fret. He still hasn't named Hilton's replacement. I think Conran's keen to get it over with so he can get paid.'

'I like enthusiasm,' said Rohm. 'It's surprising how easy it is to kill prominent people if you go about it in the right way. It wouldn't be difficult to kill the President.'

'You're really enjoying this,' said Bale. 'You think it's a game.'

'I am and it is,' said Rohm. 'It adds variety to my normal business affairs.'

Chapter 24

Cape Town

'Conran says you'd rather be chasing the killers than checking the allegations of corruption,' said David Strauss. It was after work and he and Adam Fairley were having a drink in the Nightcap.

'I would,' said Fairley. 'Ravelling through bank transactions is not what I'll easily acquire a liking for. I'm used to a bit more action.'

'What did you think of Steiner?' asked Strauss. 'That's a good looking woman he's got with him. She didn't say much but I don't think she misses anything.'

'She wouldn't have to pay me to go down on her,' said Fairley. 'Steiner must have something going for him but as you heard me say he'll have to be very good to find the guy behind it.'

'Who says there's only one?' said Strauss looking at Fairley. 'There has to be more. It's too much for one guy to dream up.'

'I meant there's one person doing the work,' said Fairley. 'I'll bet he's the best available and I don't think he's local. Two bullets in each of the four victims, so tightly grouped they looked as if they'd gone through the same hole. That's good by anyone's standards.' He drank the last of his beer and got up to go. 'I admire such ability. I wonder who he is. It would be interesting meeting him. Let's go.'

Chapter 25

Cape Town

When Steiner and Kirsty Callard reached Brown's Hotel, they booked in, took their bags to their room and went downstairs to the lounge.

'This is really nice,' said Kirsty. 'It's not cheap. When are you going to discuss money with the DSO? They got the last job free and it was probably the most important in their short history.'

'When Smith asked me to help I owed him a favour and didn't feel I could ask for payment. When the file copy was intercepted by Kallis, Smith seemed to give in and didn't ask me to do anymore.' He drank some tea. 'I'll see what happens in this case.'

'I don't really care,' she said. 'The most important thing to me is being with you.' She looked at her watch. 'Let's take a walk. It will soon be time for you to meet the ministers.'

Chapter 26

Cape Town

At five the DSO driver met Steiner in the lobby of Brown's Hotel.

'I've been asked to take you to the residence of Colin Dredge,' said the driver as they walked to the car. 'Anthony Hamilton will also be there.'

Steiner nodded and twenty minutes later they reached Dredge's home, a magnificent house in the Cape-Dutch style with beautiful grounds. The driver parked at the side of the building and led Steiner to the front door. He was ushered in by a servant and taken to a study where he was greeted by the two men.

'We are pleased you are here,' said Dredge. 'I'm sure you know everything we do except that the President has just appointed a new Minister of Justice, Robert Baker. It will be announced tomorrow and he is the replacement named on the list the President received.'

'What do you think of him?' said Steiner.

'He's not exactly one of the President's admirers but I think he'll fit in,' said Hamilton. 'I like the guy, but I don't know him as well as I knew Hilton.'

'He sticks to himself,' said Dredge. 'He's intelligent and an astute politician.'

'I assume he's honest,' said Steiner.

'I think so,' said Dredge. 'So was Hilton. There's something strange going on and we think we have some idea what all this is about. These people have got nothing on us that can be called corruption and that also applies to Delaware. The President will have to name the replacement for him as well. It's the only chance he has of ending this business, besides catching the killer.'

'If finding the killer could stop it,' said Steiner. 'What is this all about?'

'A year ago, Hilton came across what he felt was the existence of an insidious, corrupt organization run by some of the most powerful men in this country,' said Dredge. 'He initiated inquiries but the people he asked confirmed, without much detail to back it up, that Hilton was right and that five leading industrialists were involved.'

'And he confided in you and Delaware,' said Steiner.

'Yes,' said Hamilton. 'Hilton had no hard evidence and without it he could not ask the police or DSO to carry out an in-depth investigation. But he kept at it, using the same people. This time he felt he was getting somewhere tangible and was talking about bringing in the expertise of the DSO. Apparently he had a very good friend in the DSO in Durban, a man named Peter Smith.'

'I know Smith fairly well,' said Steiner. 'He told me he had met Hilton in Durban the day before he was killed.'

'That's correct,' said Dredge. 'Smith had agreed to get some of his best people to investigate. Hilton needed the experience they could bring and I think he was sorry he didn't approach Smith earlier.'

'Do you think the four of you are on the list given to the President because of what Hilton was doing and that he confided in you?' asked Steiner.

'We think that's a strong possibility,' said Dredge. 'We can't think of another reason.'

'When Hilton referred to the five industrialists did he mention any names?' asked Steiner.

'No,' said Hamilton. 'He simply said he would keep us informed when he heard something from Smith.'

'He must have told Smith,' said Steiner. 'I'll ask him. Don't the two of you fear for your own safety? My brief is to find who's behind all this, not to offer any sort of security.'

66

'We appreciate that,' said Dredge, 'and we are not scared of these people. Each of us has a twenty-four-hour guard and we're either in public places or at home. As well as the guard we have the latest high-tech security devices fitted by consultants. Weisz mentioned a safe-house but these people would just wait until we came out. The only answer is to leave things as they are until they are caught.'

'What about Delaware?' said Steiner. 'Did he feel safe after Hilton?'

'He was careless,' said Dredge. 'He should never have released his guard at night and certainly not have opened the door to a stranger, whoever he claimed to be.'

'So you're satisfied with your security and prepared to stick to your routine,' said Steiner.

'We don't hide from threats,' said Hamilton defiantly. 'It's not in our nature.'

Steiner got to his feet. 'Thank you for seeing me. I'm sure Bruce Weisz will keep you abreast of developments. I'll see myself out.'

Chapter 27

Houghton, Johannesburg

'I'm glad you came,' said Andrew Rohm. 'I've something that'll be of interest to you.' It was late afternoon.

Seated near him was Johan Teichmann, former head of operations in the disbanded group of no name. 'You sounded in good spirits over the phone,' he said. 'When are you are going to get rid of Dredge?'

'Three days from now,' said Rohm, 'but that's not what I want to tell you. You once told me that there is one man you'd like to get hold of, James Steiner.'

The two men had been at school together and had through the years become very close friends. Although Rohm had not been actively involved in the group, he had heavily supported it financially and had lost a large sum of money when it had collapsed. Teichmann had never been prosecuted. He had always made sure nothing from his past could be pinned on him. He knew about the plan Rohm and his friends had devised to remove the heat from their operations and that Rohm was working through Paul Bale. He had also been told that Bale was using someone in the DSO.

'Yes, that's right,' said Teichmann, straightening his back, his eyes fixed on Rohm.

'By that you meant you wanted him in a box,' said Rohm. 'A few days ago Paul Bale told me that Weisz had asked Peter Smith of the Durban DSO to find an agent to find the people behind the killings. Weisz remembered Steiner from the group business and wanted Smith to get him, which he did. Steiner and his girlfriend Kirsty Callard, as she now calls herself, are now in Cape Town and he's on the case.'

'This sounds almost too good to be true,' said Teichmann. 'Thank you for that. I now have the chance I've been waiting for.'

'When Bale told me he was here I asked him to get Steiner and Smith on the assassin's list,' said Rohm. 'I'd also like to see the man put down. A lot of the men prosecuted were good friends of mine.'

'No,' said Teichmann. 'I want to issue the instruction and keep it separate from the other business. I'm the one who's directly involved. I'll never forget Steiner's phone call to me after he'd got both files. He said he was going to give them to Smith and that I should learn to behave myself.'

'I can understand your dislike for him,' said Rohm, concealing a smile. 'There's also the girl. She was married to Jan Krige and dumped him for Steiner. You said she asked him to help her find the files and for that bears prime responsibility for bringing our people to trial and having them convicted.'

'Yes,' said Teichmann, 'and I'm sure she was at the farm when Krige and John Kallis were killed by Steiner.'

'Perhaps she helped him,' said Rohm, inadvertently fuelling Teichmann's hatred. 'I'll phone Bale and tell him to cancel his instruction to the guy in the DSO. Do you know someone who can do the job?'

'Yes,' said Teichmann, unemotionally. 'I'm going to play a little game with our James Steiner, like the one he played with me. It will involve his woman and mean the end of their continual interference in our affairs. Smith will be dealt with as well.'

'You haven't told me who's going to be your lead player,' said Rohm.

'Earlier, I mentioned the name John Kallis,' said Teichmann. 'He was one of my men in the GROUP and I said he was killed by Steiner. I knew his brother Marc

Kallis reasonably well and at one point I thought of asking him to join the group. I didn't.'

'Why?' asked Rohm.

'I don't like admitting this but I didn't think I had the strength to control him,' said Teichmann. 'Marc was like his brother when it came to intelligence, physical prowess, mental strength and hunger. But that's where they diverged. Even though John could be unorthodox he was never in the same class as his brother regarding those winning attributes of controlled aggression and sheer ruthlessness.'

'Do you think that makes him a good killer?' said Rohm.

'Yes, in part,' said Teichmann. 'But he has the rest as well. When he was at Witwatersrand University studying law he lived in Johannesburg's Hillbrow, the equivalent of Soho in London, and was regarded as an invincible streetfighter. He led a gang for kicks and once a year they used to visit Durban where they engaged in street fights with the best, the guys who controlled the city and the beach. It was as if it was an annual event, pre-arranged. Kallis was always the winner.' He drank from the gin and bitters Rohm had put next to him. 'After university Kallis went to London. He held a good job for two years and then went to China where he studied *tai chi* under a famous master for five years. He was also interested in *muay thai*, Thai boxing, and went to Bangkok for a year. He fought in the ring and his fights were a mirror image of those in the street. He was always the winner against hard, experienced professionals. Death in the ring is simply an occupational possibility. He returned to London, spent a while there and then back here. He works for a law firm in Pretoria, Du Bois, Randt and Partners. They're near the old group offices.'

'Would he take such a job?' asked Rohm, wondering why he hadn't heard of Marc Kallis before.

'He would, for one very good reason,' said Teichmann. 'He was very close to his brother and was manic when he heard he'd been killed. He swore then that if he ever got a lead on the killer he would destroy him.'

'Do you know if he's got a criminal record?' asked Rohm. 'People who have a passion for violence are often associated with crime.'

'Not to my knowledge,' said Teichmann. 'I would take him anyway. I'll do what is required to get rid of Smith and Steiner.'

'It looks as if you and Kallis will be satisfied,' said Rohm, thoughtfully. 'You both want the two of them dead for the same reason, hatred. When are you going to contact him?'

'As soon as I leave here,' said Teichmann. 'I'll let you know when he starts work.'

Chapter 28

Cape Town

'I don't know where you're going to start,' said Kirsty. 'You're looking for someone who has never been seen, a phantom.' She and Steiner were having a drink in the hotel bar before dinner.

'No one is that,' said Steiner. He stared at the glass of water on the counter. 'I have a feeling that I am not going to have to look for your phantom or the people behind him. It's the feeling I had in London. I'm meant to come out here.'

'What do you mean?' she said. 'They're not going to appear suddenly and say 'I'm guilty, take me'.

'Of course they're not,' said Steiner, smiling at her description. 'But I think they'll still come to me, and it won't be out of concern for my health.'

'You worry me,' she said, taking his hand.

'Don't be, I'm not' he said. 'I'm going to phone Smith and ask him for the names of those industrialists given to him by Hilton.' He looked at her, shaking his head. 'It's a shot in the dark.'

'It's certainly that,' she said. 'Even when you get the names you can't do anything with them. You can't simply burst in and accuse them of being behind the killing of two government ministers.'

'Let's have something to eat,' he said, getting off his stool. 'The break I need will come. I hope it's not too late.'

Chapter 29

Johannesburg

After leaving Andrew Rohm, Teichmann phoned Marc Kallis from his mobile phone and arranged to meet him at a club in the centre of Pretoria, Nocturne, in thirty minutes. He arrived early, found a table away from the bar and waited. Kallis soon appeared, a tall, powerful man who walked with consummate ease.

When they had ordered drinks, Kallis drank some and moved his chair a little nearer to the table. 'I sense something has got you going. Am I right?'

'Pretty close,' said Teichmann. 'I've got a job for you. I think you'll enjoy doing it.'

'I haven't heard anyone say that for quite a while,' said Kallis. 'I'm listening.'

'Do you remember the names Smith and Steiner?' asked Steiner. 'If you don't, I might have to go elsewhere.'

Kallis' brown eyes darkened. 'Where are they?' he asked, his voice low, sending a chill through Teichmann.

'Steiner's in Cape Town,' said Teichmann. 'Smith is still in Durban. He was asked by the DSO in Cape Town to come up with an agent to do some work for them. Steiner's the agent.'

'Are you telling me this for my benefit or for yours?' said Kallis.

'Yours and mine,' said Teichmann, candidly. 'But I'd like you to kill them. I'll give you a substantial sum of money, 200 grand in pounds sterling. It would look good in your UK bank account.'

'When do you want it done?' asked Kallis, reclining slowly.

'I would like it completed as soon as possible,' said Teichmann. 'I want to forget about them. That will only be

73

possible when they don't exist.' He looked down. 'Steiner also has a woman with him.'

'I'll try and isolate her while I deal with him,' said Kallis. 'I'm not killing her.'

'You might change your mind,' said Teichmann. 'When your brother was killed on the farm the owner of the place Jan Krige was also present. He was doing work for me and was also killed. His wife Kirsty Krige, now Callard, was there as well but she had joined forces with Steiner. She's the one with Steiner now.'

'You certainly know how to come up with the surprises,' said Kallis. 'Was she involved in the deaths of her husband and my brother?'

'It's entirely possible,' said Teichmann. 'I say that because John was killed by a blow to the side of the neck, which only Steiner could have delivered, and Krige by a bullet in the head. If Steiner had had a gun he would have used it. She must have had the gun and I think she used it on her husband.'

'You could be right,' said Kallis. 'I'll find out. Even if I don't kill her I might use her to get Steiner. How do I recognize them?'

'He's about six-one, dark hair, 185 pounds, a lean powerful physique and good looking,' said Teichmann. 'There're not many like that around. She's around five-seven, dark, long hair, very attractive. I'd give a lot for a night with her.'

Kallis thought for a moment then said: 'Who's on the farm now?'

'It's deserted, not operating,' said Teichmann. 'Why do you ask?'

'Just interested,' said Kallis. 'It's where John was killed. Where are they staying? I'll also need to know where I might find Smith, his office, home, and also a photograph if you have one.'

'Steiner and the girl are at Brown's Hotel just outside Cape Town. I'll send Smith's details to you in the next hour on your AOL address. I have a photo of him at the trials. Alternatively, you can come with me now.'

'Send it by email,' said Kallis. He finished his drink. 'I'm now on the job. I'll stay in contact. I'll be on the late plane tonight.'

Chapter 30

Houghton, Johannesburg

After speaking to Teichmann, Rohm phoned Bale at his home.

'I've just had a meeting with Johan Teichmann,' said Rohm. 'I told him about Steiner being on the case and that I'd asked you to get your man in the DSO to eliminate Smith and Steiner. He didn't like that and said he would arrange for it to be done. Apparently he knows just the guy.'

'I've already asked Conran,' said Bale, 'but I'll stop it. I'll ring him.'

Chapter 31

Cape Town

Paul Bale phoned Conran and told him the change of plan. 'The guy must hate them even more and wants to keep it in the family,' he said.

'I haven't initiated anything,' said Conran. 'I'll just leave it. At this rate we'll have hitmen running all over town. I hope he keeps his distance. We don't want them bumping into each other.'

'I'm sure it won't come to that,' said Bale. 'They won't meet if your man sticks to the ministers.'

Chapter 32

After an early breakfast Steiner phoned Peter Smith at his home in Durban.

'I'm still no closer to a lead than when I last saw you,' said Steiner after they had exchanged greetings. 'I'd like to get some details of those who might be connected. I met the two ministers Dredge and Hamilton yesterday afternoon and they said that Hilton had asked you to investigate the activities of five businessmen.'

'He did,' said Smith. 'I didn't tell you because there was no obvious link. Maybe there is a connection but we might only know that when the people I've asked to investigate report back to me. That will take time.'

'Which we haven't got,' said Steiner. 'But I'd like whatever you've got, even if it's only who they are and where they live.'

'I'll email the stuff Hilton gave me to your address here,' said Smith. 'You'll see that the apparent leader of these men is Andrew Rohm. You might not have heard of him but I certainly have. He's probably the most influential businessman in this country and when he speaks people listen, including the President. I don't want to sound callous, but you might only get a lead when the next minister is killed. As a matter of interest the President has just named Hilton's replacement. He's on the list, Robert Baker. I'm surprised he didn't do the same for Delaware.'

'I'll be in touch,' said Steiner. He replaced the receiver and looked at Kirsty.

'I need inspiration,' he said. 'You're very good at that.'

She was about to speak when the phone rang. Steiner picked it up. 'James Steiner.'

'You don't know me,' said a man. 'I heard you're in Cape Town.'

'Who are you?' asked Steiner, turning to face Kirsty.

'I'd rather not say over the phone,' said the man. 'I'll tell you when we meet. You won't be disappointed.'

'Where and when?' said Steiner, knowing that he had to examine every chance.

'There's a hotel, The Northumberland, at the far end of the city's main street,' said the man. 'Meet me there at eight and come alone. I'll be in the front reception room, black chinos and a white shirt.'

'I'll be there,' said Steiner. He terminated the call.

'What's all that about?' asked Kirsty, walking over to him.

'Some guy wants to meet me at a bar in Adderley Street. He said he's got something to tell me concerning this case.'

'Is that all?' she asked.

'I'll look into anything that might give me a break,' said Steiner. 'It's interesting. I've met the people who know I'm here. Did one of them tell this guy? If not, who did?'

'Could it be a trap?' asked Kirsty.

'I'm not close to anything,' said Steiner. 'I can't be a threat and if they wanted to neutralize me they wouldn't choose a public place.'

'Be careful,' she said. 'Phone me when you meet him. The car is out the front but I think you should use the driver and ask him to wait for you.'

'I will,' said Steiner. 'I'll ring him now. Don't worry about me. Smith is sending me an email with the names Hilton gave him. Perhaps you can print it out on the machine downstairs.'

She put her arms around him and kissed his lips. 'I love you so much. Take care of yourself.'

Chapter 33

The President's office, Cape Town

'When are you naming Delaware's replacement?' said Barry Tyson. 'And when are you replacing Dredge and Hamilton?' He looked at the President, seated across the desk from him.

'They gave me no timetable,' said the President, 'and I'm not going to act like a startled rabbit and replace all of them immediately. I didn't think they would kill Delaware so soon but it reinforces our belief that they're after all four. But I'll do as required and name Delaware's replacement, Peter Cochrane, on Monday. On Tuesday I'll replace Dredge and Hamilton. I was hoping Weisz could have come up with something by now.'

'Why don't you insist and stick them in safe houses or at least reinforce the guards?' said Tyson. 'I think they're sitting ducks.'

'They are stubborn, proud men,' said the President, 'and they're as safe as they want to be with one man for security. I can't force any more people on them. Besides, Delaware was partly to blame for his own death by releasing his guard during the night.' He got up and walked to the door. 'Give Weisz a ring on Monday and see what he's got to say.'

Chapter 34

Durban

Peter Smith sent the details Hilton had given him to Steiner. He thought about what Steiner had said and then phoned Bruce Weisz on his home number in Cape Town.

'Bruce, Peter Smith,' he said when he heard Weisz's voice.

'I've been meaning to call you,' said Weisz. 'There're a couple of issues we need to discuss about people we're after who have fled to your area. Perhaps we can meet up. It'll be easier.'

'That suits me,' said Smith, 'not only because of that but also the killing of the ministers. When you asked me if I'd heard about Hilton's murder I didn't say he'd come to see me in Durban the day before on the way back to Cape Town. I didn't think it had any connection but I believe now that what he gave me might well help you. Briefly, he believed that five prominent business leaders are together involved in serious organized crime. He gave me their names and an idea of the stuff that had aroused his suspicion.'

'That could be behind all this shit,' said Weisz. 'I'm glad you contacted me. What did you do about it?'

'I assigned a small team to it,' said Smith. 'Hilton came to me because we knew one another at university. It's no reflection on you. You told me you had an agent Adam Fairley looking into the allegation of corruption against Hilton. I think that's a waste of time because you'll find nothing. You should concentrate on the list Hilton gave me, in particular the apparent boss, Andrew Rohm. Fairley could work with my people or I could pull them off and leave it entirely up to you.'

'Very interesting,' said Weisz. 'Why do you single out Rohm?'

'According to Hilton he is heavily into the most lucrative forms of organized crime, drugs, trade in endangered species, bribery, which includes contracts for the supply of military weapons, and diamonds. With drugs it is primarily cocaine. His network covers the Republic, Europe and, through extensive links developed previously, the UK.'

'How is he involved in cocaine?' asked Weisz. 'That's the really big drug. Demand for it has increased considerably in recent years while that for heroin has remained the same. Cannabis and ecstasy has gone down.'

'I'll read some of what Hilton sent me on this,' said Smith. 'It'll give you an idea of the supply and distribution structure Rohm uses and the potential value. He wears it like a glove and has been a key player in establishing it. You are probably aware that Colombia produces 600 tonnes of cocaine per annum, eighty per cent of the world's supply. This is produced as freebase cocaine and crack cocaine, commonly called rock, and insufflation – snorting, sniffing or blowing – is the most common form of ingestion. Freebase and crack are adulterated or cut from cocaine hydrochloride salt, a pearly-white powder and the purest form of cocaine. The salt is produced by macerating leaves from the coca plant with water acidulated with sulphuric acid and evaporating the water after maceration to produce a pasty mass of impure cocaine sulphate salt, the intermediate step to full CocHCl. A large percentage of this goes by small planes from Colombia to Venezuela and from there by larger aircraft to West Africa, mainly Ghana and Guinea-Bissau. The president of Venezuela, while pretending to be a mediator in solving the chronic problems between the Colombian government and Farc, the Revolutionary Armed Forces of Colombia, the oldest guerrilla movement in the world, surreptitiously supports

Farc who essentially control cocaine production in Colombia. He recently expelled the US Drug Enforcement Administration from the country and he allows his military to let the drug pass freely through Venezuela.' Smith drank some water, lit another of his high-tar cigarettes and then continued.

'From West Africa the cocaine is shipped to Europe and South Africa. The Republic's extensive coast line makes it easy for cargo and fishing vessels carrying freebase cocaine and crack to get through. Luxury yachts are also used and seldom searched because of status and who owns them. This applies to the UK and Europe. Portugal and the autonomous north-western Spanish province of Galicia are the EU Schengen zone entry points. Light aircraft and boats take it to the UK's east coast, places like Essex and Norfolk. Mules using international flights are widely employed and their services readily procured for peanuts. The twenty-seven states in the EU, many without interconnecting border controls, and corrupt officials in African countries, make trafficking easy for anyone with brains, good organization and the right contacts. Rohm has it all at his disposal and runs the business from South Africa and London. Neither the movement nor the distribution of drugs is a problem for him because he is so well organized. At a street value of fifty pounds sterling per gram of cocaine the fiscal return can equal the GDPs of many developing nations. It was estimated recently that the total street value of cocaine in Europe is 7.5 billion pounds per annum. The UK has 800 000 users and Africa a lot more. Rohm is an extremely rich man and as well as London and South Africa has houses in Monaco, Paris, Los Angeles and Tokyo. To say he is spoilt for choice is putting it mildly. I'll send the rest to you.'

'All very interesting,' said Weisz, 'the maceration of an innocent coca leaf to the production of a lethal white powder and those who make a fortune out of the process. It is incredible to think some people use their intelligence to devise and engineer such a basic process knowing it brings such devastation. What about the animal products and the other stuff?'

'On animal products it is easy with a good organization like Rohm's to get what you want in Africa illegally and distribute it,' said Smith. 'In 2000, a global threat assessment by the US concluded that the illegal trade in animal parts and endangered species was second only to drugs in the profits it could turn. A small rhino horn in powdered form can, in the right market place, Asia, Europe and North America, fetch 20 000 pounds sterling. Big cat pelts can go for 10 000 pounds each. Monkey brains, big-cat carcasses, elephant feet, tails, horns and teeth have enormous value. Profits from the trade run from fifteen to twenty-five billion US dollars a year according to the WWF.' He ran his finger along his lips.

'The arms deals he strikes are massively lucrative. As soon as the major suppliers put in their bids, Rohm and his people step in. They make sure that their preferred bidder, the one who is prepared to pay the most in bribes, knows what the others have bid so they can adjust their bid accordingly. They are then awarded the contract because they have the lowest price. It is so simple it is almost a joke. The diamonds are called blood diamonds because they are frequently used to finance revolutionary movements or terrorists. Like the drug mules, all you need are people at the hard end in the mines to take the risk and carry the stones through the checks. In fact the risk can be small if you bribe the people who are conducting the checks to let you pass.'

He stubbed out his fag. 'By now you of course realize that one word describes all this and Rohm can spell it backwards. It is corruption and it's not only Rohm's ball game. Africa's economy is based on it.'

'Does Interpol have anything on Rohm?'

'No, he's certainly not listed on their database,' said Smith. 'There's a lot more. Hilton's people were pretty thorough.'

'Yes, but without evidence,' said Weisz. 'We'll talk further. Would you like to come here?'

'That sounds fine,' said Smith. 'I'll fly down first thing on Monday and come to your office.'

'I'll be there,' said Weisz.

Chapter 35

Cape Town

At seven-thirty Steiner met his driver in the hotel lobby. He gave him instructions and they left for the car parked at the front.

Standing idly next to a new Audi saloon, Marc Kallis watched them. Teichmann's description was perfectly adequate. When the car had disappeared down the winding drive, he crossed to the hotel, entered and casually walked to the desk served by a young girl.

'I'm here to see James Steiner and Kirsty Callard,' he said. 'Do you know if they're in?'

'I saw him go out,' she said. 'I think she's still in their room. I can't see her down here.'

Kallis smiled disarmingly and leant forward. 'I would like to surprise her,' he said. 'I'd appreciate it if you could give me the room number.'

'I wouldn't give that to some people,' she said, drawn to his handsome features, 'but for you it's 117 on the first floor. Are you sure you don't want me to ring her.'

'No, that'll be fine,' said Kallis. 'Thank you. I can't wait to see the look on her face.'

Kallis left the desk, climbed the stairs to the first floor and went down the passage to room 117. He knocked twice and was about to repeat it when Kirsty opened the door.

'Kirsty Callard?' said Kallis.

'Yes,' said Kirsty. 'Who are you?'

As soon as she said the words she knew she was in trouble. She made to close the door but it was too late. Kallis pushed her back into the room, shutting the door in one easy movement.

'Make a sound and it'll be your last,' he said, smoothly taking her arm and leading her further into the room. 'I'm not here for fun and I advise you to cooperate.' He released her arm.

'What do you want?' she said. 'I don't even know you.'

'I've heard of you,' said Kallis. 'You were present when your lover James Steiner killed my brother. My name is Marc Kallis.'

She sat down on the bed, calming herself. 'Your brother was a killer. Didn't you know?'

He laughed evenly. 'He was not. I heard that you shot your husband and killed him. That wasn't a very nice thing to do.'

'That's a lie,' she said. 'Tell me why you are here.'

'I've come to take you away with me,' he said. 'You'll need a change of clothes and personal items. We've got a long drive ahead of us.'

She got up and stared at him defiantly, knowing it wouldn't help. She was powerless. 'Why?'

'I want Steiner to come for you,' said Kallis, 'so I can have the two of you in the place where you killed my brother. This time you won't be doing the killing. I will, of Steiner and maybe you. You're equally guilty and my only hesitation is that you're a woman.'

'The farm,' she said. 'I'm not going back there. And you want to kill us? You're insane.'

'Do you want to get your things or should I?' he said.

'And how are you going to get me out of the hotel?' she asked. 'You can't drag me out.'

'I don't intend to,' said Kallis. 'We'll simply walk out like good friends through the rear exit into the garden and then round to the car park at the front. I'm primarily interested in getting Steiner and if you interfere with my plans it'll be your end.' He drew a silenced semi-automatic Beretta *90two* 9mmx19 Luger/Parabellum pistol from behind his belt and waved it at her. 'Have I made myself clear?'

87

She walked over to the cupboard, extracted a change of clothes, soft shoes and put them into a canvas bag. She added toiletries from a shelf and faced him. He would do as he pleased and for now there was nothing to be gained by resisting.

'Does that satisfy you?' she said.

'For now, yes,' said Kallis. 'Let's go, and bring your keys for the house. I don't want to have to break in. It's not good manners.'

They went from the flat, used the rear fire exit to leave the building and soon reached the car.

'Get in,' said Kallis, opening the co-driver's door.

Kirsty complied and in five minutes they were on the N1 freeway from Cape Town to Johannesburg.

'This is going to be a long drive,' said Kallis, stating the obvious. 'It'll be around fifteen hours.'

'What are you going to do when we get to the farm?' asked Kirsty. 'Steiner will never go there. You're wasting your time.'

'He'll come,' said Kallis confidently. 'He didn't bring you all the way to South Africa just to turn his back on you. From what I hear the two of you are inseparable. He'll come running as soon as he knows where I'm holding you.'

She closed her eyes. She had been right. Someone would come for Steiner and that was Kallis, even though he had nothing to do with the killing of the ministers.

Chapter 36

Cape Town

Steiner was a little early for his meeting with the man and when he arrived at the Northumberland he found a quiet seat in the mostly deserted front lounge. At eight-thirty he knew he had been duped; for what reason he didn't know. He felt a bit of a fool but under the circumstances he would do it again.

He left the place, met the driver outside and they headed back to Brown's Hotel. He thought about phoning Kirsty but knew he would soon be with her. When they reached the hotel he ran inside, looked to see if she was downstairs and, when he didn't see her, went to the room. She wasn't there and he had a feeling of unease. Someone had taken her and had cleverly got him out of the way.

Steiner sat on the edge of the bed. There was no sign of a disturbance. Whoever had come for her knew exactly what they were doing. They would soon contact him. He was the prime target and for the first time wondered if Kirsty's disappearance had anything to do with the case. He had assumed the phone call was linked to the killings but now he didn't think that was the case. He got up, realizing that his mind was jumping ahead, without being certain she was nowhere around. Perhaps she was in the grounds and the man on the phone was genuine, even now waiting for him at the bar.

Steiner went downstairs and before going outside crossed to the young girl at the desk.

'My girlfriend Kirsty Callard seems to have vanished,' said Steiner. 'She's not in her room.'

'She was here,' said the girl. She thought for a moment. 'A man was asking for her shortly after you went out. He wanted to surprise her.'

'What happened to him?' said Steiner.

She looked a little embarrassed. 'We couldn't see her down here and I gave him your room number. He went up the stairs.'

'Did he give you his name?'

'No,' she said. 'But I'd easily recognize him.'

Steiner was painfully aware his first thoughts were confirmed. The man had simply walked in, gone up to her room and taken her. It couldn't have been easier.

'Thank you,' he said. 'They must have gone out. I'll wait for them in my room.'

'I'm sorry you missed them,' she said. 'He was tall, blond, in his late-thirties. I'll always remember his smile.'

'I don't know him,' said Steiner. He left her and returned to the room. What had he got Kirsty into? The man would soon contact him.

Chapter 37

Kirsty Callard's farm, near the Kruger Reserve

Marc Kallis's estimated time for the journey to the farm was close. He and Kirsty arrived at ten-thirty that evening.

'Home sweet home,' said Kallis when they got out of the car at the front of the house. 'Bring the keys. You told me you have them.'

Kirsty hadn't been to the farm since the death of her husband. She'd instructed her lawyer to ensure the staff and workers were released, the house cleaned and the barns locked. She had some fond memories of the place and never thought she would again revisit it with a man who wanted her and Steiner dead. She had told Kallis she had the keys on her ring and she wouldn't have to watch him smash his way in.

She followed him to the front door, unlocked it and entered. She noticed the small stain of blood from Jan Krige's fatal wound had been removed and the lounge was clean and tidy. She faced Kallis. 'What now?'

Kallis sat in the chair nearest to the doors. 'You can go and sleep,' he said. 'I'll sleep here but before I do I want to look around and then phone your boyfriend. I want to get him moving so that I can finish this business and get out.'

'What are you going to tell him?' she asked, his last words emphasizing his deadly intent and filling her with foreboding. Steiner would be gunned down mercilessly when he came.

'Exactly what has happened,' said Kallis. 'I'll tell him that if he doesn't make an appearance you'll be killed.'

'And if he doesn't?'

'I'll kill you,' he said. 'He won't see or hear from me again until we meet at a place of my choosing. I want a bit of foreplay before I add him to my score. Killing him without it wouldn't give me enough satisfaction. I want to see him sweat, here or elsewhere.'

'What's the reason for bringing me here?' she asked. 'You could have done all this in Cape Town.'

He stretched out his legs. 'It's a case of choice. This is my preference because it's where you and Steiner killed my brother and your husband. If that is denied me I'll go to Steiner. In truth, whichever way I get him is irrelevant as long as I do.'

She walked to the window. 'Who told you that James Steiner and I killed your brother and Krige?'

'That's of no concern to you,' said Kallis. 'It's irrelevant.'

'So there is someone behind all this,' said Kirsty. 'I didn't think you were doing this on your own.'

'I didn't say that,' said Kallis, becoming cautious.

'I think someone's pulling the strings,' said Kirsty. 'How did you know Steiner and I were in Cape Town?'

'You're a persistent bitch,' said Kallis. 'That's typical of women and a good reason why some men hit the bottle.'

'It could only have been through the DSO,' said Kirsty.

'Enough of this shit,' said Kallis. 'Show me around this place.'

'After that, I want to be present when you phone Steiner,' she said. 'The phone has not been disconnected.'

'I don't mind if you stay,' he said, getting up. 'I want the cell phone in the pocket of your jeans. It's just a precaution.'

She took out the mobile and gave it to him. He put it on a table and pointed to the passage door. They walked through the house and in five minutes returned to the living room. He went to the house phone, rang Brown's Hotel and asked to be put through to James Steiner's room.

Chapter 38

Cape Town

James Steiner spent the rest of the day in his room. He thought of speaking to Weisz and Smith about it, but didn't. There was nothing they could do that he couldn't and the only course of action was to wait. A call from those responsible was inevitable.

He was lying on the bed, after having eaten sparingly from a late meal delivered to the room, when the phone rang. He let it ring three times and then answered. 'James Steiner.'

'Steiner, I have your woman. My name's Marc Kallis.'

'Where is she?' said Steiner as if the name meant nothing to him.

'We're at her farm near Kruger,' said Kallis. 'I'm sure you remember it. It's where you killed Jan Krige and my brother.'

'I thought I'd heard the name before,' said Steiner. 'What are you doing with her?'

'I'm waiting for you to come and collect her.'

'Why not bring her back here?' said Steiner. 'We can then see what's on your mind.'

'You're pretty slow,' said Kallis. 'I want you standing in this room when I kill you.'

'I'll meet you,' said Steiner, 'but I don't want Kirsty involved.'

'You've no real choice,' said Kallis. 'Either you come or the girl dies.'

'Let me speak to her.'

'Here she is,' said Kallis. 'It won't change what I've said.'

Steiner heard Kirsty take the phone. 'Kirsty, how's he treating you? I got you into this.'

93

'I'm alright and you didn't,' she said. 'James, don't come. He'll kill me whatever you.....' Steiner heard the phone being taken from her.

'Steiner, I'll be waiting for you,' said Kallis. The line was cut.

Steiner replaced the handset. He guessed it would take thirteen hours to drive to the farm from Cape Town. That meant flying to Johannesburg and hiring a car. He looked at his watch. It was too late for the last plane. It would have to be the first flight in the morning. He thought about phoning Weisz but decided there was no point. This was a private matter and unrelated to the case which had brought him to South Africa.

Chapter 39

Kirsty Callard's farm

After Kirsty had gone to bed, Marc Kallis phoned Teichmann on his mobile number. 'I've got the girl,' he said when Teichmann answered.

'Where are you?' asked Teichmann. He was in his pyjamas and about to go to bed.

'We're at her farm, Jan Krige's place before they got him,' said Kallis. 'I picked her up at the hotel and we drove here.'

'Why the hell have you taken her there?' said Teichmann. 'Where's Steiner? He's the one I want.'

'He'll soon be on his way to get her,' said Kallis confidently. 'I decided to use her as bait to get him up here. He killed my brother in this room and I think it appropriate that he spills his brains on the same floor. I haven't decided what to do with her. If I kill Steiner I'll probably kill her. But it's not easy to kill a beautiful woman, especially in cold blood.'

Teichmann thought for a moment. Although a bit bizarre, he could understand Kallis's reasoning. It seemed perfectly logical; get Steiner away from Cape Town, kill him and leave no trace of his disappearance. He could imagine the frustration it would cause the DSO, their appointed agent investigating the execution of the ministers simply evaporating. Kallis was smart.

'You've obviously contacted him,' he said. 'When do you expect him?'

'I don't think he'll drive,' said Kallis. 'That means a plane. I spoke to him thirty minutes ago and that rules out tonight. I think he'll fly up first thing in the morning to Johannesburg and hire a car. The earliest flights are at six.

With a flying time of two hours and a car ride of three I expect him to arrive at around eleven.'

'What then?' asked Teichmann, glad he wasn't Kallis. 'He's not going to just walk in with his hands up.'

'I'm sure he's not,' said Kallis. 'All I want is for him to come. I'll be waiting and take it from there.'

'What have you told the girl?' asked Teichmann.

'She asked me how I knew they were in Cape Town,' said Kallis. 'I told her it's no concern of hers.'

'I'm glad you didn't mention me,' said Teichmann. 'If you had, you would certainly have to kill her because the DSO would inevitably find out and be all over me. I might just as well have been one of those guys in the white file. I still think you should silence her.'

'I can look after myself,' said Kallis.

'Remember, after Steiner you still have to get Smith,' said Teichmann. 'I'll then transfer the money into your London account.'

'I'll keep you informed,' said Kallis. He put down the phone.

Chapter 40

Pretoria

Teichmann phoned Andrew Rohm at his home.

'I've just had a call from Marc Kallis,' he said when Rohm answered. 'He's accepted the job and has taken the girl to her farm near Kruger. He's using her as bait to pull in Steiner.'

'When did this happen?' asked Rohm

'He picked her up at the hotel and has just arrived,' said Teichmann. 'At first I wondered what he was doing but he said he wants Steiner to die where he killed his brother. A bit strange, but that's the way he feels. I don't have a problem with that. I'm sure he'll get the job done and move on to Smith.'

'What about the girl?' asked Rohm.

'That's up to him,' said Teichmann. 'If he kills Steiner he'd be wise to kill her. But all I really want is Steiner and Smith dead.'

'Has Kallis informed Steiner?' asked Rohm.

'Yes,' said Teichmann. 'He expects to see him in the morning.'

'If something goes wrong and Steiner finds out you're involved he'll come after you,' said Rohm, thinking ahead and protecting himself. 'I think you should give me Kallis's cell phone number in case that happens. Did he use the phone on the farm or is it disconnected?'

'It was the land line,' said Teichmann. 'I'd rather you didn't contact him but I'll give you the number and that of his cell phone.' He gave Rohm the numbers.

'I wish him luck,' said Rohm disingenuously. 'Please keep me informed. I expect the third guy to be liquidated on Tuesday and I'd like to know where Kallis is with Steiner and Smith. I assume you have an appropriate passage to give the press before they find out and print their own stuff.'

'It's ready,' said Teichmann confidently. 'I'll ring you when I know more.'

Chapter 41

Johannesburg

After speaking to Teichmann, Rohm remembered Paul Bale saying Hilton had met Peter Smith in Durban. As he thought about it and that Steiner might find out about Teichmann being behind the plan to kill him, he became uneasy. Rohm didn't know why Hilton had met Smith but it was not a courtesy call. To him there was a good chance that Hilton was asking Smith to investigate his affairs in the light of what Hilton believed he had uncovered. It was a chance Rohm could not take, particularly when coupled with the possibility that Steiner might overpower Kallis when he reached the farm.

Rohm went to the phone and rang Kallis on his cell phone. Kallis answered.

'Marc Kallis?' said Rohm.

'Yes, who is it?' said Kallis. Only a few people knew the number and they were friends or close associates who would've recognized his voice.

'My name is Andrew Rohm. I'm an old friend of Johan Teichmann. He told me he had asked you to take care of James Steiner and Peter Smith.'

'I thought my dealings with him were confidential,' said Kallis. 'What's he playing at?'

'I'm sure he hasn't told anyone else,' said Rohm. 'I'm on your side and he told me he'd just spoken to you at the farm. I've something to offer you that I don't believe you'll refuse.'

'I'm not interested in anything else,' said Kallis. 'I've got a specific job to do and I don't want outside interference while I'm doing it. Teichmann wouldn't like it either.'

'Please hear me out,' said Rohm. 'Teichmann told me you have Steiner's girlfriend with you and that you are using her to lure him to his death. I also believe that after you kill Steiner, and probably the girl, you are going to Durban to get Smith. I also want to see Steiner and Smith killed and before Teichmann said he wanted to do it I had taken steps to have both men removed. I only called my people off because Teichmann has had previous contact with Steiner and, I suspect, hates him and Smith more than I do. They were largely responsible for the demise of the group.'

'Get to the point,' said Kallis, his interest aroused.

Rohm was prepared to let the tone of condescension pass. 'I would like to make sure that if there is the slightest chance you can't kill Steiner this time you leave him, inform me and Teichmann, and go straight for Smith.

'Does Teichmann know you are phoning me?'

'No,' said Rohm. 'If he did he might be a little annoyed but he would come to realize that I'm protecting him as well as myself.'

'Why don't you just ask me to pull out now?' asked Kallis.

'I think you've got a very good chance of killing Steiner and I'm prepared to take the risk,' said Rohm. He thought for a moment and then said: 'Did you tell the girl about your intention to go for Smith after you'd dealt with them?'

'No,' said Kallis. 'I'm not stupid.'

'Good,' said Rohm, not sure he had heard the truth. But he couldn't do anything about it if Kallis had lied. 'I'll give you 500 grand in sterling if you play along with what I've just said to you. And I don't want Teichmann to know about this. It's between you and me. Do you agree.'

'Yes,' said Kallis. 'Is there anything you can tell me about Steiner?'

'No,' said Rohm, 'except that he knows how to kill. He's wiped out some pretty tough characters and he's intelligent.'

'I've met that type before and I'm still here,' said Kallis arrogantly.

'I believe you have,' said Rohm. 'I'll wait for your call.' He replaced the phone.

Chapter 42

Sunday, 9 August
Kirsty Callard's farm

Kallis slept on the sofa in the front room. He woke at four and thereafter his pattern of sleep was erratic until he got up at six-thirty and washed in the second bathroom, away from Kirsty's bedroom. He made some coffee in the kitchen and returned to the front of the house, certain that Steiner was in the air. His thoughts dwelt only on him, a man he knew nothing about except that he had killed his brother, an act for which he would die.

At eight he woke Kirsty and told her to get up. She left her bed, showered and joined him, taking up a seat across the room.

'What are you going to do now?' she said. 'I'm sure you've managed to come up with another of your little plans.'

'He'll soon be here,' said Kallis, fixing a silencer to his pistol and placing it next to him on the sofa.

'And then you'll just pump lead into him,' she said, looking through the window at what she could see of the deserted track. 'It always amazes me how people like you, your brother and the other thugs in the group deliberately choose the dark side of hell so that you can get the satisfaction of taking human life. It's a drug, an opiate from which you can never abstain.'

'Not only attractive but quite a little philosopher,' said Kallis. 'I don't crave what you call the dark side of hell. People like you and your boyfriend lead me into it.'

She smiled sardonically. 'You're so beautifully deranged I have to admit I find it entertaining,' she said, staring at him. 'Wait until you see Steiner in action. He's quite something.'

'Nothing like what I'm used to,' he said. 'Now shut up. If you don't, I'll make sure I'm screwing you when he arrives. Just imagine the effect that would have on him.'

His words sent a chill through and she was reminded of the hideous experience when Koch was trying to do exactly that when her husband had arrived. She looked away. She had gone too close to the edge and decided to keep quiet. Everything now depended on Steiner.

Chapter 43

Cape Town

At six in the morning Steiner caught the South African Airways flight to Johannesburg's OR Thambo International Airport. Two hours later he hired a Mercedes Benz saloon at the airport and joined the main road to Pretoria.

After reaching the city he started on the final leg of his journey to White River and Kirsty Callard's farm, wondering how many more times he would be on the same road. On each previous occasion the drive to the farm had not been for pleasure or because he enjoyed the intoxicating scenery of the predominantly wild land on either side of the road, but because he was heading for something that carried the possibility of being killed. He was still alive but for how much longer he didn't care to think about. Clear strategic and tactical thinking, and reliance on his training in the *do*, was now of the essence. He thought about Marc Kallis and judging by what he had done and his manner on the phone he was not unlike his brother. But in Marc's case he sensed there was something more, something deeper. He sensed that Kallis was not only canny and streetwise but that he had spent time overseas. A faint accent on some words betrayed this but there was, significantly, a calm about him that led Steiner to believe the man had been trained in some esoteric discipline, one that was not merely learning strict rules of behaviour at a private school. Steiner was also starting to believe that Kallis would not gun him down on sight if avoidable but would want some form of exchange, verbal or physical, as a starter.

In a little under three hours Steiner reached White River and without stopping came to the turn-off to the farm, the sign Krige still hanging lugubriously from a short post. He was now about two kilometres to the farm and he started along the graded dirt road. When he saw the main gate to the farm, some 200 metres in front of him, he parked the car among some trees near the road. If anyone saw it they would not be Kallis. He had thought of driving up to the front door but preferred a quieter approach before he showed himself and confronted Kallis.

He left the car, went over the nearest length of fence and ran through the undergrowth to the ridge, parallel to the track that led to the house. Vegetation on the side of the ridge concealed him adequately as he moved quickly along it. When he neared the building he halted and crouched, studying what lay before him. His position offered a view of the side elevation and front of the house, an Audi parked near the verandah steps, and, as expected, he saw no one.

Steiner thought about what he'd felt earlier, that Kallis would want to deride him verbally before killing him. He now was also sure that he had little chance of suddenly appearing, taking Kallis by surprise and subduing him, which he would have to do before he could free Kirsty and leave. As he was about to move he saw a man through the window of the lounge cross the floor. The sighting was brief but it was enough to tell him where he would find Kallis, sitting where he had a view of the front and the other entrance, the passage to the kitchen, Kirsty with him, his bait. When they met it would at first be a waiting game, each assessing the strengths and weaknesses of the other, like two Japanese swordsmen of old confronting one another. But Steiner, from his training, chose not to wait for an opponent to move physically before delivering the killer strike. Instead he would wait only until the mental commitment or opening, *suki*, presented itself and intuitively compelled him to close in and nullify the threat.

Steiner rose and started weaving through the bushes towards the front of the house. When he reached flat ground, fifty metres from the front corner of the building he slowed, walked to the verandah steps and up to the open doors. What he saw was expected, Kallis and Kirsty seated, well apart, quietly waiting.

'Welcome,' said Kallis, remaining in his seat. 'You're on time.' He took the pistol, got up and walked into the centre of the room.

Steiner looked at Kirsty and then back to Kallis. 'Put your gun down and leave. You're out of your league. I'll let you pass freely.'

Kallis hadn't seen such calm strength in anyone for a while and he felt the first stirring of excitement. He felt no fear, and even without the gun he would not feel fear. Fear was an alien emotion and he wouldn't let it cloud his judgement now. He was aware of what Rohm had said on the phone and instinctively knew he had to forego the prelude and finish his business.

'I'm not leaving,' he said, his words like ice. 'I came a long way for this meeting and my patience has at last been rewarded. You killed my brother and your woman killed her husband. I'm here for revenge and that means you are both going to die.' He lifted the pistol and slowly started squeezing the trigger.

A split second before the pin detonated the charge and released the bullet at 400 metres a second, Steiner moved. In a blur of speed he sprang forward, doubling over, pirouetting on his left foot like a ballet dancer and covering the space between them. When he had turned through 180 degrees and was less than two metres from Kallis, he delivered a back kick to the chest that drove Kallis ignominiously against the passage door. Kallis reeled, but with the agility of a circus acrobat went straight for Kirsty, still in her seat. Steiner, surprised at the way Kallis recovered, could only watch as he wrenched Kirsty to her feet, pulled her in front of him and held the gun to her head.

'Stay back,' he rasped, his dark eyes fixed on Steiner. 'Any move and I'll blow her apart.'

106

Steiner was motionless, wondering how he had not dropped Kallis. 'Don't harm her,' he said. 'This is between the two of us.'

Kallis knew that luck had been on his side. Steiner's move had been perfectly executed and it was only rapid reflex action by him before the kick landed that had enabled him to avoid the full impact. Steiner was extremely fast and he wanted to see who was better. He was sure that no man he'd met before was in Steiner's class. His thoughts again went to Rohm's words of caution, the reward that awaited him, and he knew that he would have to wait until he and Steiner met again, which he now was certain would happen. If he left with the girl and dropped her some way off he would have a clear start and if he moved quickly be gone without interruption. Steiner would also lose time before he reached his car, obviously not on the farm.

'I'm leaving with her,' he said. 'You'll find her on the main road to White River, well away from a phone. We'll meet again and I won't be careless.'

Steiner looked at Kirsty. 'I'll soon be with you. Take care, my love.'

Kallis walked Kirsty sideways to the front doors, on to the verandah and down the steps to his car. He pushed her behind the wheel through the co-driver's door and got in next to her. They were soon in a shroud of dust as they sped to the gate and the road beyond.

As they were going down the track, Steiner was thinking ahead. Kallis wouldn't harm Kirsty and he'd probably do as he said, leave her at the side of the road to White River, in the middle of nowhere with no visible sign of help. Phoning her would have to wait because if she was still with Kallis when the phone rang he would probably remove it, if of course he hadn't already. He quickly looked around the room and saw Kirsty's cell phone on one of the tables. Clearly, phoning her was out and the only thing he could do was get his car and go after her. As he was closing the doors he realized that Kallis would have seen the car and unless he was a fool immobilized it. He set off down the track to the gate, thinking of Kirsty, the woman he loved.

Chapter 44

White River road, near Kruger

After passing through the gate Kallis told Kirsty to drive slowly. Steiner's car had to be parked nearby and he wanted to find it. They soon saw it.

'Pull up and turn off the engine,' he said. He took a folding knife from the cubby hole and opened his door. He grabbed her by the arm and drew her towards him. 'Come out this side.'

They got out and still leading her, he walked to the nearest front wheel. With her next to him, he knelt, extracted the knife from the sheath and stabbed the blade into the tyre wall. Satisfied, he led her round to the second front tyre and did the same to it.

'That will hold up your lover,' he said. 'What a nice surprise after such a long journey, two flat tyres and not a garage in sight.' He pushed her back to the Audi and they left the scene. At the main road they turned left towards Pretoria.

When they were half-way to White River, thirty kilometres from the farm and in the middle of a long stretch of tar with no buildings in sight, wild bush interspersed with trees lying dormant on either side, Kallis got Kirsty to pull over and get out. He left the car and she walked round to him.

'This is where we part,' he said. 'If I'd killed Steiner I would have killed you. Consider yourself lucky. I've a feeling the three of us will meet again.' He got into the car and drove off towards Pretoria.

Chapter 45

White River road, near Kruger

When Steiner reached the Mercedes Benz his fears were confirmed when he saw what Kallis had done to the tyres. He phoned directory enquiries in Pretoria and after getting the number of the dealer where he had hired the car, he arranged for a car to be sent out to meet him on the road his side of White River. He told them to pick up Kirsty and put her on the phone to him if they saw her. He then left the car and started walking. Pretoria was 340 kilometres from White River with another sixty kilometres to the farm turn-off. At 120 kilometres per hour the car would take just over three hours to reach him and less time to Kirsty if Kallis had released her.

Steiner had walked for three hours, nearly twelve kilometres, on the road to White River when he received a call on his mobile from the dealer. The car had found Kirsty and they were driving towards him. The man put her on.

'James, it's me,' she said. 'Where are you? I've just been picked up. We're thirty kilometres from White River. Kallis has gone.'

'You're about ten minutes from me,' he said. 'I'll see you soon.'

Shortly after the call, Steiner saw a Mercedes approaching, the only car on the stretch of road, and knew it was Kirsty. The car drew up.

She sprang out of the door and into his arms. 'Are you alright?' she cried.

'Yes,' he said, embracing her and running his hand through her soft hair. 'It's great to see you. We'll talk later.'

As he moved to speak to the driver she said: 'I've got to tell you something. I think someone else is involved, someone connected to the group.'

'Did Kallis tell you that?' he said.

'No,' she said. 'But I'm certain he's not doing this alone and it's not a coincidence that he wants to avenge the death of a group operator who is also his brother.'

'We'll discuss it when we've changed the tyres of the car,' he said. He spoke to the driver. 'I'll direct you to the car.'

The driver nodded and they drove on to where Steiner's car was parked. After the tyres had been changed, the driver left for Pretoria.

'Where're we going now?' asked Kirsty when they were inside the vehicle, resting her head on his shoulder.

'We must lock up the house,' said Steiner. 'We'll discuss what to do next when we're there.'

Chapter 46

Pretoria

Three hours after leaving Kirsty at the side of the road, Marc Kallis reached his flat in the centre of Pretoria. It was in a prime location, spacious, three bedrooms, and he had bought it on his return from London.

After making something to eat, Kallis reflected on what had happened that morning. He had been reluctant to leave without dealing with Steiner, a man of obvious ability who had had dedicated training, probably in the Oriental martial arts, but he did not regret his decision after the conversation with Rohm. He now had to contact both men to keep them satisfied. He dialled Teichmann's mobile number.

'Kallis here,' he said bluntly, when Teichmann answered. He was at home. 'Steiner arrived but I decided to back off. I wanted to toy with him but he's no novice. I'm prepared to wait until after I've got Smith.'

'I was hoping you could deal with him and the girl this morning,' said Teichmann. 'How have you left things and where are they now? I can see on my phone you're at your flat.'

'Yes, I am,' said Kallis. 'I left Steiner at the farm and cut the tyres of his car on the way out. I took the girl with me and dropped her off on the main road, fifteen kilometres from the farm.'

'When are going to get Smith?' asked Teichmann.

'I'll go to Durban first thing tomorrow,' said Kallis. 'I might have a chance during the day but I think it'll be in the evening when he's at home. That might also mean his wife. I should be able to get his movements from his secretary.'

'Good luck,' said Teichamm, reassured by the confidence in Kallis's voice. 'Let me know when it's done.'

As soon as Teichmann had gone, Kallis phoned Andrew Rohm.

'It's Kallis,' he said when he heard Rohm answer. 'I didn't kill Steiner and got out. He turned up as expected but I underestimated him. He's not easy to put down. I've already told Teichmann.'

'Why didn't you stay and finish it?' asked Rohm.

'I remembered our conversation,' said Kallis, 'and didn't want to take the risk. I decided to go for him after Smith. I cut his tyres and left the girl at the side of the road to White River.'

'So you're going for Smith tomorrow,' said Rohm.

'Yes,' said Kallis, 'exactly when I don't know. I'll have to get an idea of his movements.'

'What if he's not in Durban?' said Rohm. 'I'd like it done tomorrow.'

'I'll get him,' said Kallis.

'Tell me when he's gone and your plans for Steiner,' said Rohm. 'I want him out of the way.'

'How does he interfere with you?' asked Kallis. 'When I first spoke to you I got the feeling that your motive for wanting Steiner dead was not only revenge.'

'It has nothing to do with you,' said Rohm, pointedly. 'You're getting paid to do what I say. If you have difficulty with that tell me.'

'I was just interested,' said Kallis. Rohm was right. All he had to do was the killing. 'I'll phone you tomorrow.'

Chapter 47

Kirsty Callard's farm

'Now tell me more about what you said on the road,' said Steiner when he and Kirsty were seated on the verandah. 'I've been thinking about it and you could be right.'

'I asked him who was behind all this and how he knew you and I were in Cape Town,' she said. 'He certainly didn't like the questions. When I said he could only have found out that we were here through the DSO, he clammed up.' She drank some coffee and then continued. 'I don't believe Kallis is acting alone and doing this only because he wants revenge for the death of John Kallis. I think that someone in the group who cannot forget what you did to them is exploiting Kallis's desire for personal revenge to get satisfaction. Kallis wants revenge and because he was not involved couldn't care a shit about the files and the prosecutions that followed after the DSO got hold of them. But someone does and for that reason they want you dead, not because you wiped out John Kallis, Krige and the others.'

'You did Krige,' said Steiner. 'I hope it doesn't become a habit.'

'I have no regrets,' she said, 'and I'm not another Bonnie.'

'I hope you're you not,' he said. 'That would make me a Clyde.'

She laughed. 'Now tell me what you think?'

'I agree with you,' said Steiner. 'Johan Teichmann, the head of group operations, immediately comes to mind. When you told Kallis he could only have found out we were here from the DSO is perfectly logical since there is no one else. If that is true then Teichmann, assuming he's

114

behind it, knows about DSO operations regarding the ministers and that I am working for them.'

'Then Teichmann knows who is behind the killings,' said Kirsty.

'It's possible,' said Steiner, 'but I can't be sure.'

'Could it be Teichmann?' she asked.

'No,' said Steiner. 'This points to the businessmen named by Hilton. I think Teichmann gets his information from them and they could only have found out by having direct access to the DSO. I don't know how but I doubt it's through a plant. I could understand it if it was the other way round, like the Cartwright case when Bryant of the DSO was undercover in the group. Anyone joining the DSO and other agencies like MI6 is going to be subjected to intensive vetting and the people behind a plant have to know exactly how to prepare their candidate. I think the link to the DSO is an outsider who holds their trust.'

'We've missed something,' said Kirsty. 'If Teichmann wants you dead for the damage you caused by getting hold of the files and giving them to the DSO, then it's not only you he wants.' She got up and walked towards him. 'Who was behind you and is just as guilty?'

'Peter Smith,' said Steiner. 'You're absolutely right. I hadn't thought of him.'

'And Kallis could be on his way to him as we speak,' she said.

Steiner went to the phone. 'I must warn Smith. Kallis is being paid for killing me and him.' He dialled Smith's home number. He answered after several rings.

'Peter, James Steiner. I'm glad I got hold of you.'

'Where are you?' asked Smith. 'It sounds as if something's wrong.'

Steiner briefly described the events involving Marc Kallis and when he had finished said: 'Kirsty and I are now at the farm and have been discussing all this. We think that Kallis is after me not only because he wants me dead for killing his brother but because someone linked to the defunct group, who also wants me killed, is playing on his sentiments and using him. Some haven't forgotten the files and it's not a coincidence that Kallis suddenly popped up a day after we arrived. The only way these people could have found out I'm here is through the DSO and that suggests they know I'm working for the DSO on the government case. Does that mean they are behind the deaths of the ministers?'

'Very clever,' said Smith, 'and I wouldn't be surprised if they are behind the murders. Who is this someone in the group?'

'Who else but Johan Teichmann,' said Steiner. 'He'll never forgive me for giving you the files. But the reason for this call to you and not Weisz is that we believe Kallis is also after you and could be heading your way now.'

'I think that's stretching things a bit,' said Smith. 'I don't think Teichmann even knows I exist. I've certainly never seen him.'

'He knows about you,' said Steiner. 'I was just the dog serving a master. Teichmann would have been at the trials and someone could have pointed you out to him as the person behind the convictions. You were also named in the press.'

'Don't worry about me,' said Smith dismissively, still unconvinced. 'What are you going to do now? I suggest you see Weisz. After you phoned me yesterday I contacted him and suggested the people I've assigned the job of looking into the affairs of the businessmen join forces with Adam Fairley. I'm going to Cape Town tomorrow to discuss some things with him and we'll go through it then. Fairley's wasting his time trying to find out if the allegations of corruption against Hilton are true. He'll come up with nothing.'

'When will you get back to Durban?' asked Steiner, still convinced Kallis had Smith on his list.

116

'In the afternoon,' said Smith. 'I've got a lot on at the moment.'

Steiner knew there nothing more he could say about Kallis. Smith was not the first to ignore a warning that his life was in danger. 'I'll ring you when I've spoken to Weisz. Enjoy your trip.'

When Smith had gone Steiner sat down and looked at Kirsty. 'He doesn't believe Kallis will go for him,' he said. 'He's going to see if Weisz wants to use his people to investigate the activities of the businessmen. That would mean getting Fairley to work with them and forget about checking the allegations of corruption against Hilton. Smith's going to see Weisz tomorrow in Cape Town.'

'You've done what you could,' said Kirsty. 'What's next? I think you should ring Weisz or wait until we get back to Cape Town.'

'I'll ring Weisz now, tell him briefly what has been going on and that I want to see him later today,' said Steiner. 'When I do I'll say that I think Smith's life is in danger. Regardless of what he says, I'm going to Durban.'

'What are you going to do there?' said Kirsty. 'Walk around in Smith's shadow so that you can catch Kallis before he commits the act?'

'I'm not sure,' said Steiner. 'I just want to be in the area. I might go and see if I can get some sense into Smith. I wouldn't be able to live with myself if anything happened to him now.'

'Ring Weisz and let's get seats on a flight to Cape Town,' said Kirsty. 'Remember, you are working for him. If he doesn't think you should go to Durban and you do, you'll be disobeying him. I know you like your independence but that wouldn't go down well.'

Steiner phoned Weisz and summarized what had happened. Weisz agreed to see him later at his home and Steiner booked seats on the five-thirty afternoon flight from Johannesburg.

Chapter 48

Cape Town

After speaking to Steiner, Bruce Weisz phoned John Conran at his house and updated him.

'Steiner wants to see me when he gets back here,' he said. 'That'll be later this afternoon and I'd like you to be present. Steiner thinks this might be connected to the government case and I'm also going to ask Adam to come in.'

'Perhaps things on the case are about to turn our way,' said Conran, phlegmatically. 'I'll be in the area. Ring me on my cell phone when he arrives.'

When Conran had gone, Weisz phoned Fairley and relayed what he'd told Conran. Fairley agreed to meet them when Steiner appeared.

Chapter 49

Cape Town

After leaving their hire-car in Johannesburg, Steiner and Kirsty flew to Cape Town. On arrival they went to Brown's Hotel. From their room, Steiner phoned Weisz at his office.

'Bruce, James Steiner,' he said when Weisz answered. 'We're at the hotel. When can we meet?'

'Say about thirty minutes from now,' said Weisz. 'I've asked Conran and Fairley to join us if that's all right by you.'

'That's fine,' said Steiner. 'I'll see you then.' He replaced the receiver and turned to Kirsty. 'I'll see him at eight. He's asked Conran and Fairley to be there. I said that's all right but my mind goes back to what we said earlier about a link to the DSO. Such a link means knowing someone who works for the DSO, one of their agents.'

'Yes,' she said. 'Weisz, Conran and Fairley obviously know we're here and they're closely involved. We were also introduced to David Strauss but you've not seen him again. If Weisz is running a tight-lipped outfit then it's unlikely that others know about us. How does that sound?'

'At the moment we don't know anymore,' said Steiner. 'Anyone could be the direct or indirect link to the outsider I mentioned before, the one who has their trust. By indirect I mean that they referred to our involvement casually or inadvertently to someone who then told the outsider. But whatever it is, I'm about to meet Weisz, Conran and Fairley and I'll have to be careful what I say. Weisz has probably told them a bit about what happened and named Kallis.'

'Being careful is the difficulty,' said Kirsty. 'In a few words you can virtually tell them everything and you can't just sit there saying nothing.'

Steiner thought for moment and then said: 'This is how I'll play it. I'll repeat what I've already told Weisz, which is a man named Marc Kallis tried to kill me and then for some reason bolted. Such information is of little value and the DSO is hardly going to run off looking for Kallis. I might look a bit foolish but that's all they'll get until I know who I can trust.'

'So you won't tell them about our extrapolations,' she said.

'No,' said Steiner. 'I'm merely touching base with Weisz, that's all.'

'What about Smith?' she asked.

'I'll go to Durban as planned,' said Steiner. 'Weisz hasn't said anything to me about payment and that means I'm a free agent doing him a favour. I can take a break and go to Durban when I like. If something serious happens Weisz will be the first to know and I'll say I went on impulse with no time to alert anyone.'

'The ever-independent James Steiner,' said Kirsty smiling. 'What do you mean by serious?'

'You know the answer to that,' he said. 'It means Kallis killing Smith.'

'I'm going with you,' she said. 'If you get into trouble I want to be there.'

'I knew that was coming,' he said, leaning across and holding her hand. 'You are not going this time.' He got up and walked to the window. 'We're booking out of this place tomorrow. We'll make our own choice.'

'When are you leaving?' she asked.

'Get me a mid-morning ticket,' said Steiner. 'He looked at his watch. 'I'll go and see Weisz now.'

Chapter 50

Cape Town

When Steiner reached the DSO he was shown to Bruce Weisz's office by the security guard. Conran and Fairley were already there.

'It sounds as if you've had a hectic weekend,' said Weisz when they were all seated. 'Let me have it again. I'd like these guys to hear it from you.'

Steiner briefly described the events that had taken place from the time he had received the phone call from Marc Kallis to the call he had made to Weisz from the farm. He omitted any of the conclusions he and Kirsty had drawn.

'It's an interesting story,' said Weisz, 'and I don't think it's a coincidence that Kallis appeared so soon after you arrived here. Do you think there is a link between this and the work you are doing for the DSO?'

'Kallis made it clear that he wanted to kill me for killing his brother,' said Steiner, not being drawn. 'He appeared to be acting alone and only for that reason. I don't know how he knew I was here.'

'Did you kill his brother?' asked Weisz. 'Smith never gave me the details of how you got hold of the files.'

'I did,' said Steiner, 'after he tried to kill me. But that's got nothing to do with how he knew I'm here.'

'I was only confirming his alleged motive,' said Weisz. 'I wanted to eliminate anything else. There's nothing the DSO can really do about all this but I'm glad you told me about it. Kallis might still rise again and provide a link to your present case.'

'I phoned Peter Smith before I called you,' said Steiner. 'He told me he's coming down to see you in the morning.'

'Yes he is,' said Weisz. 'We have some things to discuss but he also suggested the people he has

121

investigating the five businessmen join forces with Adam and that we should forget about checking the unsubstantiated corruption charges against Hilton.' He looked at Fairley. 'Forgive me. I was going to tell you after this meeting. Before Hilton died he met Smith in Durban and asked him to investigate the activities of five prominent industrialists who he thought were heavily involved in organized crime. He said one man, Andrew Rohm, deserved special attention and cited him as the leader of their cartel.'

'That's very interesting and fine by me,' said Fairley. 'I'd very much like to see what he suggests. I think Hilton was clean.'

Weisz addressed Conran. 'What do you think of all this?'

Conran looked at Steiner. 'I am curious as to why Kallis pulled out with Kirsty Callard as a hostage when he was in a position to fill you full of lead. Do you have any idea?'

'The only thing I can think of is that he was surprised I went for him when he had his gun on me,' said Steiner. 'He might be the type who takes great delight in emphasizing the guilt of his chosen victim before killing them. Perhaps he felt robbed and was prepared to wait for another chance.'

'But he might have felt that he had something more urgent to attend to,' said Conran.

'That's a possibility,' said Steiner, 'but I can't think of what. He revealed nothing except the desire to destroy me.'

'We simply don't know what was in his mind except for that,' said Weisz. He faced Steiner. 'What are you going to do now on this case?'

'I can only examine the details Hilton gave Smith on those five men,' said Steiner. He glanced at Fairley. 'I think it would be good if Smith's people joined forces with Adam and I'll have to work closely with them. I think those men are definitely behind all this.'

'I'll let you know what Smith and I decide after our meeting tomorrow,' said Weisz. 'We'll take it from there. I think we can call it a day.'

Chapter 51

Pretoria

After speaking to Teichmann, Marc Kallis poured a drink and turned on the television. He was an avid rugby fan and enjoyed watching the last of the weekend fixtures on Sunday afternoon. After the games he switched to films. He watched a double-bill and when it was finished he thought about Peter Smith. His plan was to fly down on Monday morning, phone Smith's office to determine his whereabouts during the day and then act accordingly, either when Smith left the office or at his home. He had a photograph of Smith from Teichmann and his home address, a house up on the Berea where he lived with his wife. Kallis knew Durban reasonably well from his visits during university holidays, and the fights with local beach gangs, when he was always victorious, were a satisfying memory.

Kallis thought about Steiner and Callard and wondered what they were doing. By now they were probably together, an ineffectual force as far as he was concerned, only their word against his, and making their way back to Cape Town. He thought again about Smith and then it came to him. The perfect time to get him was before or as he left for work in the morning; he cursed himself for not having thought of it before. He could even have gone to Durban earlier and got Smith this evening but it was too late for that now. He had been too set on the plan he had made when he also had other things on his mind.

It was eight-thirty. Kallis went to the phone, reserved a seat on the ten-fifteen evening flight from Johannesburg to Durban and packed a small bag. It contained a change of clothes, personal items, his silenced Beretta *90two* pistol and two extra clips each filled with 9mmx19 Luger/Parabellum ammunition. He left the flat at nine.

When Kallis arrived in Durban he hired a car and drove to the city centre. He booked in at the Royal Hotel in Smith Street and ordered something to eat on room service. He then poured a Scotch and phoned Smith's home number. A woman answered.

'Hullo, I'm trying to contact Peter Smith?' said Kallis softly. 'Perhaps I can phone him at work tomorrow.'

'He's here now,' said the woman. 'I'm his wife. Do you want me to call him?'

'No,' said Kallis. 'I won't disturb him. I really wanted to make sure he's in town so that I can see him.

'He's flying to Cape Town at six-thirty in the morning on business,' said Mrs Smith. 'He'll be back after lunch. Shall I tell him who is calling?'

'I'll phone him then,' said Kallis. 'Thank you.' He replaced the receiver, glad he'd made the call and wondering why Smith was going to Cape Town. It could only be to do with the DSO. It now meant being at Smith's house no later than four-thirty to eliminate the risk of missing him.

After his meal Kallis showered and went to bed. He could feel the excitement taking hold.

Chapter 52

Monday, 10 August
Durban

At four o'clock, when it was still dark, Kallis rose and dressed in a navy shirt, denim jeans, jacket and loafers. He booked out of the hotel, went to his car parked in the street and soon picked up the old main road leading to the interior. He left the road at the university exit and in minutes was in the heart of the Berea, one of the most prized residential areas in Durban, and a road down from Acacia Avenue where Peter Smith lived. He stopped the car. The area was deathly quiet and he didn't want to draw attention to himself, unlikely as most people would be asleep in bed. After a while he drove to the end of the road, turned the corner and went up to the start of Acacia Avenue. Smith was at number 32. He went slowly along, saw the house, two storeys and set back at the end of a fifty-metre drive, and pulled up at the far end of the road. He turned off the engine and thought for a moment. Access to the property was easy, no heavy gates and wrought-iron balustrades like other similar areas in Johannesburg, and he decided to go into the grounds and wait there, rather than in the car. He thought about the servants, if Smith had any, and he knew he'd have to get rid of them if they appeared uninvited.

Kallis left the car and after sticking the silenced Beretta inside his belt under the jacket walked along to Smith's house. He went through the gate up past the side of the building and to the rear. The garden was well-vegetated and two willow trees partly blocked the servant's quarters some forty metres from the house. He paused, listening, the silence infinitely peaceful, and then went to the kitchen door. It was locked and after a moment he went and found

126

a vantage point under the awning attached to the adjacent double garage. From there he had a clear view of the path to the quarters and the back elevation of the house. He sat down, expecting to wait for an hour before there were signs of life. If it came from the house he'd have to knock on the door to get in and hope whoever was inside thought he was a servant. If he was interrupted by a servant he'd simply let them open the door and then dispose of them.

Chapter 53

Cape Town

Shortly after Kallis started his wait under the awning in Peter Smith's garden, Steiner got out bed, put on a gown and took a seat near the window. For the past hour he had lain awake thinking of Smith and the belief he had that Kallis was going after him. The only consolation he now had that nothing would happen to Smith before he reached Durban was that Smith would be in Cape Town. Since Kallis had first rung on Saturday morning he had given little or no thought to the job he had been asked to do for the DSO. He knew he couldn't stay in Durban indefinitely, certainly no more than a couple of days, and that was frustrating. It wouldn't look good if a third minister was killed and no attempt was made on Smith's life. He couldn't be at Smith's side constantly, a nursemaid, and Kallis was a clever operator who would only strike when he was reasonably sure he could get in and out without being stopped. In short, Kallis held all the cards, like the person assassinating the government ministers. He wondered where that person was now, when he was planning to kill again and the real people behind him. He and Kirsty could be way off the mark thinking there was a possible connection to Teichmann and Rohm and it could be people that they had never heard about, perhaps political enemies of the ANC and, by definition, the government.

Steiner had been at the window for close to an hour when Kirsty woke up and joined him. She was wearing a nightshirt to the middle of her thighs and the most attractive woman he'd ever known. She sat on his lap, resting her cheek on his head and the feel of her full body immediately dispelled the thoughts that had occupied him. He ran his hand up her thigh and drew her closer, kissing her softly on the cheek, slowly taking his lips to hers. As his hand went to her proud breasts and played with her nipples she slid off his lap and said: 'Let's go back to bed. You can have what you want there. There's no hurry and you'll think of me while you're away.'

Chapter 54

Durban

It was five-thirty when Kallis, resting in a half-sleep, lifted his head off his arm and looked down the garden where he had heard a sound. In seconds a young, black male dressed in regular servant's clothes and bare-footed appeared and walked towards the house. Kallis, relatively concealed, waited until the servant reached the door. When the servant produced a set of keys from the pocket of his shorts, Kallis drew the Beretta and hanging it at his side moved with the speed of a cat. In a few long strides he drew close to the black and in a harsh whisper said: 'Stay still and give me the keys.'

Startled at seeing the white, the servant took a step back and lamely held out the keys. 'Who are you?' he managed in a subdued tone.

Kallis took the keys, placed the muzzle of the gun against the black's chest in front of the heart and with meticulous deliberation fired twice, killing him as he was about to scream. As the body slumped, Kallis held it and lowered it to the ground. He dragged the body off the stone slabs round a trellis and dumped it out of sight. He waited a moment then went to the door, unlocked it and slipped inside. He was in a scullery. There was only silence and after adjusting to the dark passed through the kitchen into a hall from which a flight of stairs led to the bedrooms above. Three open doors in the hall revealed at a glance a large sitting room at the front, a dining room behind it and a study with banks of books on shelves reaching from waist height to the ceiling.

Kallis checked his watch. It was five-forty and he wondered what had happened to Smith. It was a good thirty minutes to the airport. He was about to go into the study to wait when a passage light went on at the top of stairs. He heard someone walking and then a door being closed.

Kallis stepped inside the study and after ten minutes a person came to the stairs and started coming down. Kallis took a quick look and saw a middle-aged woman in a nightdress. She could only be Smith's wife and he let her reach the hall and walk into the kitchen. When he heard water running from a tap he went swiftly to the stairs.

On the first floor Kallis saw a long passage flanked by a series of rooms. One of the rooms was open and the light illuminated a swathe of the passage carpet. All was quiet and he went swiftly to the open door, peering carefully round the edge when he reached it. On the far side of a double bedroom Peter Smith, his back to Kallis and standing fully dressed in front of a mirror, was adjusting his tie. Kallis stepped into the room and said: 'Peter Smith, Marc Kallis.'

Smith went still and then turned, his hands slowly going down to hang at his sides. 'What the hell do you want?' he said.

Admiring Smith's calm, Kallis said: 'I want you for being behind the murder of my brother John and for destroying the lives of people I know.'

'And you're the man on the farm,' said Smith. 'James Steiner said you might turn up but I didn't think you would.'

Kallis walked further into the room. He liked it when his adversaries showed spunk. 'You're the one who won't be turning up anywhere,' he said. 'Steiner's next. He's out of his league, he and the girl.'

'So you've met her as well,' said Smith. 'Did you find her attractive?'

'I'll have her after I've dealt with him,' said Kallis. 'I'm sure it'll be a pleasure.' He levelled the Beretta at Smith.

'Who are the people you know?' said Smith. 'I think they're using you to do something they couldn't. It's not a

131

coincidence that avenging your brother's death and punishing those who upset your friends are together at the top of your agenda.'

'If you must know, they're from the group,' said Kallis. 'But I'm here and you're going to die.'

'So you don't think that your brother and his masters in the group were murderers,' said Smith.

'Peter, you're running late.' Both men heard the call from Smith's wife.

Kallis turned slightly towards the door and Smith took his chance. He bent low, reaching smoothly under his pillow, his fingers taking hold of a small revolver and jerking it free. But before he could bring the gun to bear, Kallis took a giant step forwards, savagely cutting down on Smith's extended arm, breaking his grip on the weapon and sending him to his knees.

'Nice try,' gutted Kallis, 'but not good enough. He aimed the gun and fired twice, the bullets penetrating Smith's brain, driving him back in a heap, a sack of waste, his mouth a rictus in death.

For a moment Kallis looked at Smith. He then walked to the door was about to go through into the passage when he heard someone coming to the room. Without stopping he entered the passage and as expected saw Smith's wife. She came to a halt, raised her hands to a mouth and stared at him. He moved closer to her and said: 'If you hadn't seen me I was going to take a chance and let you live. Now there is no option.' He shot her twice through the heart and watched as she dropped, first to her knees and then slowly onto her side. He'd never wanted to kill a woman.

Kallis left the house the way he'd come in, locking the door and throwing the keys into a bush; anything to give him more time. The job had been done and he was satisfied. With Smith expected to be in Cape Town he had a start of a few hours, during which time he would be back in Pretoria. It was then a case of fitting in Steiner.

In thirty-five minutes Kallis reached the airport and two hours later after collecting his car at OR Thambo Airport in Johannesburg he was in Pretoria.

Chapter 55

Cape Town

After breakfast Steiner and Kirsty booked out of Brown's Hotel and drove into the city. They looked at a few hotels they liked and reserved a room at the Mandarin Hotel near the beachfront, in a side road off the main street.

'This should do for a few days while I find out where I'm going on this case,' said Steiner. He and Kirsty had just been shown their room.

'I'm sure something will come up,' said Kirsty. 'Kallis is not the type to be put off and neither are those we think are behind him. If it is Teichmann and he is connected to the people behind the murders of the ministers, they will know all about what happened on the farm and someone somewhere is surely going to raise their head. That could be the lead you want.'

'Yes,' said Steiner. 'But while I'm waiting I must have another go persuading Smith his life is in danger. Whatever he chooses to do after I've seen him is up to him and I can't do anymore. I can't spend more than a day in Durban. I don't want Weisz on my back.'

'What will you do when you return?' she said.

'I'm going to pay Teichmann a visit,' said Steiner, 'and tell him that I know he was behind Kallis. I'll soon find out the truth and I'm prepared to bear the consequences if I'm shown to be wrong.'

'How will you find out the truth?' she asked.

'Don't worry, I'll be gentle. But I'm aware that you'll get nowhere if you don't act on your convictions.'

She looked at her watch. 'It's time you were going,' she said. 'I'll drive you to the airport.' She put her arms round him. 'Take care of yourself.'

Chapter 56

Pretoria

Shortly after reaching his flat Marc Kallis rang Teichmann on his mobile.

'Johan, Marc Kallis. Smith is finished. I'm back in Pretoria.'

'Excellent,' said Teichmann. 'Were there any hitches?'

'Smith's wife and his servant got in the way and I had to kill them,' said Kallis as if he had just come in from the local cinema. 'There's certainly nothing on me.'

'So now it's Steiner,' said Teichmann, now impressed by the way Kallis operated. He had wondered if he'd made the wrong choice after Kallis had missed out on Steiner at the farm. 'When do you plan that?'

'I'll give it some thought today,' said Kallis. 'I want to be sure this time. He's more of a challenge than I gave him credit for.'

'That's good thinking,' said Teichmann. 'He is certainly not an amateur. The way he worked his way through some of the best men in the group proves that.' He was quiet and then said: 'There is a chance Steiner will come after you even though he can't prove anything. That might give him the advantage. I think you should stay somewhere else, a hotel perhaps, until this is over. What do you think?'

'I think I will,' said Kallis after a moment's thought. 'I'll stay in hotels until Steiner's removed. I'll tell you where I am when I decide on how I'm going to get him. I'm going to Cape Town and I'll phone you from there.' He replaced the handset and poured a drink. He phoned Andrew Rohm at home.

'Marc Kallis,' he said when Rohm answered. 'Smith will not upset you again.'

'That leaves Steiner,' said Rohm. 'He's the one I really want.'

'I've just spoken to Teichmann and I'll work out a plan for Steiner and his girlfriend today,' said Kallis. 'I'll first have to find out if they're still staying at Brown's Hotel. I see no reason why I can't finish him off in the next twenty-four hours. I'm going to Cape Town. I'll stay in hotels until this business is over and the dust has settled. You have my mobile number.'

'That suits me perfectly,' said Rohm ambiguously. 'Keep me informed. If you can't get me here you can get me on my mobile.' He gave Kallis the number.

Chapter 57

Durban

When Steiner reached Durban he hired a car and drove into the city. It was nearly twelve and he found a place to wait in a coffee bar. He bought a copy of the Natal Mercury, flicked through the first few pages and then thought about Kallis. He was now certain that at some time during the day Kallis would arrive in Durban and try to kill Smith. If he was Kallis, the first thing would be to get some idea of Smith's movements during the day by contacting his office and plan accordingly. Kallis would know where Smith lived and it really came down to getting him in the office car park, which could carry more risk than he wanted, or when he got home. As he thought about it he ruled out the car park because there was no access to it from the street by foot and office security wouldn't let anyone in without a pass.

After an hour in the coffee bar Steiner walked around the city centre and along the esplanade. He had fond memories of the place but had no desire to return. He was now firmly committed to life in London and running seminars for business people on the value and development of mind and body coordination. It was two-thirty when he phoned Smith's office number.

'Janice, James Steiner,' he said when Smith's secretary answered. 'I'm trying to get hold of Peter.'

'James, I'm glad you phoned,' said Janice. 'Peter's not here and he didn't go to Cape Town as planned. I spoke to Bruce Weisz thirty minutes ago. I've tried his house but there's no reply. I think he must have been called away on something urgent. That happens in this business.'

'Have you tried his mobile phone?' said Steiner. 'I know he was going to Cape Town and expected him back by now.'

'I have but there's no answer,' she said.

Steiner thought for a moment and then said: 'I'll ring you again in thirty minutes. You can also phone me on my mobile. I'm going up to his house. His maid might know something.'

Steiner went quickly to his car. For the first time he felt he'd left it too late. He picked up the old main road to Pietermaritzburg and left it at the Ridge Road turn-off, the most direct route to Smith's house in Acacia Avenue. He had been there once before and had met Smith's wife Julia, a charming, attractive woman in her early-fifties, a few years younger than Smith. He soon reached the road he wanted, drove slowly along it and stopped fifty metres from the house. Smith's car wasn't in the driveway which meant he either hadn't used it or he was not there. The area was deserted, not unusual he thought for the time of day, and he went at a half-run through the gate and up to the front door. He pressed the bell and when no one came he went round the back to the kitchen door. He tried it, found it locked and ran down the path to the servant's quarters. The door to the only room was also locked and he started back to the house. He was a few metres from it when he saw the servant's bare feet poking out from behind a shrub. He went to it and when he saw the body with blood on the chest his worst fears were confirmed.

Knowing he wouldn't find the keys on the man, Steiner went to the door, burst it open and entered the house. He looked quickly in the ground-floor rooms and then went up the stairs. When he reached the passage he saw Julia lying on the carpet and, sure that she was dead, went to the open door. In the far corner he saw the body of his ex-boss. He went over and knelt next to it. It was a sad moment in his life. Kallis didn't waste time. He was ahead of the game.

Steiner left the body, went down the stairs and found a phone in the hall. He rang Bruce Weisz in Cape Town.

'Bruce, James Steiner. I'm afraid Peter Smth's dead. He was murdered.'

'Where are you?' said Weisz. 'Now I know why he didn't turn up.'

'I'm at his house,' said Steiner. 'His wife Julia and the servant have also been shot dead.'

'I know who you think did it,' said Weisz. 'I thought you were holding something back at the meeting yesterday. You believed Kallis would go after Smith and that's why you phoned him before contacting me. Am I right?'

'Yes,' said Steiner. He decided to take a chance and trust Weisz. 'You said yesterday that you didn't think it a coincidence Kallis knew I was here. You asked if I thought there was a link to the work I'm doing for the DSO. I didn't say it then but I believe there is a link. That means he is getting his information from someone who has connections in the DSO and who also wants me out of the way. That person was using Kallis.'

'So someone in the DSO is directly or indirectly passing on information to an outsider,' said Weisz.

'Yes,' said Steiner. 'And the outsider is in some way connected to the people who are killing the ministers.'

'Who do you think is the DSO man?' asked Weisz.

'If anyone can answer that it is you,' said Steiner. 'I've only met Conran, Fairley and Strauss.'

'I trust them,' said Weisz, without elaborating. 'Tell me more about this outsider. Surely you have a better idea than any of us of this person's identity. You were deeply involved in the Cartwright case and the workings of the group. Kallis' brother was a group operator. Could this person be an ex-member of the group?'

'Yes,' said Steiner. 'We'll talk about it when I see you in Cape Town. Can you arrange for your people to sort out the mess here? The bodies have to be removed. You'll find

Smith in the upstairs bedroom, his wife in the passage and the black servant in a flower bed near the back door.'

'I'll do that now,' said Weisz. 'When will you be back?'

'I'll get the earliest flight and phone you,' said Steiner. 'Kirsty and I have changed hotels. We're now in the Mandarin off the main street. It's not far from the DSO.'

'I don't blame you,' said Weisz. 'I can meet you there this evening. You probably don't know but the President named Delaware's replacement this morning. He is Peter Cochrane. I believe he is going to replace Dredge and Hamilton tomorrow. It will be very interesting to see if that stops the murders. Dredge and Hamilton still refuse to be shifted to safe houses and have extra guards. It's a case of hubris on their part.'

'Let's hope it protects them,' said Steiner. 'I don't think it will. I'll ring you later.' He put down the phone. He'd taken a chance with Weisz but now after the conversation he felt he'd done the right thing. He needed friends who had authority and he liked dealing with Weisz.

Steiner phoned SAA, booked a seat on the five o'clock flight to Cape Town and left the house for the airport.

Chapter 58

Cape Town

Weisz thought about what Steiner had said after speaking to him. It was not Smith's death that occupied his thoughts but the possibility that someone in the DSO was revealing what was going on in the agency to an outsider. Smith was history and there was no point in dwelling on him. Weisz thought about Conran, Fairley and Strauss. He had told Steiner he trusted them. Strauss was not involved in the government case and knew nothing about Steiner's movements. He had known Conran for four years and he didn't know a more dedicated and loyal agent, one who ruthlessly went after society's arch-criminals and who he could trust with his life. Fairley was new in South Africa and had excellent references from New Scotland Yard. It was highly unlikely that he had had the time and inclination to form links with the underworld and betray his new employers. As he thought about it, the more Weisz felt he could trust both men and that if there was a leak it came from someone else, a person to whom they had casually mentioned Steiner's presence. He called Conran and Fairley into his office to update them on what was going on.

'I've just had a call from Steiner,' said Weisz when Conran and Fairley were seated. 'He is in Durban and some thirty minutes ago found Smith, his wife and their servant dead at his house. All three had been shot.'

'Steiner anticipated it,' said Fairley. 'I didn't think he was being entirely open. It could only have been Kallis.'

'It certainly was Kallis,' said Weisz 'I have no doubt that he'll resume where he left off and hunt Steiner. I'll be seeing him later when he returns to Cape Town.'

'That doesn't tell us anything about the ministers,' said Conran, 'but it will distract Steiner enough to make him ineffective. He can't look after his own life and chase after an assassin in an unrelated case at the same time.'

'I can only wait and see,' said Weisz. 'I want him to carry on as before. It's too late to find a replacement now and you two are busy. I'd like you to keep this to yourselves for the time being. I wanted to keep you up to speed.'

Chapter 59

Cape Town

When Conran got back to his office after seeing Weisz he dialled Paul Bale's direct number at work. The NDPP answered.

'Your friend's assassin is busy,' said Conran casually. 'He had a go at Steiner yesterday, failed, and a short while ago killed Peter Smith of the DSO, his wife and their servant at their house in Durban.'

'I didn't think he'd move so soon,' said Bale. 'Perhaps he needs the work.'

'I think it's the money,' said Conran.

'That's what I mean,' said Bale. 'We're not talking about chicken feed. What a sum for a few hours' work.'

'He'll now return to Steiner and be doing us a favour,' said Conran. 'It'll keep Steiner guessing and dilute the concentration he can give to my guy.'

'Yes, that's one way of putting it,' said Bale. 'I assume you heard all this from Weisz. Steiner must know the identity of the guy.'

'His name is Marc Kallis,' said Conran. 'Steiner killed his brother when he was acquiring the files from the group. Steiner thought Kallis might go after Smith too and he went to Durban. He found Smith dead and told Weisz.'

'This is not good for the person I'm representing,' said Bale. 'If Steiner knows who is behind Kallis it could lead to him.'

'I don't think Steiner does know,' said Conran. 'He didn't say as much when I saw him yesterday in Weisz's office. But I heard something else that is very interesting. Before Smith died he told Weisz that Hilton had visited him in Durban and asked him to investigate five eminent businessmen regarding serious organized crime. Hilton named Andrew Rohm, who we've all heard of, as the leader. Is he the man you're representing?'

For a while Bale didn't answer. There was no harm Conran knowing about Rohm and it could make him even more useful. 'Yes,' he said, 'but that doesn't make Hilton innocent. Hilton was using Smith to deflect the heat from his own illegal activities.' He felt a bit of a fool. Conran would have soon found out. He changed the subject. 'Is your guy ready for tomorrow?'

'He would have told me if he wasn't,' said Conran. 'I see that Delaware's replacement has been announced, Peter Cochrane. I believe the replacements for Dredge and Hamilton will be named tomorrow. The President is doing as requested but it might not save Dredge if your friend wants all four dead regardless.'

'I'm following orders,' said Bale. 'You're getting paid a considerable sum for doing the same thing. Don't forget that.'

'I won't,' said Conran bluntly. 'I'll tell you when it's done.'

Chapter 60

Cape Town

When Conran had gone, Bale phoned Rohm.

'I've just had a call from John Conran,' said Bale. 'Teichmann's guy Marc Kallis has been busy. He missed Steiner but managed to kill Smith in Durban.'

'So I've heard,' said Rohm. 'Who told Conran?'

'Weisz,' said Bale. 'Steiner went to Durban because he thought Kallis would make a try for Smith. He found Smith, his wife and the servant dead and informed Weisz. If Steiner knows Teichmann is behind Kallis he will soon be on his doorstep to put it mildly. That could blow everything apart.'

'I've spoken to Kallis,' said Rohm, feeling pleased with himself. 'He assured me that neither Kirsty Callard nor Steiner knows about Teichmann. The business at the farm is their word against his and I'm sure he didn't leave any tracks in Durban. He's far too clever to make that sort of mistake. He will simply resume where he left off regarding Steiner and wrap things up in the next twenty-four hours.'

'I hope you are right,' said Bale. 'There is something else. Before Hilton died he asked Smith to investigate you and your friends' business activities. Smith told Weisz and was going to see him about it.'

Rohm's earlier fear was justified but he wasn't going to show it. 'They will not find anything on me or my colleagues,' he said. 'They're not in our class.'

Bale had expected the reply. 'Does Teichmann know you have spoken to Kallis?'

'No,' said Rohm. 'It will stay that way until I'm sure everything has been satisfactorily concluded. I hope things are on schedule for tomorrow.'

'Conran gave me his assurance,' said Bale. 'He also told me that the replacement for Dredge will be announced tomorrow.'

'As you know that won't affect anything,' said Rohm. 'Just tell me when Dredge is dead and I'll look after Kallis and Teichmann.'

Chapter 61

Cape Town

When Steiner reached Cape Town he went directly to the Mandarin Hotel. He found Kirsty seated in the main reception area reading a book. She got up and held out her arms when she saw him.

'I'm so glad to see you,' she said as they embraced. 'I can't help being worried about you. Did you see Smith?'

'Smith's dead,' he said. 'His wife Julia and their servant were also shot dead. Kallis was well ahead of me. I didn't think he'd go after Smith first thing this morning.'

'So they were killed at Smith's house,' she said. 'I wonder if Kallis knew Smith was coming to Cape Town.'

'I think he did and made sure he got him before he left for the airport,' said Steiner. 'Smith's secretary told me that Weisz had phoned, saying Smith hadn't arrived. She hadn't been able to contact Smith and I went straight to the house.'

'What did you do after finding the bodies?'

'I phoned Weisz and gave him the news,' said Steiner. 'He'll take care of things. We spoke for a while and I think he agrees with us that there is a link between Kallis and someone in the DSO. He also believes there is an outsider. I'm going to see Weisz later, either here or at his office. I'll ring him. Would you like dinner now or after I've seen Weisz?'

'See Weisz first and get it out of the way,' she said. 'I don't want him hanging over us now you're back.'

Steiner phoned Weisz and arranged to meet him in the hotel in thirty minutes.

Chapter 62

Cape Town

When Weisz arrived at the Mandarin Hotel, he and Steiner found a quiet table in the hotel bar and ordered drinks.

'I think things are beginning to move,' said Weisz when they had been served, 'and if I dare say so it rests on Kallis's primeval desire to avenge his brother's death. I now believe Kallis is fuelled by someone, your outsider, who has links, perhaps through someone else, to a DSO agent.

'That's the line I'm going to pursue,' said Steiner. 'When Kirsty and I were reunited on the farm after Kallis drove off with her we both thought that Smith was in danger and that's why I phoned him. He didn't buy it and I decided then to go to Durban. I didn't say that when I met you, Conran and Fairley because I didn't know who I could trust.'

'Well you can trust me for what it's worth,' said Weisz. 'I think you can trust those two but in this world you never know until they prove it. I can't believe it is Strauss. I trust you because Smith brought you in reluctantly at my request and completely from the cold. Now back to the outsider. Who do you suspect?'

'Johan Teichmann, former head of operations in the defunct group,' said Steiner. 'Do you know him?'

'I heard about him during the trials,' said Weisz, 'but I never met him.'

Steiner went on. 'I think Teichmann knows who is behind the ministers and that they have a source in the DSO, exactly how and in what form I don't know. I believe that those behind the ministers are the five businessmen named by Hilton, specifically Rohm, and that Hilton was killed because he got too close to them.'

'And you're going to start with Teichmann,' said Weisz.

'Yes,' said Steiner. 'But keep that to yourself for now. I have met him before and he would know Marc Kallis. I'd work on that and see what I can get out of him. It would be a big break for us if he reveals what we suspect about Rohm.'

'What will you do when you see Teichmann?' asked Weisz. 'Kallis would have kept him updated on what happened at the farm and with Smith. He will be prepared for your visit. If Kallis didn't tell you or Kirsty about him you will be acting on pure supposition and he'll simply laugh you out of court.'

'I'm aware of that,' said Steiner. 'I'll play my hand accordingly.'

'I won't ask anymore,' said Weisz. 'Don't tell him you are working with me. Smith was pretty good at denying your existence.'

Steiner laughed. 'I'll not let you down. If we're finished I want to see Kirsty.'

'I heard she was married to Jan Krige,' said Weisz. 'She seems to be quite a girl.'

'Yes,' said Steiner. 'She divorced him.'

Chapter 63

Cape Town

'Bruce Weisz now knows as much as we do,' said Steiner. He and Kirsty were in their bedroom at the Mandarin Hotel.

'You decided to trust him,' said Kirsty. 'What made you do that?'

'My intuition,' said Steiner. 'I don't have the same feeling yet about Conran and Fairley but that might change. If I'm to resolve this business it helps to have someone with authority inside the agency I'm working with.'

'When are you planning to see Teichmann?' she asked.

'Tomorrow morning after the replacements have been named for Dredge and Hamilton,' said Steiner. 'That might come in useful when I'm with him.'

'One of them might be dead by then,' she said. 'The President will have a lot to answer for if that happens. He could have acted more swiftly.'

'If I hadn't gone after Smith I would have tackled Teichmann yesterday,' said Steiner. 'I had no choice but I'll still find it hard if another minister is killed and I feel I could have prevented it.'

'Don't you want me along?' she said, her lovely lips parting in a smile.

'I do but only when I think it's not dangerous,' said Steiner.

'You took me along when you went after John Kallis and my husband,' she said.

'I asked you to go round the back,' he said. 'I didn't expect you to show yourself and take part in the action.' He held her. 'Actually, I'm glad you did. I was in trouble. How would you like to go out for something to eat?'

'I'd love to,' she said. 'There're a few nice restaurants nearby.'

Chapter 64

Colin Dredge lived in a large house near Stellenbosch. It was set in five acres of ground and the garden was the envy of most who were invited to visit the place. As well as oak and jacaranda trees, a small fruit orchard, shrubs and flower gardens, the grounds boasted a well-sized swimming pool and two all-weather tennis courts. The front of the property was adorned by a wrought-iron balustrade and double gates, and the remainder of the perimeter, bordered by natural forest and farm land, was demarcated by barbed-wire fencing. Dredge and his second-wife Janet, an attractive woman twenty-five years younger than him, lived alone. They had two servants, each with quarters set apart from the house at the rear. They were both dedicated professionals and for that reason had decided not to have children.

When Hilton was murdered, Dredge had reluctantly accepted the appointment of a personal bodyguard, an ex-policeman named de Villiers. As Dredge spent most of his working days in the houses of parliament where security was stringent, he only needed de Villiers to drive him to and from work, at seven and six-thirty, and to conduct random checks of the premises at night. The man used a small office next to the garage to rest between patrols. At weekends, de Villiers was at the house during the day and another man at night.

At five-thirty, a little before dawn, a man dressed in black parked his car a few hundred metres down the public road from the house and walked to the gates. He could just see the building through the trees and after a moment in the shadows climbed over the gates, entered the grounds and slowly moved up the right flank until he had a full view of the front and left side elevations of the house and the garage. When he had received a note on the property he had carried out a brief survey and what he saw wasn't new to him. He went closer and found a concealed position fifty metres from the garage. He sat down and waited.

At six-thirty, lights went on in the house and just before seven de Villiers appeared at the front of the garage. He opened the double doors, revealing a new Mercedes Benz 500 SL coupe, a car that most could only dream about, and then went onto the verandah and to the front door. The door opened and Dredge came out. He greeted de Villiers and followed him down the steps and along to the car. As soon as they disappeared inside, the man in black left his position, swiftly closing the distance to the garage. When he got there, de Villiers standing by the open rear door of the car and Dredge about to take his seat, a silenced Beretta 90two 9mmx19 Luger/Parabellum semi-automatic pistol appeared mercurially in his right hand. Before they could react the man said: 'Dredge, this is not personal.'

The man levelled the gun and fired twice into the head of each man, their mouths half-open, expecting sound that never came, the bullets fusing together, the tiny popping noises almost one. The bodies, momentarily held in mock suspension, finally fell to the concrete floor, the arms splaying to their sides in unison like those of a conductor giving a virtuoso performance in front of a packed house.

For a moment the man looked at what he had done, cold satisfaction lighting his face, three ministers dead and one left. He turned, left the garage, and returned the way he had come in. He soon reached his car and after a U-turn went from the area, leaving only silence to accompany the first light of dawn.

153

Chapter 65

The President's office
Cape Town

Dredge's maid found the bodies of the two men thirty minutes after they were shot. She ran to the house and woke Janet who after seeing the damage for herself rang the police. The President was notified and his head of security, Barry Tyson, informed Weisz at the DSO.

'So they've struck again,' said the President. 'These people were going to get him regardless of whether I comply with their demands. What did Weisz have to say for himself?' He and Tyson were alone in his office.

'He thinks they are close to getting the people behind all this,' said Tyson, 'but he wouldn't elaborate. We'll have to give him some slack. We're not spoilt for options. Are you still going to name the two replacements?'

'No,' said the President. 'I don't want the public or my ministers to think I'm obeying a set of instructions. I'll wait a couple of days. When these men are caught they'll pay heavily for this.'

'You should insist that Hamilton's moved to a safe house,' said Tyson. 'He must be made to understand that they are going to kill him and that he has to be in a box.'

'For how long?' said the President. 'He'll have to come out eventually and they'll get him then. Stay on Weisz's back. I want a daily progress report from him. There's another press briefing later today.'

'Yes,' said Tyson. 'He got up and looked at the President. 'If there is not an arrest very soon it won't only be the media demanding answers. The opposition parties and members of your own party the ANC will start to clamour for your resignation. Your head will be on the block. You are on the edge of the abyss and if these people nail Hamilton you're finished. There is not even a suspect.'

Chapter 66

Cape Town

Steiner and Kirsty had just got of bed when the phone rang. Steiner answered and was surprised to hear Weisz on the line.

'They've got Colin Dredge,' said Weisz. 'He and his police guard were shot dead in his garage forty-five minutes ago. I'm going over there now but there won't be any evidence. When are you going to see Teichmann?'

'The President won't name the replacements now Dredge is dead so I won't wait,' said Steiner. 'I'll fly to Pretoria this morning.'

'Good luck,' said Weisz. 'Let me know how you get on. The President's on my back.'

'I'm not surprised,' said Steiner. 'This stuff hits the headlines everyday and people are starting to call for him to go. I'm not sure he'll manage to keep them at bay when Dredge's death is announced. He has no answers and at the very least needs a group or someone to blame. I'll be in contact.' He replaced the receiver and looked at Kirsty. 'You can guess what that was about. Dredge's dead, shot at his home forty-five minutes ago.'

'I'm sorry,' said Kirsty. 'I'll book your seat to Pretoria. Teichmann's our only chance.'

Steiner nodded and started for the bathroom. 'Thank you,' he said. 'Let's have breakfast before I leave. I don't like working on an empty stomach. I had enough of that in Japan.'

She smiled. 'It didn't do you any harm.'

Chapter 67

Cape Town

'Colin Dredge is dead,' said Conran when Bale answered his direct line at work. 'His bodyguard had to go with him.'

'I'll tell my friend and let you know when to let your guy loose on the next one,' said Bale. 'We're nearly at the end of all this.'

'Did you pass on what I told you to Rohm?' said Conran.

'Yes,' said Bale. 'Kallis had already told him. He was also assured by Kallis that Callard and Steiner don't know who is priming him. I don't think he's surprised the DSO plan to investigate his affairs. And if they are it doesn't worry him'

'Such confidence,' said Conran. 'So he's in direct contact with Kallis.'

'I believe so,' said Bale. 'But the guy who assigned Kallis doesn't know that.'

'Do you know the name of the person?' asked Conran.

'No,' lied Bale, 'Anyway, it's of no concern to you. Just keep on doing your job. The less we know about the others in all this the better.'

'Let me know when to move,' said Conran. 'I need the money.'

Chapter 68

The President's office
Cape Town

'Hamilton is staying put,' said the President. Tyson had just returned to his office after speaking to Weisz. 'It is what I expected. He refuses to bow down to murderers. I have to accept his wishes but he doesn't object to two guards on him round the clock with immediate effect. Pass that on to Weisz.'

'I'll do it now,' said Tyson. 'He'll be giving us a twelve-hour report, morning and evening from today.'

Chapter 69

Cape Town

After the call from Conran, Paul Bale rang Rohm in Johannesburg. When Rohm answered he said: 'I've just heard from Conran. Colin Dredge is dead.'

'I'm pleased,' said Rohm. 'When I first thought of this I didn't think it would actually happen. I'm still surprised at how easy it is to kill these people.'

'You only have to look at John Kennedy, his brother Robert, Machel of Mozambique, Ghandi, Bhutto and others to know that,' said Bale. 'Ronald Regan and the Pope were lucky.' He paused then continued. 'I don't think the President will announce the replacements this morning as expected. He's got too much pride for that.'

'The strategy of ours is primarily to give the President a chance to replace four of the most powerful men in the cabinet with the people we want,' said Rohm. 'This has been made perfectly clear to him and at some stage he has to put in the guys we want because we're playing the tune. I'm certain they'll be named in the next few days. It restricts my operations when I do not have allies in government and that includes the President.'

'I told Conran I'd let him know when to complete the process,' said Bale. 'When do you want it done?'

'My reasoning is this,' said Rohm. 'There'll be pressure on the President to stick Hamilton in a safe place and he has to show that he is trying. If he manages to persuade Hamilton to give up his freedom - something very important to Hamilton as it was to the others - it will have to be done immediately otherwise there's no point. If it's not done this morning they're not going to and we can choose our time, Thursday or Friday. See if you can find

out what happens and let you know. I'll make a decision
then.'

Chapter 70

Pretoria

Steiner caught the ten o'clock flight to Johannesburg, hired a car at the airport and reached Pretoria at eleven. He firmly believed a meeting with Teichmann was the best chance he had of finding the person who was killing the ministers. He could also try and find out where Kallis lived and pay him a visit but Kallis was essentially a pawn with only Teichmann's name to offer him, if he could get it out of him. If his efforts with Teichmann failed for whatever reason the only real remaining course of action was to have a go at Rohm.

When Steiner reached Teichmann's road he parked a short distance from the house and walked to the side gate. He entered, went round to the front door and pressed the bell. A black servant opened the door.

'May I see Johan Teichmann?' said Steiner, noting the empty reception room.

'Is he expecting you?' asked the servant. 'He's very busy at the moment.'

'I want to see him now,' said Steiner. 'Show me to him.' He moved past the servant.

The servant hesitated, looked round nervously and then said: 'Follow me.' He walked past Steiner to the passage and went along it and to the open door of a large study. Steiner had been there before. Seated at his desk and staring at a computer screen was Teichmann. He turned his head, showing surprise when he saw Steiner.

'I didn't think I'd see you again,' he said. 'I heard you were living in England. What brings you back to this part of the world?'

Steiner waited for the servant to depart and then walked into the room. 'You know the answer to that,' he said. 'You

161

know very well that the DSO asked me to investigate the killings of the government ministers. I'm sure you know that Colin Dredge was added to the list this morning.'

'I don't know what you mean,' said Teichmann, leaning back in his leather-bound chair, his demeanour calm. 'Someone's been feeding you fairy stories.'

'I'll start at the beginning,' said Steiner. 'When you heard I'd arrived, you asked Marc Kallis to kill me for being instrumental in bringing the group to its knees and incarcerating many of your friends listed in the white file, File A. I know you're behind Kallis because he told me when he tried to kill me on the farm. He'd also told my friend, Kirsty Callard. Kallis blew it, or rather bottled out for some reason, and went on to kill Peter Smith in Durban.' Steiner walked closer. 'The only way you could have known I and Callard were in Cape Town was through the DSO, directly or indirectly.'

Teichmann laughed briefly, a guttural inflection. 'You're pissed off because I was innocent. Your boss couldn't find me in the file and that drove him crazy. I've never heard of Marc Kallis. I only know a John Kallis, the man you murdered, an act for which you should have been prosecuted and convicted. You also killed Jan Krige, or was it his wife?'

Steiner was quiet, his eyes on Teichmann. He knew it would come to this. His eyes dropped to the desk. He took two steps forward and before Teichmann could move, picked up the mobile phone lying close to Teichmann's hand. Steiner smiled and said: 'I think this might tell me something.'

As he pressed the button for contacts, Teichmann came angrily to his feet. 'That's mine,' he rasped. 'You've no right to storm in here, accuse me of something of which I have no knowledge and grab my phone. I'm calling the police.'

162

'Sit down,' said Steiner brutally, looking at the little screen and scrolling down. 'Make a move to your phone and I'll take you apart.' He read more and then said: 'That's strange, there are two numbers listed for a Marc Kallis.' He grinned mockingly. 'Maybe there're two of them.'

'So what does that prove?' said Teichmann defiantly. 'His brother might have given it to me in case I couldn't contact him. I don't remember.'

'You also received two calls from one of Marc Kallis's numbers, the land line,' said Steiner. 'It has a Pretoria code and is probably where he lives. One of the calls was on Sunday and the other yesterday.' He scanned further and said: 'You received a call on Saturday evening from a number I recognize, Kirsty Callard's farm. The only people there at that time were her and Kallis.' He put the phone in his pocket. 'I saw another name I recognize but we will come to him later. Do you want to cooperate?'

'I don't know who made those calls,' said Teichmann. 'The man didn't give me his name and I cancelled them. Now give me my phone and get out.'

'You sound pathetic,' said Steiner. 'What's your connection with Andrew Rohm? He's on your phone contact list.'

'A lot of people know and have heard of Rohm,' said Teichmann. 'He's an international businessman and so am I.'

'I'm going to phone a friend of mine,' said Steiner. 'I'll then decide what to do with you.' He walked round the desk to within a few feet of Teichmann and pointed to the computer. 'But before I do that I want to look at your recent emails, those sent and received.

'You've got a nerve,' said Teichmann. 'That's confidential data and I'm certainly not going to let you read it.' He started to stand up, his hopes rising.

But before he could lift himself off the leather, Steiner took him by the biceps and held him. 'You have another chance,' he said. 'Give me access to those emails.'

Teichmann knew from what he had heard that Steiner was not averse to killing. He had left enough dead men in his wake. He looked up at him. 'I'll get you in,' he said. He faced the machine, clicked on the service provider and typed in his password. In seconds he was connected and he sat back in the chair. 'There, satisfied?'

Steiner leaned over and clicked on emails sent. A current list going back two months appeared. Staring at him was the name of Marc Kallis. He opened the email, read it and swung Teichmann round to face him. 'That is Peter Smith's death warrant,' he said. 'I see you also wish Kallis good luck in killing me and Callard. You have been busy.' He looked at the screen and went down the list. There were no other names he recognized.

'That doesn't prove anything,' said Teichmann, his spirit diminishing.

'I think it does.' said Steiner. He pulled Teichmann out of the chair, led him round the desk to the open space of the study and pushed him into a chair. 'Any move from you and I'll go to work,' he said. He moved a few metres away, took out his mobile phone and rang Bruce Weisz at his office.

'Bruce, Steiner,' he said when Weisz answered. 'I'm with Teichmann in his study. He's not very cooperative but I've found a couple of things that will be of interest to you.'

'That was fast,' said Weisz. 'I didn't expect to hear from you so soon.'

'I found two numbers for Marc Kallis on his mobile and two calls from one of them yesterday and Sunday,' said Steiner. 'On Saturday evening Teichmann also received a call from Kirsty's farm. Only she and Kallis were there.' Steiner looked across at Teichmann. The man was motionless, as if made from wax. Steiner continued. 'Now comes the big one. I got Teichmann to give me access to his computer email account, specifically messages that had been sent. Five days ago he sent Kallis Smith's contact details including a photograph and wished him luck in killing him and me. I also found Andrew Rohm's name on his mobile. What do think?'

'Rohm's well known and Teichmann's a businessman,' said Weisz. 'Unless there is something more on that it means little. Regarding the other stuff, Kallis didn't kill you and you had a go at him on the farm even though we both know it was self-defence. Kallis not only walked away from you but he also released Kirsty unharmed. The email Teichmann sent to him and the phone calls we believe he made to Teichmann, one from the farm, wouldn't convict him of anything. You might as well accuse him of urinating in his garden.'

'What about Smith?' asked Steiner.

'We both know he did it but there are no witnesses,' said Weisz. 'It is an isolated incident even though Teichmann's email refers to it. In short, we've not got anything damning against him and the same would apply if we went and picked up Kallis.'

'So I have to let him go,' said Steiner. 'We're where we started and no closer to Rohm.'

'Yes,' said Weisz. 'You'll also have to return his mobile if you've got it. We've both been through this before but we'll get him. I hope we don't run out of time.'

'I'll contact you when I get back,' said Steiner. He cut the call and walked over to Teichmann. 'I'm letting you go this time,' he said, 'but I'll be back. Whenever there are circumstances like this the guilty are always finally caught. Their desire for crime is congenital.'

Teichmann came to his feet, a look of triumph on his face. 'You're a cold-blooded killer who has been denied his prey,' he said. 'I hope you and your lover rot in hell. Now get out.'

Steiner extracted the mobile from his pocket and placed it on the desk. He had noted the number earlier. He smiled. 'We'll meet again.' He went from the room and left the property. When he reached the car he headed for the airport.

Chapter 71

Cape Town

Bruce Weisz put down the phone and looked at Conran, seated on the other side of the desk. 'That was James Steiner,' he said. He got up and went to the cabinet against the wall. 'Would you like a drink?'

'Why not,' said Conran. 'It's nearly lunchtime. I'll have a Scotch.'

Weisz poured two drinks and gave one to Conran. When he was seated he said: 'There is a part of this affair I haven't told you or Adam about. It's no great secret but Steiner and I thought there was a chance it might provide a breakthrough.' He twirled the liquid into a vortex, let it settle and drank some. He went on. 'After the sortie at Callard's farm and the death of Smith, Steiner was sure there was someone behind Kallis who had another reason for wanting him and Smith killed. He and I discussed this last night when he got back from Durban and concluded that the likely person had been involved with the old group and wanted revenge for the conviction of those exposed in the two files. Steiner felt that this person could only have learned of his and Callard's presence in Cape Town directly or indirectly from the DSO. With Andrew Rohm a possible suspect in the deaths of the ministers and possibly aware of DSO progress in solving the case, Steiner thought that this person or outsider could have got their information through him. From Steiner's past experience with the group, the obvious person was Johan Teichmann. Do you know him?'

'I've heard of him,' said Conran. 'He was one of the group leaders. Why did Steiner pick him?'

'Teichmann directed the efforts of John Kallis, Marc's brother, and Jan Krige,' said Weisz. 'Apparently he was really incensed when Steiner killed them and another group guy John Dalton.'

'I'm not surprised,' said Conran. 'I think I'd have been. You are going to tell me Steiner went after him and that's why he phoned.'

'Yes,' said Weisz. 'He went to see Teichmann this morning in Pretoria and accused him of being behind Kallis. Teichmann denied it. Steiner then looked at his mobile and found two numbers for Kallis. Under calls received he found two from Kallis's mobile, yesterday and Sunday, and one from Callard's farm on Saturday night. Only she and Kallis were there. After getting access to Teichmann's emails on his computer, Steiner found one sent recently to Kallis containing details of Peter Smith, including a photograph, and wishing him good luck in killing Smith, Steiner and Callard.'

'It all sounds impressive but there is no hard evidence,' said Conran, 'either of Kallis murdering Smith or Kallis trying to kill Steiner. Even if flight records show that Kallis was in Durban when Smith was killed it doesn't prove he did it. Kallis can also claim that Steiner attacked him on the farm and his escape with Callard as hostage was the only non-violent way of preventing harm to himself. He later released a perfectly healthy Callard, hardly the act of someone who was out to kill her.'

'That's what I told Steiner,' said Weisz. 'I'm afraid we're still at square one, no assassin and no lead. What a position to be in with the President howling for an arrest. He's really starting to feel the heat.'

'I assume Steiner is letting Teichmann go free,' said Conran.

'Yes,' said Weisz. 'We were hoping he would give us a break on Rohm. We're not even sure he is the big man behind the assassin. If Steiner walked in on him as he did with Teichmann and accused him of being the mastermind, all hell would break loose. The DSO would be taken to the

168

cleaners. I've just heard from the President's security chief Tyson that Hamilton refuses to move to a safe house. I've been told to arrange for there to be two guards on him round the clock instead of the one he wanted when all this started. Tyson also wants a report every twelve hours beginning now. I might as well use the same empty page and just change the time and date.'

Conran laughed. 'We've done our best. Something will come up. I just hope it's not a dead Hamilton.'

'I'll speak to Steiner when he gets back,' said Weisz. 'He's moved from Brown's Hotel to the Mandarin in the city. It won't be long before he gets fed up and returns to London. He is not employed by the DSO and it can be argued he's doing us a favour.'

'You should pay him something,' said Conran. 'He's got to live.'

'I agree,' said Weisz. 'I'll sort it out. Smith didn't give him anything for the group job. Apparently Steiner owed him a favour and he went after Cartwright's killer for nothing. When the white file didn't show up and a black file suddenly came into the equation, Steiner was persuaded to go it alone. He disappeared for a few days and casually walked in one morning with the originals of both files.'

'Who then persuaded him to get the files?' asked Conran.

'It was the woman who later became his lover, Kirsty Callard,' said Weisz. 'I'll bet he's into her every night. With his training I'm sure he's got the strength.'

'And every morning,' said Conran. 'Who wouldn't? I don't think he would've needed much persuading. What do you mean by training?'

'Smith once told me that Steiner's a seventh *dan* black belt in Japanese karate, the *gojuryu* style to be exact,' said Weisz. 'Very few get anywhere near that grade and those in Steiner's class are often referred to by the Japanese as *kami*, one who is divinely inspired, and their movements

169

are beyond technique, driven purely by intuition, the unconscious mind. The prime aim of training is the development of intuition or, as some call it, the *zen* mind.'

'Sounds heavy stuff,' said Conran.

'According to Smith, not when you see him perform,' said Weisz. 'Steiner's movements are pure silk, far removed from the typical thug or street-fighter and infinitely more lethal.' He picked up his phone. 'I'll call Fairley in and tell him what I've told you. You'll remain the only two who know.'

After the conversation with Weisz and back in his office, Conran thought about what he'd heard. Steiner, with nothing else to go on, would not give up on Teichmann and Kallis, the latter probably still out to get him. How Steiner went about it was anyone's guess but he would probably do it without telling the DSO, as he had done when he'd gone to Durban to block an attempt on Smith's life by Marc Kallis. Whatever approach Steiner took, it was clear to Conran that Teichmann was a potential leak that under pressure could expose Rohm's grand scheme. If that happened, it had to lead to Bale and then to himself.

Chapter 72

Pretoria

Steiner's visit was not what Johan Teichmann had expected, and it took a while after Steiner had gone for him to regain confidence and assess his position clearly. Steiner, even though he had left after talking to Bruce Weisz, a call he hadn't disguised, would not give up and at some stage he would be back. Teichmann was sure Kallis hadn't given Steiner his name but it had been naive on his part not to think that Steiner would deduce that he was behind Kallis. He recalled Kallis saying he was going to Cape Town to follow up on Steiner and he now wanted to keep him informed and tell him about the visit. There was no need to tell Rohm. Although Steiner had seen Rohm's name on his mobile, he was not connected to anything. It was a little after noon when he phoned Kallis on the man's mobile.

'Marc, it is Teichmann,' he said when he heard Kallis. 'Where are you?'

'I'm at a coffee bar in Cape Town,' said Kallis. 'I was about to phone you. Steiner has booked out of the hotel.'

'Don't they know where he's gone?' said Teichmann.

'No,' said Kallis. 'I'll find out. I get the feeling you have something on your mind.'

'Steiner came to my house this morning,' said Teichmann. 'He accused me of being behind you.'

'Something told me he would show up again,' said Kallis. 'It's all the more reason for me to nail him quickly. What did you do?'

'Not a lot,' said Teichmann. 'He's not the kind of person you play with. He found your two calls to me, yesterday and Sunday, and one on Saturday from the phone

171

on the farm. He also found the email I sent you about Smith's details.'

'Where's he now?' asked Kallis calmly. He had learnt early on in his life to control his emotions and not let them get in the way.

'He phoned his boss Bruce Weisz and after a brief exchange apparently decided he had nothing on me,' said Teichmann. 'He left after returning my mobile.'

'He won't give up,' said Kallis. 'It's even more reason to get rid of him quickly. When he is faced with this he is the sort who breaks the rules. He'll come back but this time he won't be asking for permission from Weisz. He might even go after me.'

Teichmann chilled at the words. 'What do you suggest? There's no place to hide. Whatever I do he'll simply wait and then pounce.'

Kallis liked Teichmann feeling the squeeze. Men in positions of power, politicians, often lost sight of the real world. They had others doing the dirty work for them. 'Sit tight,' he said. 'I'm sure Steiner will return to Cape Town, if he's not already here. He'll touch base with Weisz. This will give me a day or two to get him. Remember, he also has the other job to concentrate on and this business with you and me is separate and isolated. I'll ring you this evening and let you know how I'm getting on.'

Chapter 73

Cape Town

Paul Bale was in his office at the NPA when his phone rang. He picked it up. 'Bale.'

'Paul, John Conran. I've just heard something from Weisz that should interest you and Rohm.'

'Let's hear it,' said Bale, impatiently. 'I hope it's not bad.'

'Steiner concluded after recent events involving Marc Kallis that a man Johan Teichmann is backing him,' said Conran. 'Do you know that?'

'Yes,' said Bale, deciding to tell the truth. 'I only found out a day or two ago. It doesn't affect you.'

'But Teichmann knows Rohm?' said Conran, 'and it could affect me. I'm at the sharp end and the chance of someone catching me makes me very nervous

'What have you heard?' said Bale, unapologetically.

'Steiner paid Teichmann a visit this morning,' said Conran. He told Bale about the email and phone records Steiner had found.

'That wouldn't stand up in court,' said Bale.

'I agree and so does Weisz,' said Conran. 'But it is still uncomfortably close and if Steiner has another go at Teichmann he might spill it all. Steiner is not the type to admit defeat when he thinks he is right.'

'Where's Steiner now?' said Bale.

'He's returning to Cape Town,' said Conran. 'He's staying at the Mandarin Hotel. If Kallis still wants him he can forget about finding him at Brown's Hotel.'

'Thank you for phoning me,' said Bale. Conran. 'I'll pass this on to Rohm. He won't be happy. I'll also try and get a decision on Hamilton.' He replaced the handset and leaned back in his chair. Conran was right. This was too close for comfort. He phoned Rohm at home and when no one answered tried his mobile. He got through.

'Andrew, Paul Bale. I'm sorry to disturb you. I've had a call from John Conran.'

'You didn't disturb me,' said Rohm. 'I'm leaving the gym. What does Conran want?'

'He's just been speaking to his boss Weisz,' said Bale, and passed on details of Steiner's visit to Teichmann.

Rohm thought for a while then said: 'It's certainly not enough to prosecute Teichmann and Kallis, let alone convict them,' said Rohm, 'but it doesn't sound good. I'm sure Conran knows by now that we're together in all this and that I know Teichmann. Am I right?'

'Yes,' said Bale. 'There was no way of him not finding out. But Conran is on our side and not of concern here. Steiner is not the sort to give up on something when he believes he is right. He'll definitely have another go at Teichmann. He will also think that Kallis will try again to kill him and he might reverse things and go after him. Either way, Teichmann and Kallis are potential time bombs as far as we go. They both know you and you've probably told Teichmann about me.'

'I did,' said Rohm. 'Things weren't so complicated then.' He thought for a moment. 'You are quite right in what you say. I'll deal with it. I'm not going to let this stuff spoil the party.'

'What will you do?' asked Bale.

'You're in as much danger as I am,' said Rohm tersely. 'What do you think should be done?'

'Get rid of Teichmann and Kallis,' said Bale. 'That would wipe the slate clean.'

'Kallis is valuable to me,' said Rohm. 'I want Steiner dead. Kallis is the only one I know who can do it. Besides that, it won't be easy to find someone with the ability to kill Kallis. Teichmann poses a much greater threat and is expendable.'

'Teichmann's a friend of yours,' said Bale.

'Friends are great as long as they are not a threat,' said Rohm. 'Let's call it self-preservation.'

'I assume you'll ask Kallis to do the job.' said Bale, noting Rohm's cold, detached logic. 'He'll end up being a rich guy after all this. It will have to be before Steiner starts moving again. For the record, Steiner has moved to the Mandarin Hotel in Cape Town.'

'Don't tell Conran anything about this,' said Rohm. 'The less he knows the better.'

Chapter 74

Cape Town

When Steiner reached Cape Town, he went to the hotel. Kirsty was reading a book in the front reception room and he went to her. 'I hope that's interesting,' he said when she looked up.

'Disappointing,' she said, getting up and throwing her arms round him. 'I'm sure you've got a far more exciting story to tell.'

'No,' he said as they sat down. 'I went to see Teichmann. It revealed what we suspected but there is not the evidence to convict him or lead me directly to the people behind the killing of the ministers.'

Steiner told her what had happened with Teichmann, including the conversation with Weisz. When he had finished he said: 'Unless I go and beat the truth out of Teichmann, which is not my style, we're back at the beginning.'

She rested her head on his shoulder and held his hand. 'When are you going to see Weisz?'

'I'll give him a ring now and arrange a meeting,' said Steiner. He took out his phone and rang Weisz. He soon answered.

'Bruce, Steiner. I'm at the hotel. When would you like to meet?'

'I'm here all afternoon,' said Weisz. 'Come in when you like. I've spoken to Conran and he agrees there is not a lot we can do on that front. But we've got to come up with something.'

After the call Steiner turned to Kirsty. 'I'll see him later. Have you had lunch?'

'No,' she said. 'We can go to the bar if you like.'

They went to the bar and found seats. 'It's not Teichmann and Kallis that I'm bothered about,' said Steiner after they had ordered sandwiches and drinks. 'I'm sure Rohm is the top cat and I need a lead that takes me to him. Weisz won't be able to tell me anymore than I already know and he has to work strictly to the rules. If he doesn't he'll be lucky if he ends up on the street without a job.'

'What about the information we think is coming out of the DSO?' said Kirsty. 'Did you say anything about that to Weisz?'

'I did when I met him here last night,' said Steiner. 'He trusts the guys we've met, Conran, Fairley and Strauss. If he's right, the only way anything about me could have got out is through one of them casually telling a colleague. These guys talk amongst themselves and it could be anyone.'

'It's far-fetched to think there is a long-term plant sitting in the DSO waiting to gather snips of information to pass on to the outside,' said Kirsty. 'I think it is a person closely involved with the case, a person who knows the identity of the top cat as you call him and is feeding him. Do you trust Weisz?'

He looked at her. 'I think I do,' he said. 'But I could be wrong. The only person I completely trust is you.'

'You're so sweet,' she said, kissing him on the cheek. 'Let's eat our sandwiches and go upstairs. There's no hurry to see Weisz.'

Chapter 75

Pretoria

When he reached his car outside the gym and after speaking to Paul Bale, Rohm sat in the seat and thought about the call. Teichmann was clearly a danger and had to be killed. He had served his purpose by bringing in Kallis and getting him to kill Smith. Steiner was only important if he upset Rohm's plan to eliminate the ministers and have them replaced, and that work was nearly complete. Kallis could go back to Steiner if he wished after removing Teichmann. Rohm took his mobile from his bag and phoned Kallis.

'Marc, Andrew Rohm,' he said when Kallis answered. 'I assume you're in Cape Town. How are things going?'

'The sun is shining but that's about all,' said Kallis. 'Steiner and his woman have left the hotel. They didn't leave a forwarding address and it could take a while to find them. Teichmann rang me earlier and he didn't know.'

'I haven't spoken to him since you were on the farm,' said Rohm. 'Is he worried about you?'

'He was worried about himself,' said Kallis. 'He hasn't phoned you? He had a visit this morning from Steiner.'

'I've heard,' said Rohm. 'I want to talk to you about that. I believe Steiner is now staying at the Mandarin Hotel but I would like you to forget about him for the time being and come and see me in Johannesburg.'

'It sounds as if you and Teichmann are playing different games,' said Kallis. 'You obviously have your own sources.'

'We always were,' said Rohm. 'Smith and Steiner were the only common element and I let Teichmann get on with it when he insisted on recruiting you. I only intervened when I wanted to speed things up and set my own priorities.'

'From what you say, Teichmann doesn't know anything about you wanting me to leave Steiner and fly back,' said Kallis. 'It would be nice to know who's really calling the shots.'

'I am from now,' said Rohm. 'You will find out why when you see me. If Teichmann calls you again, tell him you're still looking for Steiner.'

'Where do you want to meet?' said Kallis. 'I'll get a flight as soon as I can.'

'Come to my house in Houghton,' said Rohm. He gave Kallis the address.

Chapter 76

Cape Town

Steiner left the Mandarin Hotel at a little after five and walked the two-blocks to the DSO. He was shown up to Weisz's office.

'Welcome back,' said Weisz as he showed Steiner to a chair. 'I'm sorry your visit didn't yield more.'

'I know he's behind Kallis,' said Steiner, 'but it might be a good thing that we can't pin Smith's death and the business at the farm on him now. I think Rohm is directing the killing of the ministers and if Teichmann is free he could show us the way in.'

'Let's hope you're right,' said Weisz. 'What are we going to do now?'

'I think you should get hold of the people Smith assigned to the job of investigating Rohm and his crew and put them in touch with Fairley,' said Steiner. 'I can send you the stuff Smith received from Hilton if you haven't got it.'

'Thanks,' said Weisz. 'Smith was going to give it to me when he came down here. I will contact the people in Durban and tell Fairley.'

'What about tapping Teichmann's land-line and mobile?' said Steiner.

'Tapping needs to be authorized by a court,' said Weisz. 'It is only approved when evidence shows it is not possible to detect criminal or subversive activity in less intrusive ways. The law often requires that the crime investigated must be of a certain severity. Again, the issue here is evidence but I can try. Whatever happens, I think Teichmann will be very careful from now concerning calls he makes on his phones. I can see him sneaking out and using the public system.'

'I don't expect it to give us much but you know what they say about beggars,' said Steiner.

'The President has asked us to increase the guard on Hamilton to two,' said Weisz. 'Hamilton refuses to go to a safe house.'

'Two men won't stop the guy doing this from getting through,' said Steiner.

'It must be frustrating for you,' said Weisz.

'My head won't roll if there isn't an arrest pretty soon,' said Steiner. 'It will be yours. Does anyone else know what we discuss?'

'Conran's up to speed,' said Weisz. 'I trust him completely and even though he's not on the case he puts a lot of thought into it. He's a very good agent.'

Steiner got up. 'I'm sure he's good,' he said. 'You can get hold of me at the Mandarin.'

Chapter 77

Johannesburg

Marc Kallis caught the 4 o'clock afternoon flight and arrived at OR Thambo Airport at five-thirty. An hour later he reached Rohm's house and was shown in by the maid. Rohm was in the second reception room overlooking the rear garden and a large swimming pool.

'That was quick,' said Rohm as he pointed to a chair. 'I want to get this business over as soon as possible. Would you like a drink?'

'No, I'm fine,' said Kallis. 'It must be important to pull me off Steiner's trail. You have my attention.'

Rohm poured himself a glass of cold water and sat down. 'Steiner's visit to Teichmann did not make me happy,' he said. 'He might not have got the hard evidence he wanted but his suspicions would have been confirmed and he will not give up. If he believes he is right he won't wait for his boss in the DSO to authorize another go.' Rohm drank some water and continued. 'Even at this moment he could be preparing for another visit and this time he'll pull out all the stops. When he does, Teichmann will squeal and reveal everything, not only about you but also me.'

'Why didn't you leave me to fix Steiner while I was in Cape Town?' said Kallis. 'I could have ended it tonight even if it meant catching him in his room and killing them both.' He stared at Rohm. 'It sounds as if you want to prevent Teichmann from spilling his guts. How do you intend to do that?'

Rohm walked to the French doors. He faced Kallis and said: 'Remove him so he can't cause any damage. In other words kill him.'

'So that's why I'm here?' said Kallis.

'Yes,' said Rohm. 'You will be extremely well paid for an easy job.'

'He's a friend of ours,' said Kallis.

'Friends are expendable when they become dangerous,' said Rohm. 'With Teichmann out of the way we can finish our work unhindered. Remove Teichmann and you are nearly there. It would just leave Steiner.'

Kallis thought about asking Rohm about his other work but decided against it. He was getting well paid, even more with Teichmann in the bag, and he could hardly be called a close friend of Teichmann's. 'What's the package and when do want it done?' he said. 'I hope you haven't got others you also want dead. I don't want this work to become a habit.'

Rohm liked Kallis. He was clever but there was something simple and unblemished about him. 'The package is 300 grand in pounds sterling,' he said, 'and if Teichmann hasn't paid you for Smith and Steiner I'll pay that as well. When you were at the farm I said I'd pay you to speed things up. I haven't forgotten and you'll also get that. I'll need your bank details. It has to be a foreign account.' He moved away from the doors. 'I'd like it done tonight. I think you will find Teichmann at home.'

Kallis came to his feet. Rohm was one of the most ruthless men he'd ever met. 'I'll contact you when it's done.'

'Please do,' said Rohm. 'I'll show you out.'

Chapter 78

Cape Town

'Weisz wants me to go to Durban and meet the guys Smith assigned to the job of investigating the people on Hilton's list,' said Adam Fairley. 'Steiner sent him a copy of the details Hilton gave Smith.' It was seven in the evening and Fairley and John Conran were having a drink in the Nightcap. They had finished work for the day.

'It's a pity Smith couldn't deliver them himself,' said Conran. 'Did Weisz fill you in on Steiner's visit to Johan Teichmann? I hadn't heard of him before Weisz told me.'

'He did,' said Fairley. 'Neither had I heard of him. It make's sense and I'm sure Steiner's not pleased he didn't get something conclusive. I also think the big fish is Andrew Rohm but short of detaining and torturing him he will stay out of bounds. He has enormous political clout and influential friends at the top level. What do you think about Steiner's belief that there is a leak of information inside the DSO? How else did Teichmann know Steiner and Callard were in Cape Town? It had to be someone who has an idea what the DSO is doing regarding the ministers' case and could not help hearing that Steiner was here.'

'I don't think there is a leak,' said Conran. 'Steiner's groping in the dark. He needs something to justify his existence.'

'He doesn't need to justify anything,' said Fairley. 'He is effectively an independent agent passed onto us by Smith at the request of Weisz.'

'If you think about it, how could this insider, if there is such a beast, have got hold of that information?' said Conran. 'The only people who knew are us, Strauss and Weisz, and I'm certain we haven't passed anything on to a colleague.'

'It might not be a colleague as such,' said Fairley. 'Weisz sometimes reports to the NPA and speaks to the police. He asked the police to stick a bodyguard on each of the ministers, now increased to two.' Fairley thought for a moment and then said: 'I've heard you in conversation with Paul Bale the NDPP. Did you say anything to him about Steiner?'

Conran was caught off-guard. For an instant his expression changed. He cursed himself for the momentary relapse but didn't think Fairley had noticed. 'I've never discussed this case with Bale,' he said evenly. 'I haven't spoken to him since this business started with the murder of Hilton. The last time was the prosecution of a guy caught trafficking drugs along the coast. Anyway, Bale is after all the NDPP and if we can't trust him to be discreet, who can we? Do you ever speak to people outside the DSO?'

'No,' said Fairley. 'I've met Bale once and no one else outside these walls, not even the police. Weisz's too canny to say anything of significance about our operations. I'm inclined to agree with you. Steiner's got it wrong.' He finished his drink and held up his glass. 'That's enough about work. Would you like another?'

'Thank you,' said Conran. 'We'll leave all that stuff to Steiner. He'd better come up with something quick.'

Chapter 79

Pretoria

After leaving Rohm, Marc Kallis returned to his flat in Pretoria. It would be the last time for a few days and he wanted to pack some things to see him over the period. It was a little after nine when he was ready to go to Teichmann's house, a good time because the servant would have been released for the night and Teichmann would probably still be up. He wanted it that way, although not essential, because it helped if Teichmann let him in and he didn't have to bother working past the alarm system which would have been activated.

Kallis put on his dark jacket and grabbed his bag with the silenced Beretta inside. After double locking the flat he went to his car in the street and was soon on the main road that bypassed the centre of the city and came close to the area in which Teichmann lived. When he filtered off the road he was several streets to the north of where he wanted to go. He knew the area fairly well and in minutes was at the start of Teichmann's road. He parked the car in a side-street and stuck the pistol inside his belt a little to the rear of his right hip. With the relaxed stride of someone out on an evening stroll he went into the road and towards the house. When he came to the garden gate, concealed from the house by fruit trees, he went through and round to the front of the building. The curtains of the large reception room were drawn and the lights were on. He halted and then went on to the verandah and to the double glass doors. He rang the bell.

For twenty seconds Kallis heard nothing and then came Teichmann's voice from the other side of the curtains. 'Who's that?'

'Marc Kallis. The job's been done. I'm sorry it's so late.' Kallis inhaled deeply, silently.

'Just a minute,' said Teichmann, excitedly. 'I have to turn off the alarm.'

Kallis waited patiently and then the curtains were partly opened. Teichmann was still dressed in day clothes and when he saw Kallis he unlocked the doors and slid them a few feet apart. He held out his hand in welcome. 'Marc, that's fantastic news.'

Kallis shook Teichmann's hand and followed him as he led him into the room. 'I didn't think I'd finish it so quickly,' he said. 'I had a bit of luck.'

'In what way,' said Teichmann showing him to a seat. 'I felt you were going to need it.'

'I tried Brown's Hotel again,' said Kallis. 'I thought Steiner must have left something that told them where he could be contacted. The girl on reception gave me the Mandarin Hotel. She was surprised the previous woman hadn't done the same.'

Teichmann could hardly suppress his excitement. 'Don't keep me waiting.' he said.

'I won't,' said Kallis. 'He came to his feet and walked over to Teichmann. He was in his favourite chair, his fingers clasped together in front of his chin, a happy smile parting his lips. When he was a few paces from him, Kallis brushed aside his jacket, drew the Beretta, levelled it smoothly as if he hadn't a care in the world and fired twice. The slugs hit Teichmann between the eyes, his mouth half-open and his eyes showing the first hint of fear. His head fell slowly forward in death, his torso convulsing in a final attempt to stave off the inevitable moment.

For a while Kallis stared at the body of the man who had trusted him. He felt no remorse. He had learned that there was no place for it, or sentiment, when something that posed a threat to his existence had to be eliminated. He stuck the pistol behind his belt, closed his jacket and left the room. Seconds later went from the premises through the side gate to his car. After placing the Beretta in his bag he drove from the area and picked up the main road leading away from Pretoria to the east. Earlier, he had booked a room in a small family hotel ten kilometres from the city.

When Kallis reached the hotel he booked in and went to his room. He washed his face in cold water, poured a Scotch and then phoned Andrew Rohm at home. The man answered.

'It's Kallis. Teichmann is no more. I left his place thirty minutes ago.'

'Where is he?' said Rohm.

'In the reception room,' said Kallis. 'Are you going to collect him?'

'No,' said Rohm. 'There's no need. I'll leave it to the local police.' He was confident Kallis hadn't left anything incriminating. 'Where are you?'

'I'm in a small hotel ten kilometres from Pretoria,' said Kallis. 'Do you want me to go after Steiner?'

'Let them first find Teichmann,' said Rohm. 'Lie low for a while. I want to see the reaction from the DSO before you move. I'll ring you.'

Chapter 80

Johannesburg

When Andrew Rohm had asked Kallis to meet him in Johannesburg so that he could ask him to kill Teichmann, he had been giving more thought to when Hamilton should be killed. Rohm had told Paul Bale to plan a hit on Hamilton on Thursday but he was having second thoughts and now after hearing from Kallis that Teichmann was dead he saw no reason why it shouldn't be done earlier. He believed the President was playing games with him in not replacing the ministers and even though he thought it would soon happen he was becoming impatient. The President was in no position to do anything other than what was requested of him and he had clearly held back in announcing Delaware's replacement, probably because of his pride. Rohm also had business to deal with and on Friday was meeting his friends at his estate near Paarl in the Western Cape. It was ten-fifteen and he phoned Paul Bale at home. Bale soon answered.

'Paul, Andrew Rohm. I hope this is not too late for you.'

'Andrew,' said Bale. 'No, I've got a lot on. You've got news.'

'Teichmann is dead,' said Rohm. 'It was done an hour ago.'

'That's what you wanted,' said Bale.

'It's what we both wanted,' said Rohm. Bale was being patronising and he didn't like it. He would have been the first to squeal if Teichmann had blabbed. 'I want you to get Conran to remove Hamilton now. There is no sense in waiting until Thursday. The President is messing around and I don't like it.'

'If you do that he will not replace Dredge and Hamilton with the people you want,' said Bale. 'They'll be out of the way but you might get worse.'

'Hilton was investigating me for quite a spell and there was the danger he and the others, if he confided in them, would strike gold,' said Rohm. 'With Hamilton and the other three out of the way I will have achieved the most important part of my plan. But I'm not forgetting the second part. As I once told you, we would like very much to have our people in powerful cabinet positions and having come so far we'd like to see it completed to our satisfaction. To make sure we get the last two replacements specified, I want you to send a letter to the President telling him that we're going to expose the corruption of some of his black cabinet ministers and pass our stuff on to the NPA. We have had damning evidence of this for a long time but we were prepared to let it ride because they kept to themselves, content to get fat without interfering in the affairs of others. Such exposure would make the President's position untenable and he would have to leave his office in disgrace, possibly facing charges himself. I don't think the public would be surprised to read the allegations in the national and international press. The President would also start to fear being exterminated.'

'If you did that we would be hunted down like dogs,' said Bale. 'The DSO and the police would stop at nothing.'

'Don't be hysterical,' said Rohm dismissively. 'You of all people should know that conviction relies on motive and evidence, of which there is none in our case.'

Bale felt denigrated but Rohm was clever and confident. He was like any successful businessman, keen to finish what he had started. Bale also wanted it all completed and knew that if they wanted to kill the President and get away with it they could. 'I'll try and get hold of Conran now,' he said, 'and ask him to put his guy on to it. It'll probably be

190

done sometime tomorrow. They are keen to receive their money.'

'I'll rely on you to see it's done and that the President gets the letter,' said Rohm. 'On Friday I'm going to my estate in Paarl for a few days, maybe a week. I want a break and there are things I need to settle. I've invited my friends to join me when I get there. You have my address down there and my phone numbers.'

When Rohm had gone, Paul Bale phoned Conran at home.

'Rohm wants your guy to hit Hamilton before Thursday,' said Bale. 'Do you think you can manage that? He wants to see an end to all this and thinks the President is messing about.'

'I'll see what I can arrange,' said Conran. 'If I'd known earlier it might have been possible tonight. I think you can count on it being sometime tomorrow.'

'Thank you,' said Bale. 'Please let me know when it's over.'

Chapter 81

When Johan Teichmann's maid found his body at six-thirty in the morning, she immediately phoned the local police. With no obvious valuables stolen, the solid gold Rolex Oyster Pepetual still on his wrist, 2000 rand and credit cards in his wallet, they concluded it was a contract killing and contacted the DSO office in Johannesburg. Bruce Weisz heard about it soon afterwards and called Steiner at the Mandarin Hotel. He reached him in his bedroom

'Who knew I went to see Teichmann?' said Steiner when he'd been told about the killing.

'Conran and Fairley,' said Weisz. 'Conran was in my office when you phoned from Teichmann's house. I told Fairley later.'

'Do they know Teichmann's dead?' asked Steiner.

'Not yet,' said Weisz. 'I'll tell them after this call.'

Steiner made no comment. Weisz's trust in them was clearly the same and he had nothing on them that would change it. He then said: 'It's not a coincidence that someone suddenly popped up and put two bullets in Teichmann's head. If it's not from our side, Teichmann must have told someone about my visit, someone who is or is in contact with the killer. Initially, Teichmann asked Kallis to kill me. My visit was all the more reason for him to urge Kallis to finish the job in case I returned. The only other person I can think of is Rohm. But Teichmann would be too proud to tell him that his efforts to remove me might have backfired and that I was now after him, if he'd let Rohm in on it in the first place. Rohm would only regard him with contempt, a man who had screwed up. I can only conclude that Teichmann told Kallis about my visit and put pressure on him to finish me off.'

'Would Kallis have turned on the person who was paying him?' said Weisz. 'If he hadn't already been paid, which is likely, he wouldn't get his dough. And Kallis also wants you dead because you killed his brother.'

'Well, someone knew about my visit and thought Teichmann posed a risk,' said Steiner. 'We're still left with nothing.'

'I'm afraid you're right,' said Weisz, 'and the person who did it is still out there. I'll have a word with Fairley and Conran. Thank you for the stuff Hilton gave Smith on Rohm and his friends. I'm going to send Fairley to Durban to speak to the people Smith assigned to the investigation. I'll let you know if we come up with anything. We sure need to.' After the call, Weisz buzzed Conran and Fairley and called them to his office.

'I've just heard that Johan Teichmann was last night shot dead at his home in Pretoria,' said Weisz when the two men were seated. 'The motive was not robbery.'

'I assume we don't know who did it,' said Fairley. 'Does Steiner know?'

'Yes,' said Weisz. 'I've just spoken to him. 'The killer has to be someone who knows Steiner visited Teichmann. They removed him from the equation because they felt he might be put under further pressure and squeal. Marc Kallis is the only one we know of who is in close contact with Teichmann. Rohm's name is on Teichmann's mobile but that could mean anything. Many in South Africa have heard of him.'

'Kallis is not the type who would panic on hearing about Steiner's visit and proceed to kill his paymaster,' said Conran. 'This means we have nothing to go on.'

'Precisely,' said Weisz. He looked at Fairley. 'I've spoken to a Garth Banks at the DSO Durban office. He was leading the small team set up by Smith to investigate the affairs of Rohm and his mates. I told him you'll contact him and fix up a meeting, either up there or down here.' He faced Conran. 'I'm thinking of releasing you from some of your work so that you can give Steiner a bit of help when he wants it.'

'He won't,' said Conran. 'He's too independent. I know the breed. Did he ask for help when he went after Cartwright's killers? No. But I'll help if asked.'

'Fine,' said Weisz. 'I'll speak to him later today and see what he's doing.'

Chapter 82

Cape Town

'Teichmann only had himself to blame,' said Kirsty after Steiner had told her the news. They were still in their bedroom. 'What did he expect, a peaceful life.'

'I don't think anyone ever expects that will happen to them, whatever they're involved in,' said Steiner. 'Even though it doesn't help me, it means I don't have to pay him a return visit.'

'Is that what you were going to do?' she said.

'Yes,' said Steiner. 'I felt he was the only person I could get anything from. Kallis is not high enough up the tree and I can hardly start with Rohm.'

'What are you going to do now?' she asked. 'As we speak, someone out there could be moving in on Hamilton. When he is killed these people will go to ground, having achieved essentially what they wanted.'

'Essentially,' said Steiner. 'What is that? Are these people so magnanimous and determined to want to replace four allegedly corrupt men – an allegation apparently without foundation – with others they nominated who are without blemish? Also, was Hilton really getting too close to justify killing him? Smith didn't think so. But my only work now, with nothing to go on, is to be near Hamilton, try to prevent him from being killed and hopefully grab the killer.'

'Does Weisz know you want to do that?' said Kirsty.

'No,' said Steiner. 'And I'll keep it that way.'

'I want to help you,' she said. 'I'm sick of sitting in this place while you're out there. Keeping watch on someone is a lonely job especially when you don't want to be seen.'

Steiner walked over and kissed her. 'This time I'll let you,' he said 'I was waiting for you to ask. Two are needed for this job, one watching while the other gets some sleep. It will be a case of taking it in turns.'

'I hope you know where Hamilton lives,' she said. 'If you don't you'll have to find out from Weisz and he'll suspect you're up to something.'

'Weisz's already told me,' said Steiner. 'I got it from him when we arrived. Hamilton's in the wine country near Stellenbosch, a few kilometres away from where Hilton and Dredge lived. Of the four, only Delaware lived in Cape Town. Hamilton lives alone in a six-bedroom house near a village called Sleepy Hollow, for some strange reason. It's in a small valley.' He looked at her, his eyes glinting. 'Did you ever see the film?'

'*Sleepy Hollow*?' she said. 'Yes, it was very good. I hope we don't meet another decapitated horseman.'

'We won't,' he said. 'I hope it's just a simple assassin. Let's have some breakfast and decide what we're going to do.'

After breakfast, Steiner and Kirsty found seats in the reception room and ordered more coffee. 'We know it will be a night job,' said Steiner. 'Hamilton will be in his office during the day and well protected.'

'And when he goes to work and returns at the end of the day?' said Kirsty. 'There have been a number of assassinations elsewhere at those times. People become complacent and don't expect anything to happen.'

'We'll have to take our chances on that,' said Steiner. 'We can't keep watch during those times without travelling with him. The killer has been operating alone and I think we can assume they'll carry on doing so. To strike a moving target takes careful planning and an organization involving more than one.'

'I was thinking more about when he actually starts and finishes each journey, at home and at his office,' said Kirsty.

'We can rule out his office for that,' said Steiner. 'The car park at the houses of parliament is underground and well guarded. But his home is different and we'll have to be in the vicinity when he moves, in the early morning when he leaves and the late afternoon or evening when he returns. Dredge was shot when he was getting into his car to go to work.'

'You spoke to Hamilton once before,' said Kirsty, 'and said you didn't intend watching over him personally. Are you going to tell him your plan?'

'No,' said Steiner, 'for these reasons. He probably won't like it and might tell Weisz. And, if he agreed to it I would be obliged to dedicate all my time to be near his house. I can't give him that commitment. Weisz would soon wonder what the hell I was doing with my time.'

'He'll wonder that anyway,' said Kirsty. 'Even if you're not being paid at the moment you're still doing a job for him. I think that at some point very soon you're going to have to suggest he bring in someone to replace you, or at the very least to assist you. It's his decision and unfair that you should carry on bearing the responsibility for finding and stopping a killer who is proving very elusive.'

Steiner thought for a while and then said: 'I'll give this two days starting this afternoon. I'll keep in touch with Weisz and remain open to anything he can suggest, even if he says he's assigning someone to help me. I might tell him later that we're sitting it out at Hamilton's place but for now I want to do that alone without him knowing. I don't want him crowding things and I've got a feeling that this killer is going to strike very soon. What do you think?'

'I'm with you,' she said, 'and don't try and leave me out. Now, what are we going to do? I think we should pay Hamilton's area a visit this morning and become familiar with it. We'll need a place where we can park the car so it's not easily seen and a vantage point for us. The time each one of us keeps watch really depends on the difficulty we might have staying awake.' She laughed. 'Don't start thinking I'll be the one who keeps defaulting. Life on the farm taught me to hack it alongside the best.'

'We'll be close together so I wouldn't worry about that,' said Steiner. 'If the car is nearby, one can sleep in it. If not, it'll mean sleeping on a makeshift bed. I'm sure you know how to prepare one. Perhaps I should do all this alone.'

'If you were alone you'd have to sleep all day and that means going to bed now,' said Kirsty. 'If Weisz phones, do you want me to tell him you're fast asleep?'

'Let's take a drive out that way,' he said. 'When we return we can get some sleep and order some food and drink from the hotel to take with us. I'd like you to phone Hamilton's office and try and find out when he leaves work for the night. If they refuse to tell you, we should plan on being in position no later than five-thirty.'

'I'll ring his office now,' said Kirsty, getting up. She went to a public phone in the foyer, looked up the number and phoned Hamilton's office at the houses of parliament. His secretary answered.

'I'm a personal friend of his,' said Kirsty. 'Do you know when he leaves work for home? I'd like to surprise him when he gets there.'

'We don't usually give out those details,' said the woman. 'How do you know him?' She knew she could get any number of convincing answers but Kirsty sounded genuine and very nice.

'He used to date my sister,' said Kirsty. 'I met him then and we became friends.'

'I believe you,' said the woman laughing. 'He usually leaves at six-thirty. The journey takes about forty minutes. Would you like to speak to him now?'

'No,' said Kirsty. 'I'll see him later. Thank you.' She replaced the receiver, joined Steiner and passed on the information.

'That gives us an extra hour,' he said. 'Let's go.'

198

Soon after leaving the hotel they joined the N1 freeway and fifty-kilometres and forty-five minutes later saw the turn-off for Sleepy Hollow. They took it and when they reached the village Steiner stopped. He looked at their map and pointed to a road on the left. 'It's down there,' he said. 'I don't think it's far. The name we're after is as you might have guessed, Hamilton. You called your farm Krige.'

'Yes, not much imagination,' she said. 'I hope it doesn't reveal anything about me. I suggested the name Krige for the farm.'

They drove down the road and after a few kilometres saw the house, set well back from the road on the other side of large indigenous trees, lawn and waist-high bushes. 'It's quite a spread,' said Steiner. 'It, along with those grounds, and in this area close to Cape Town must put its value in the millions. Does money like that come from politics?'

'No, but these people often have extensive business interests,' said Kirsty. 'And, in the case of some, they're up to their ears in vice.'

They went past the property and after another kilometre pulled over. The only place they could leave the car later without drawing attention to it was a small car park for walkers that they had passed. It was 300 metres from the gates of the house. They had noticed only one neighbouring property this side of the gates, similar in size and style to Hamilton's and well separated from it.

'It has to be that car park,' said Steiner. 'There isn't much of a view of the house from there but the car won't stand out. Actually, it doesn't matter that much because the vantage point for keeping watch will have to be inside the grounds and out of sight of the car even if it was parked at the gate. I didn't know they were so big and that the house was set so far back.'

'What are you saying?' said Kirsty. 'Is it that we both sit in the grounds, one sleeping and the other watching?'

199

'Yes, but only when I'm on watch,' said Steiner. 'When you're off, you're sleeping in the car. I'll be walking around a bit anyway, which I don't want you to do.'

'Do we know what Hamilton backs on to?' asked Kirsty. 'He has ten acres there and it must go somewhere.'

'This map is not like those produced by the UK's ordnance survey,' said Steiner. 'All we know is that this road is the address listed.' He pointed to the map. 'There's that road on the far side but I don't know if it offers access.'

'What about the guards?' she asked. 'They'll shoot you on sight.'

'Don't worry about that,' said Steiner. 'I'm sure they'll stick close to the building and there'll only be one doing the rounds at a time.'

'Let's leave that as our plan for now,' said Kirsty. 'We can make changes when the time comes. Who knows, we might have everything wrapped up shortly after we set up our stall.'

'I'm not sure about that,' he said. 'Let's return to the hotel.'

Chapter 83

Stellenbosch

Steiner and Kirsty spent the afternoon at the Mandarin Hotel and at six-thirty left for the area near Hamilton's house. When they got there they parked in the car park they had seen earlier. They were dressed in dark, casual clothing and had on soft shoes. Although it was the middle of summer, with sunset shortly after eight, they took light sports jackets with them. The temperature range was expansive and night hours could be deceptively cold.

'Now we wait for things to happen,' said Steiner, opening a canned drink after passing one to Kirsty. From their position they could see the iron front gates, three hundred metres down the road towards the village of Sleepy Hollow. On either side of the gates, a five-foot stone and concrete wall, covered sparingly by creepers, defined the front boundary. Barbed-wire fences ran down the sides of the property and separated it from the neighbours. They were relatively isolated.

'What do we do when Hamilton arrives?' said Kirsty. 'I assume his two guards will arrive with him.'

'They will,' said Steiner. 'They meet him at work and drive with him in his car. They leave together in the morning. Weisz told me they shack up in a utility room near the garage, as did the guy at Dredge's place. They have keys to the house in case of an emergency.'

'After the killer has struck,' said Kirsty dryly. 'Will they take it in turns to walk the grounds or do it together? Perhaps they'll just sit in the office.'

'I haven't a clue,' said Steiner. 'Either way, it doesn't mean a lot. The killer is cunning and two guards are not enough. When the killer arrives he'll first wait and find out the guards' routine. Once he does, he'll take appropriate

201

action and remove them. It's as simple as that.' He looked at her. 'I bet he will have some idea what to expect before he arrives.'

'Which gets back to the insider,' said Kirsty. 'Well, we can't do anything about that now. You're really saying that unless Hamilton has a few more guards, he is not adequately protected and should be in a safe-house.'

'Something like that,' said Steiner. 'But it's too late.' He swallowed some of the drink. 'If the killer comes it will be after dark and when he thinks Hamilton has gone to bed he'll strike. We're looking at any time between ten and dawn. We assume he'll get in from the front, through the gates or over the wall. We've got nothing else and even if we had we can't watch two entrances simultaneously.'

'And we'll be in the grounds,' said Kirsty. 'I don't want to be here in the car while you're out there. It'll be comfortable enough stretched out on Hamilton's beautifully manicured grass.'

'You will change your mind,' said Steiner. 'The car is far more comfortable and it is safe.'

'I suppose we'll have to jump over the wall,' said Kirsty. 'I haven't tried that height for a long time.'

'You'll manage,' said Steiner smiling. 'It'll be good for you. If you struggle, I'll give you a hand.'

She smiled, touching her tongue to her top lip and glancing at him. 'I know where that will be.'

They sat in the car talking for another hour before they saw a silver Jaguar XJR appear down the road. It was going slowly and when it reached the gates a man in the co-driver's seat got out, opened them and let it pass. He closed the gates, joined the car and it continued its journey up the drive to the house. Hamilton was in the rear seat.

'He's nearly on time,' said Kirsty. 'I wonder what goes on in his head when he comes home for the night. Perhaps he thinks he'll be the lucky one and that the killer is not after him.'

'Some people would think like that,' said Steiner. 'Unfortunately they are frequently wrong. The killer has certainly got Hamilton in his sights. We'll wait until it is dark and then jump the wall, as you so sweetly put it. Sometimes I can't believe I'm doing this. It all started with the group and those files, and Peter Smith asking me to find out what was going on.'

'You were lucky,' she said. 'If you hadn't become involved, you wouldn't have met me.'

Chapter 84

Stellenbosch

At the age of fifty-five, Anthony Hamilton was one of the younger members of the cabinet. He had only moved into politics in his mid-forties after forging a highly successful career as a criminal advocate. He had always been a member of the main opposition party, the Democratic Alliance, but when apartheid came to an end he had eschewed what he felt was weak leadership and joined the ANC. He had never married and politics was his life.

When Hilton and then Delaware were assassinated, Hamilton and Colin Dredge knew their lives were also in danger. They drew no particular conclusion from the death of Hilton but when Delaware was also gunned down they knew there was something deeper and more sinister going on. They and the dead men were close friends and a pattern was emerging. When Dredge was shot, Hamilton was certain he was on the list but, as he and Dredge had told James Steiner, he had too much pride ever to succumb to the demands of cold murderers. Not for a moment did he believe the reason given for dismissal of the four of them was corruption, simply because he knew he and his friends were innocent.

When Hamilton heard that he would now have two guards he accepted, without admitting that he was pleased. Both men were former army paratroopers and if anyone could get through them they could get through anything. On reaching his home that evening he had a double Scotch and soda, a superb meal served by his maid and then watched *Dead Man Walking* on television.

After the film Hamilton went to bed. It was in the main bedroom on the first floor. He had not had sex since getting rid of his girlfriend of two years, Emma Cosgrave, a month

before and he now regretted his decision. He had tried to get her back but she didn't want it, quite happy remaining a good friend.

At nine, an hour after sunset, Steiner and Kirsty left the car, crossed the road and climbed over the wall. They went across the lawn to the nearest trees and walked until they saw the front of the house and the detached double garage close to the house.

'What do we do now?' said Kirsty. 'Some of the lights are on downstairs in the house. I can't see the guards' room by the garage.'

'It's obscured by the house,' said Steiner. 'It's there. This is where I'll wait. Go back to the car. There is no point in you staying out here with me. We'll change at about one. If I'm not tired I'll stay with you.'

She looked at him. 'I know you,' she said. 'You are going to be here all night.'

'When you come back I'll go to the car for a couple of hours,' he said. 'After that I'll be here until Hamilton leaves.'

'I'm glad you're seeing sense,' said Kirsty. 'I'm not tired at the moment. I'll go to the car in an hour.'

They found the most comfortable spot and sat down to wait. After thirty minutes the lights in the house were extinguished and a little later they saw someone appear from the side of the garage, walk past the front of the house and disappear. 'That's one of them,' said Kirsty. 'He must have come from the room. It looks as if they're going to do as you said, take turns doing the rounds.'

'Yes,' said Steiner. 'I don't think they'll go into the house.'

They didn't see the guard again and assumed he had returned to the room. Twenty minutes later they saw a shorter man appear, presumably the second guard, and disappear down the far side of the house. The round was repeated every twenty minutes and shortly after eleven Kirsty got up and said: 'I'll take you up on what you said earlier. I'll see you back here at one. Don't fall asleep.'

'I won't,' he said. 'If anything happens I'll ring you.' She left, walking off through the trees.

The guard's routine continued and at one in the morning Kirsty returned, this time wearing her short jacket. 'I enjoyed that,' she said, sitting next to him. 'I was more tired than I thought. What have you got to tell me, something out of the ordinary I hope?'

'I'm afraid not,' said Steiner, putting his arm around her. 'You haven't missed anything. They just carry on doing the rounds.'

'I think you should go and sleep,' said Kisty. 'If anything happens I'll phone you. I promise you, you won't miss the action.'

'I'll go,' said Steiner, getting up. 'Give me a couple of hours and I'll be back.' He left.

Chapter 85

Stellenbosch

When he heard that Hamilton's death had to be brought forward a day to Wednesday, the killer wasn't surprised. From the beginning, he had believed that the schedule was merely a game when the reality was the undiluted desire to murder those who were a potential threat, whatever form that threat took. The claim that it was important to replace people who were corrupt with people you liked was empty. Whoever was chosen as a replacement could in turn be eliminated if they weren't liked, were themselves corrupt or got in the way. It would just be a little inconvenient.

As soon as the man had accepted the assignment of killing the men, he had studied his options and selected the place where he would do the job. Clearly, it was the victim's home in each case. He would be working alone and the targets could not be on the move or in a place where they were well protected, which ruled out their offices at the houses of parliament. When he had heard that there would only be one guard on each, he found it amusing and in a bizarre way an insult to his ability to kill. If he had been in charge of the men's protection, he would have insisted that they were stuck in safe-houses with two guards working together on duty round the clock. But that had never happened. The decision now to give Hamilton one more guard was risible. He lived in a large six-bedroom house set in ten acres and the belief that two men could give him adequate protection was stupid in the extreme.

For a couple of hours during the late afternoon, the man had again studied the detailed map he had acquired of the area where Hamilton lived. It confirmed the plan he had made earlier that the best way to reach Hamilton was along a foot path from the road behind his property to the back fence and into the grounds. Although he wasn't concerned about there being two guards, their presence deserved extra caution and coming in through the front carried a risk of detection he wasn't prepared to take. Neither was he going to go in unmasked as he had done before and he had purchased a black balaclava. There was always a chance that when he tried to remove the guards, which he felt was unavoidable if he wanted clean access to Hamilton, one would escape and be able to identify him later.

Now, at close to two in the morning and dressed in black, the man reached Sleepy Hollow and took the right fork in the road. In seven minutes he came to the footpath, clearly marked by a white board on a post, and parked in the ramblers' car park nearby. He left the car and set off briskly along the path, well-worn from frequent use. At first he passed between vineyards, covering tens of acres, and then he entered forest supported by dense undergrowth. He had a good idea where he was and he expected soon to see the back fence of Hamilton's grounds.

The fence appeared suddenly, strands of interlocking barbed wire supported by stakes driven into the ground, and after holding it down and going over, he moved through an orchard towards the house. He soon saw the rear elevation of the building, the lights out except one above the kitchen door, and then the detached garage. A small room formed an annexe to the garage and a light was on. The notes he had been given were brief and didn't say where the guards would be, but when he saw the lit room his first thought was that they would be using it as a base. He had time on his hands and with a little patience he knew he'd soon find out. They had to be somewhere and if they were doing their job properly they would show themselves. He waited.

He was rewarded when minutes later the door of the room opened. A man came out, looked round and started walking towards the front of the house, leaving the door slightly ajar. He disappeared and after a while showed again at the far side of the house, walking slowly, stopping every now and then to scan the building before returning to the room. The door was left wide open and the sound of words came to the trees, as if riding on the gentle breeze.

Certain that he had the two guards where he wanted them, together in one place, the man pulled on his balaclava, screwed the silencer onto the Beretta that appeared effortlessly in his hand, and walked over the grass to the room. As he neared it he saw the two guards through the window, seated, the one drinking from a cup, the other drawing deeply on a cigarette. He was at the door when the guard furthest from him looked up, his eyes opening wide. 'Who the hell are you,' he gutted.

The words were the last he spoke. Two bullets penetrated his chest, tearing through his heart, killing him instantly and sending him out of his chair, sprawled on his back. As the other guard swung round, his cigarette dangling from his lips, the man shot him twice above the left eye. Death was quick and his torso fell forward, his chest colliding heavily with the top of the table, his arms going to his head as if they could remove the pain.

For a while the man stared at his work. He felt nothing. It was what he was being paid to do and he had accepted the terms and conditions of the assignment. Payday would be soon. He stepped closer to the desk, his eyes sweeping across the surface. He knew he would require keys if he was to gain easy, quiet access to the house, but he saw none. He went to the second man he had killed, probably the one who had just done the round, and checked his pockets. His found a ring of keys. He searched further in case there was another set and did the same on the other man. Without removing the balaclava he left the room and walked across to the back door. There were three keys on the ring, a car key and two others. None fitted the locks but he was not deterred. He was sure at least one of the keys gave access. He walked from the door and round to the long verandah at the front of the house. The external lights were on, bathing the verandah in a yellow glow, and he started towards the front door.

Chapter 86

Stellenbosch

At two-fifteen when Kirsty was beginning to question what she and Steiner were doing sitting outside Hamilton's house, she saw a man appear on the verandah at the front of the house. He was dressed in black and his head was covered. She stared as the man started to move towards the front door and then came to her feet. She reached for her phone but it was not there. She had left it in the car. The man reached the door.

Realizing there was no time to call Steiner, Kirsty moved through the undergrowth and towards the house. When she reached open lawn she stopped. She was torn between waiting until he got inside, so she could close on him without being seen, and shouting out. The man opened the door and went through.

She broke into a run, not sure what she would do if she came upon him. But she had to go on. There was now no choice. The thought of Hamilton lying in bed came to her and she knew she had to alert him and give him a chance to save himself. She reached the steps leading on to the verandah, sprang up them and came to the open door. She brushed the bank of switches, turning on the ceiling lights and illuminating the hall in a blaze of brilliance. Ten metres from her was the man, about to climb the stairs going to the bedrooms. He turned smoothly, took his foot off the bottom step and faced her, his eyes glaring through the holes in the black balaclava, sending a chill through her. She opened her mouth and screamed: 'Hamilton.'

Steiner, unable to sleep, his mind on the work he had accepted, heard Kirsty scream. The sound mercilessly probed his depths and in a single, fluid movement he left

211

the car. He ran to the wall, went over it as if it had ceased to exist and moved towards the house. In seconds he saw it, the open door, the hall lights reaching out into the night, and he sprinted across the lawn, thinking only of Kirsty.

With raw speed, motivated by the strongest desire to eliminate the intrusion, the man closed on Kirsty. Before she could move out of the way, he lifted his right hand, the silenced Beretta held firmly in it, and struck her with sickening force on the side of her head. She fell, a skittle in an alley, tumbling out of control, her hands instinctively lifting to ward off the blow, losing consciousness before she hit the floor. He looked at her. He knew who she was. If she was here then so was Steiner. He went to the stairs.

When Hamilton heard Kirsty scream his name he thought he was waking from a bad dream. But it was too real to be a dream and he came out of his bed in a flourish. The scream had come from downstairs. He had to see what was happening. Where were his guards? He grabbed his dressing gown, left the room and went to the stairs. When he saw the ominous, disguised figure in the hall below him, he stopped and then started to turn. He knew the dreaded killer had found him, that what his friends and the DSO had told him would happen was coming true. He had to hide and gain time. As his hands reached for the safety of the passage, the bullets hit him in the right shoulder below his neck, driving up at an angle into muscle and bone. The force took him down before he could take a step, his head hitting the edge of the corner wall, the impact rendering him unconscious.

As the first residue of burnt powder reached his nose, the killer watched as Hamilton fell to the floor, his arms hitting the balustrade with surprising force. He knew he had missed his target, Hamilton's head, and he cursed savagely.

He had lost the opportunity and he would have to go up and finish the job. He looked at Kirsty, lying where she had fallen, perfectly still. He was about to start his ascent of the stairs when, like a visitation from hell, Steiner appeared in the opening. His reflexes superb, the man levelled the Beretta, firing twice. But Steiner, his anticipation razor-sharp, was moving before the bullets left the gun. Using the door jamb, he swung out of sight, going low.

Without a sound, the man turned and ran down the passage to the kitchen. He could not take the risk of going after Steiner. In seconds he reached the back door. The key was in the lock. He opened the door and like a gazelle ahead of a predator went into the night.

When Steiner heard the man go down the passage he rose and went through the door, immediately kneeling next to Kirsty and placing his hand under her head. Her breathing was strong and he ran his hand down her face. Her eyes opened slowly. 'Kirsty, I'm here,' he said, leaning over and kissing her. 'You're safe. He's gone.'

She put her hand behind his head and held him, not wanting him to leave her again. 'I'm sorry,' she said. 'He was too quick. Where's Hamilton, the guards?'

'I don't know,' said Steiner. 'But that can wait.' He gently touched the bruise where the man had hit her. 'Do you want to lie here?' he said. 'I'll get some water.'

'I'll get up,' she said. She pushed herself onto her elbow. 'I'm so glad to see you.'

He helped her to her feet and together they went into the reception room. She was quickly regaining her strength and sat down in the nearest chair. 'Please find Hamilton.'

He left the room, went to the stairs and saw Hamilton's still prone form on the first-floor landing up against the balustrade. He climbed to him and saw where the bullets had entered the shoulder and the cut on his head, the seepage of blood already clotting. He felt the pulse. It was weak but Hamilton was still alive. The wounds were superficial flesh wounds and he would survive. He could stay as he was until help arrived. The killer had failed to get the last of the four.

Steiner left Hamilton, went down the stairs and through to the kitchen. The door was moving gently in the night air and he looked out into the blackness. Even if he had given chase, allowing enough distance to avoid being shot, he would soon have lost him. The man knew where he was going and by now would have left the area. He poured a glass of water and returned to the sitting room.

Kirsty looked up when she saw him. 'Where is Hamilton?' she said.

'He's lying at the top of the stairs,' said Steiner, giving her the glass. 'He was shot but will live. He's unconscious. I'll return to him.'

'I'm so glad,' she said, taking the water. 'I really made a mess of that. I couldn't believe what I was seeing when he appeared on the verandah with that black mask.'

'I'd have been surprised,' said Steiner. 'I couldn't sleep in the car and I was beginning to think we were wasting our time. That's when we are most vulnerable. He was a slick operator but this time his aim let him down. Hamilton got two bullets in the shoulder. They're superficial flesh wounds.'

'The guy must have silenced the guards,' said Kirsty. 'He wouldn't have dared so brazen an entry if he hadn't and he came from that side of the house.'

'I'll go and see,' said Steiner. He left the house, quickly came to the room and found the two guards. He confirmed they were dead and returned to the house.

'He killed the two men,' said Steiner when he reached Kirsty. 'They were shot, in the head and chest. It's not difficult to admire the way this person works. He's like a machine.' He saw a phone on a small table and crossed to it. 'I'm going to ring Weisz at home,' he said. 'It's time he knew what was going on and Hamilton needs attention.' He rang the number.

Weisz answered. 'Weisz.'

'Bruce, James Steiner.'

'This must be important,' said Weisz. 'Obviously there's no peace for the wicked.'

'I'm at Hamilton's house,' said Steiner. 'He was shot but he's alright. He hit his head on something, probably the wall, and is unconscious. I'm afraid the guy who did it escaped. He knocked Kirsty cold. I was too late.'

'How is she?' asked Weisz, not bothering to ask Steiner what he was doing at Hamilton's. He was getting used to him.

'She's alright,' said Steiner. 'How do you want to play this? Hamilton needs a doctor.'

Weisz thought for a moment then said: 'I'll get a doctor and ambulance to the house. I'll need some people from forensics to have a look before the body's removed. I'll see you in about thirty minutes. I take it you're alright.'

'Yes,' said Steiner. He replaced the receiver and faced Kirsty. 'Weisz's on his way.' He walked over to her and touched her on the cheek. 'You shouldn't have approached him. If you'd threatened his chances of escape he would've killed you.'

'I didn't think of that when I saw him,' she said. 'It happened so quickly. What will you tell Weisz? You didn't elaborate on the phone.'

'I've nothing to hide,' said Steiner. 'We were right but it shows how difficult it is to stop someone who is clever and determined to see something through, particularly when the element of surprise is weighted heavily in their favour.'

'We're left with nothing,' said Kirsty. 'We still have no idea who's behind it. I think this is going to be another of those unsolved cases.'

'I think we'll get a lead,' said Steiner. 'We are close and all this has something to do with Andrew Rohm. It is too

215

much of a coincidence that Hilton went and saw Peter Smith about Rohm's illegal business affairs a day before he was murdered.'

'How long are you prepared to wait?' asked Kirsty. 'These people might think Hamilton's not worth it and be satisfied with three. They will go to ground and never be found. If Rohm is involved, he is far too smart to expose himself when he has successfully eliminated Hilton. Dredge and Hamilton said he hadn't told them anything except that five industrialists were involved in serious crime. They weren't given any names.'

'Rohm doesn't know that,' said Steiner. 'And perhaps he is not satisfied. Men like that don't give up until all their demands are met. After this the President might dig in his heals and not replace Dredge and Hamilton with the two men named in the letter. That could well be unacceptable to Rohm. If it is, we will soon hear more.'

'You haven't answered my question,' said Kirsty. 'How long are you prepared to wait?'

'If Weisz doesn't get rid of me when he arrives, I'll tell him seven days,' said Steiner. 'If nothing happens in that time we'll go and see your sons and return to London. This is not my line of work.'

'I don't think it's exciting enough for you,' she said. 'You like people you can see.' She got up and went to the door. 'Would you like some coffee?'

'Yes,' said Steiner. 'I'll come with you.' They made instant coffee and returned to the front room.

Forty minutes later Weisz arrived. He parked near the garage. Steiner went out to meet him and led the way into the house and to the front room. Kirsty was standing near the window.

'I knew I shouldn't have let the two of you out of my sight,' said Weisz after he had greeted Kirsty. 'First it's the farm, then at Smith's in Durban and now here.' He looked at Kirsty. 'James told me you were knocked unconscious. Are you alright?'

'Yes,' said Kirsty, and told him what had happened.

Weisz turned to Steiner. 'When did you arrive?'

'The man was in the passage and about to leave,' said Steiner. 'He fired at me, missed, and ran out through the kitchen. I stayed with Kirsty. Even if she had been alright, I had no chance of stopping him. I wasn't close enough and he would've gunned me down.'

'You should carry a gun,' said Weisz. 'I can't understand why you don't. I've brought a Beretta 90two with me and even if you never carry it I'd like you to take it. A very useful Burris Xtreme Tactical laser flashlight comes as an accessory. It is very small and fits under the slide, no need to carry a torch. There's also a silencer. Where's Hamilton?'

'I'll take you to him,' said Steiner. 'After that I'll show you the dead guards. I assume the others are on their way.'

'Yes,' said Weisz. 'The two from forensics weren't too happy.'

They climbed the stairs to the landing. Hamilton was still unconscious but breathing evenly. 'The killer finally screwed up,' said Weisz. 'But he still knows how to shoot. You can't get a smaller grouping than that. Let's go and see the guards.'

Steiner took Weisz out of the house and round to the guards' room. 'That's how I found them,' he said, standing aside to let Weisz enter. 'Two shots pumped into each. It reminds me of an article I read about the heyday of the Israeli hit squads in the early-eighties. They were taught always to fire two bullets into their targets. It makes sense.'

'Yes,' said Weisz. 'I remember when they were at their peak, wiping out their PLO enemies wherever they were hiding. Did you find anything on these guys?'

'I didn't look,' said Steiner. 'The killer must have got the keys from them. I haven't found them. He must have parked his car at the back of the property. He didn't come in through the front. We would've seen him.'

'Clever bastard,' said Weisz. 'I'll bet he knew there were guards. Let's go inside.' They returned to the front room in the house.

Ten minutes later, the doctor, an ambulance and two men from the DSO forensic section arrived at the house. Thirty minutes later, the on-site work was completed. Hamilton had just regained consciousness and was taken away in the ambulance to Cape Town. Weisz had spoken a few words to him but planned to see him later when he had further recovered.

'I'll notify Hamilton's family and the President's office of events when I get to work,' said Weisz. 'I'm going there now. I'll let his ex-girlfriend Emma Cosgrave know after speaking to his family; they had remained close.' He looked at Steiner. 'What do you think we should do now? We get close and then hit another blank.'

'Kirsty and I were talking about this earlier,' said Steiner. 'It's impossible to know what these people will do next. They might be satisfied with three dead men and go to ground. If they're not they could have another go at Hamilton. From Smith's notes they know Hilton was the main player and a lot depends on what they think he told the others. After my conversation with Dredge and Hamilton that was not much. Another variable is how important it is for them to get the replacements listed in their letter appointed. If the President doesn't replace Dredge and Hamilton with the required men, even if Hamilton had been killed, they might find it unacceptable. I'm also sure we are dealing with people who have a lot of pride and that can be dangerous. If they do stop now it will be virtually impossible to find them without a large slice of luck or someone in their camp blabbing.' He looked through the windows and then faced Weisz. 'There is nothing I can do with what we already know. I was hoping

218

for something tonight but Teichmann was my only real chance of a breakthrough and he's dead. I think this matter is now for the police to put on their books and investigate. If you wish I'm prepared to stay around for another seven days. After that we'll return to London.'

'I'd like you to stay on for at least the seven days,' said Weisz. 'I'll then pass this business over to the police but keep Fairley on it. I'll expand his brief. I'm also obliged to follow up on the work started by Peter Smith. Even if we can't pin these murders on Rohm, we might be able to nail him and his friends on what Hilton believed he uncovered. Let's call it a night and I'll ring you tomorrow.'

'Thank you,' said Steiner. They left the house and after Weisz had handed over the pistol, parted company, Weisz going to his car and Steiner and Kirsty to theirs.

'So it's now a case of sitting and waiting,' said Steiner as they left the car park. 'Perhaps we should go and see some sights tomorrow.'

'I'm not into that,' said Kirsty. 'I've no desire to walk up Table Mountain either. The pictures are enough for me.'

'I understand,' he said. 'I get the feeling you like the fast lane.'

'Yes, after being with you,' she said. 'As much as I liked farm life, I'm getting used to London. It's a very exciting city. What do want to do?'

'Now?' he said. 'That's easy. I want to make love to you.'

Chapter 87

It was five o'clock, an hour before dawn, when Paul Bale received a phone call at home from Conran. He had already dressed and was about to have breakfast.

'Hamilton was shot early this morning,' said Conran. 'I don't think he's dead. Steiner and his girlfriend appeared on the scene and interrupted the process. The guards were eliminated.'

'I'm not interested in the guards,' said Bale caustically. 'What exactly went wrong? Why wasn't Steiner killed? It sounds as if it was a perfect opportunity to kill both of them at the same time.'

'The woman arrived and had to be dealt with before Hamilton,' said Conran. 'She was knocked out but Steiner then turned up. The risk of being outplayed by him was enough to justify leaving Hamilton and getting out.'

'Did Steiner recognize your guy?' said Bale, feeling his frustration grow. Rohm would be enraged when he heard the news.

'No,' said Conran. 'He was wearing a balaclava. He didn't want to risk the guards identifying him later if they managed to escape. What do you want to do now? I'm afraid the totally unexpected caught him short. That could have happened to anyone. It would've helped if Rohm's assassin had got rid of Steiner before.' He liked telling Bale something he didn't want to hear.

'I'll speak to Rohm and get back to you,' said Bale. 'He wanted Hamilton killed and out of the way. He also wants the final two replacements on his list sworn in. He was going to put pressure on the President to do it now. If the President doesn't comply, the corruption of some of the blacks in his cabinet will be exposed. Rohm didn't say anything about more killing but we've still got Hamilton.' He cut the call and prepared himself for the call to Rohm. He would phone him when he got up. It was not the sort of news he wanted to give him.

Chapter 88

Cape Town

When John Conran got to work in the morning, Weisz buzzed him and asked him to see him.

'They tried to kill Hamilton early this morning at his house,' said Weisz. Conran had seated himself in his office. 'Steiner and Callard were there and the killer got away. Hamilton was shot twice but he's alright.' He gave Conran the details as he knew them.

'So we're still on home base,' said Conran, shaking his head. 'Steiner's not having any luck. What's he going to do now?'

'We've agreed that he will give it another seven days,' said Weisz. 'He'll then return to London with Kirsty Callard. Hamilton will recover, be given another guard and we'll just wait. I've informed Tyson and I don't think they'll replace Dredge and Hamilton now with those listed in that letter. The President was fuming when Delaware was killed before he could name his and Hilton's replacements. I still have to tell Fairley about this but I'll leave him to carry on with his investigation into the allegations. He is going to contact Smith's people and arrange a meeting.'

'I'll be here if you need me for anything,' said Conran getting up. 'We're dealing with some very clever people.'

Chapter 89

Cape Town

At eight in the morning, Bale phoned Andrew Rohm.

'Andrew, Paul Bale. A hit was made on Hamilton last night. I'm afraid it wasn't successful.'

'What went wrong?' said Rohm. 'The man should have been able to do it in his sleep.'

'Steiner and Callard were there,' said Bale quietly. He had expected a stronger reaction. 'She got to the scene first and the man disabled her. Hamilton appeared but the guy didn't kill him. He fired two shots but they missed the vitals. Before he could try again, Steiner showed up. His only option was to leave. If he had stayed he might have been nailed and exposed the whole thing.'

As much as didn't like the news, Rohm had learnt the hard way never to dwell on what went wrong. 'I'm not going to be put off by that,' he said. 'Hamilton will be well protected while he recovers. By the sounds of it, that should be no more than a couple of days. He'll then be open game if he carries on as before and it's up to Conran's man to choose his moment and kill him. Go ahead with the letter to the President. He will know that Hamilton is included. He is in a weak position over this and he has to comply. If he doesn't realize that he is obtuse. I'm also going to ask Kallis to put the final squeeze on Steiner. He has been around for too long.'

'I'll send the letter now,' said Bale. 'I was waiting for Hamilton to be killed. When are you going to your estate?'

'I'll go tomorrow morning,' said Rohm. 'There is no reason for me to be here while this is sorted out and you can reach me there. Everything now depends on Conran and the President pulling his finger out. Why don't you come to Paarl as well? You can meet some of my business friends. It's a lovely area and my place is in a valley near Paarl Mountain with a great view of Klein Drakenstein mountain in the east. I was interested when you told me that Hilton, Dredge and Hamilton have homes near Stellenbosch. That's the other side of the N1 from me, about fifteen kilometres south. It's a small world.'

'I would like that,' said Bale. 'I don't really know the area but I've heard it's great. Let me know when you arrive.'

Chapter 90

The President's office, Cape Town

'So at last they blew it,' said the President. Tyson had just informed him of the failed attempt on Hamilton's life. The two men were alone. 'I don't want this to reach the media.'

'I've already seen to that,' said Tyson. 'Weisz was the first to know and contacted me. He hasn't spoken to anyone else about it except two of his agents. He'll keep it that way unless you instruct him otherwise.'

'But you say Weisz was called to Hamilton's house early this morning,' said the President. 'Who called him and why did the killer fail?'

'Weisz has an agent James Steiner from the DSO in Durban dedicated to the job of finding the people behind these murders,' said Tyson. 'He was at the house when the killer struck and managed to drive him off after he'd fired two shots into Hamilton. The wounds are not serious and Hamilton will be at work in a day or two. He'll speak to you this afternoon and Weisz says he's in good spirits.'

'Well it's good to hear that Weisz's people were close to nailing the guy,' said the President. 'It's a pity he escaped. This business is on the front pages every day and the main item on television news broadcasts. The families of the dead men are also howling for blood. If Hamilton had been killed, I shudder to think what would've happened to me.'

'You would have been forced to resign,' said Tyson, simply. 'You could then retire to your farm and walk the hills with Mandela.'

The President looked at Tyson dispassionately. 'I'm relying on you to make sure that doesn't happen,' he said. 'I want you to call a cabinet meeting this morning. I have the support of those who count and it's important to keep them reasonably well informed.'

'How are the replacements for Hilton and Delaware fitting in?' asked Tyson. 'When are you going to name the last two?'

'I get on well with them,' said the President. 'I can't criticize the killers for their choice. I don't know why they were selected but I don't care as long as they don't cause trouble. I'll name Dredge's replacement as requested on Saturday but I'll let you know later if I intend to include Hamilton's. He certainly wouldn't like it, particularly now he has survived an attack on his life. He will be as defiant as ever and I don't blame him. In the meantime push Weisz to find those behind all this. I want their balls to boil.'

'I'll keep the pressure on him and call the meeting,' said Tyson. He left the office.

Chapter 91

Cape Town

After speaking to Weisz, John Conran returned to his office. The failed attempt on Hamilton's life was one thing but his mind was also on the conversation he'd had on Tuesday evening with Adam Fairley in the Nightcap bar. In particular, he remembered Fairley asking him if he had said anything to Paul Bale about Steiner and momentarily being caught off-guard. At the time he didn't think Fairley had noticed anything but later he was not so sure. Fairley's time with Scotland Yard's Specialist Crime Directorate had given him considerable experience in interviewing and delivering the conviction of some very clever criminals. In gaining that experience, Fairley would have learnt a lot about questioning technique, and reaction and hesitation when people were interrogated. Conran's creeping doubt meant there was a risk Fairley could expose him as the person passing on information to the outside. Fairley might believe he was the insider and act accordingly.

Thirty minutes later and after his second cup of coffee, Conran knew there was only one way of erasing the risk. But first he wanted to speak to Bale.

Adam Fairley liked working for the DSO. He respected Steiner but was disappointed he had not been given the job of tracking down the person who was killing the ministers. It was the type of work he'd been used to in the Specialist Crime Directorate at New Scotland Yard. He appreciated Steiner's obvious frustration at not making any real progress and he agreed that the people behind the killings were receiving information from someone inside the DSO. If there was a leak and the guilty party exposed, it could be the breakthrough needed to crack the case and it was this that now occupied his mind.

Fairley had spent a lot of time trying to get confessions out of suspected criminals. He had acquired the ability to notice the slightest change of expression and variations resulting from questions asked and constant probing. During the conservation with John Conran at the Nightcap he had not failed to see such a change when he had asked Conran about him saying anything to Bale about Steiner. Even though Conran had recovered rapidly, the lapse was still noticeable to the trained eye. This was not proof that Conran had conveyed, deliberately or not, something that could be detrimental to Steiner's progress but there was still a chance that he had and was therefore involved with the people behind the murders. If he was involved, Bale was too.

When he got to work in the morning, Fairley was told by Weisz that a failed attempt had been made on Hamilton's life in the early hours of the morning. Fortunately, Steiner and Kirsty Callard had been keeping watch on Hamilton's house and had disturbed the killer. The person had escaped. Fairley was aware that the DSO was still in the position with nothing to go on and during the day the more he thought about the conversation with Conran the more he realized that he had to act. It was at one in the afternoon when he decided to phone James Steiner.

Chapter 92

Johannesburg

After speaking to Bale, Andrew Rohm made a cup of coffee and stood at the French doors, his thoughts on the conversation. The way Steiner kept popping up was uncanny, first at Smith's house in Durban, then at Teichmann's and now at Hamilton's place in Stellenbosch. The man wouldn't go away and he began to wish that Kallis had taken the chance and killed him at Callard's farm. He was looking forward to going down to his wine estate near Paarl, a part of the world he really loved, probably more than anywhere else. He had invited the four men named by Hilton on the list he'd given Smith to join him but only two were available, John Ashley, sixty-five, head of the largest legal practice in the country, and Bryan Jones, forty-eight, an extremely bright consulting engineer, chairman of a leading industrial conglomerate. The men were married but like others in their position had mistresses. In some ways Rohm regretted breaking up with his most recent girlfriend but a change of woman was sometimes therapeutic when business demands were intense.

As he had told Bale, Rohm had decided to go down to Paarl tomorrow morning. Since the four men were part of the plan to eliminate the ministers and aware of subsequent developments involving Smith and Steiner, mostly initiated by him, Rohm had kept them, particularly Jones, informed of progress. Jones was very astute in dealing with their enemies and was ruthless. He had shown a lot of interest when he had heard about the appearance of Steiner and his interference in past activities concerning the group files. Rohm had already told Jones when he was going to Paarl but now after hearing from Bale he wanted to run the latest developments past him before seeing him. He went to his desk and rang him at work in Johannesburg. Jones answered.

'Bryan, it is Andrew Rohm. I've just had a call from Paul Bale. Hamilton has a guardian angel. He's still alive.'

'I thought you were ringing with good news,' said Jones. He was in his office on the top floor of one of the highest buildings in Johannesburg. 'What went wrong? I hope you're not going to cancel Paarl.'

'No,' said Rohm. 'Conran's guy went to Hamilton's place in Stellenbosch last night but before he could finish the job, Kirsty Callard appeared followed by Steiner. He knocked out the woman but couldn't risk it with Steiner and fled.'

'He'll just have to return and do it properly,' said Jones. 'If Hamilton was a threat he would have squealed by now but letting him live is unfinished business as far as I'm concerned. We also want the replacements for Dredge and Hamilton named. They're waiting to hear when they take up their new positions in the cabinet alongside their friends; has Bale sent the letter?'

'He'll have it delivered this morning,' said Rohm. 'What about Steiner?'

'He'll never get us but he is beginning to piss me off,' said Jones. 'He must be laughing, in between screwing the girl. You said she's enough to die for.'

'I've never seen her,' said Rohm. 'Bale heard something like that from Conran. I'm going to put a fire cracker up Kallis's arse and tell him to get rid of Steiner. As long as he draws breath, he's a dangerous threat to us. He doesn't play by the rules and Teichmann was lucky he didn't beat the shit out of him. Anyone who calmly kills five group men and a DSO informer, if we exclude Jan Krige, will never rest until he has completed his brief.'

'Why do you exclude Krige?' asked Jones. 'He was also killed.'

'It looks as if he was killed by Callard,' said Rohm. 'He was shot and it is unlikely Steiner had a gun. She was present.'

'Tell Kallis to kill them both,' said Jones. He was quiet for a moment, laughed briefly and then continued. 'Why don't you put Conran's guy on to them as well, just to make sure? You'd then be the only person in the history of the Republic who has two of the highest paid assassins chasing after the same two people.'

'Thanks,' said Rohm, 'but as tempting as it sounds it would be too complicated. I also have principles.'

'Do you know who Conran's using?' said Jones. 'Except for Hamilton it sounds as if the person knows what he's doing, if it's a man. There are some very capable women out there.'

'I don't know and I'm not interested,' said Rohm. 'I'm satisfied that someone like Conran is directing it. Unless I need direct contact with someone or they are my enemies, I'm quite happy not knowing their identity. I believe that's how Conran operates and I respect it. This is not a women's tea party. I'll let you know what I decide when I see you in Paarl.'

Chapter 93

Cape Town

Paul Bale had just come out of a meeting when he received the call from Conran.

'John, how can I help?' he said. 'It must be urgent. I've spoken to Rohm.'

'There's something I'm not happy about and I thought I'd run it by you before I act,' said Conran.

'Go ahead,' said Bale. 'I'm listening.'

'On Tuesday evening I was having a drink with Adam Fairley and he was going on about there being a leak in the DSO. It goes back to Teichmann and Kallis and how they knew Steiner was in town. Fairley knows I sometimes to speak to you and he asked me if I'd ever said anything to you about Steiner.'

'So what if you have?' said Bale. 'Even though the DSO is an independent agency it still comes under the NPA and we exchange information.'

'I understand that,' said Conran, 'but the problem arises if the person thinks the information goes further and is used to give the opposition an advantage.'

'What are you saying?' said Bale.

'When Fairley asked me the question, I was momentarily caught off-guard because I was guilty,' said Conran. 'I think I might have revealed that guilt. I know that you pass on information I give you to Rohm. If Fairley interpreted my momentary lapse as that of someone who has something to hide, he might take action.'

'In other words he is dangerous,' said Bale. 'I see what you mean. There is of course the chance that he didn't notice anything to make him suspicious. The question is dare we take the risk.'

'Yes,' said Conran. 'I don't think we should. If he goes to Weisz, Steiner or even the President's security officer about his suspicion it could blow us apart, including Rohm.'

'What do you suggest?' said Bale.

'He'll have to be removed,' said Conran.

'That means through you,' said Bale. 'I don't know anyone and I can't ask Rohm to find someone. You realize I'll have to tell him.'

'I understand that,' said Conran. 'Since it was my lapse I'll see it's done. There will then be no comeback unless he has already set the wheels moving.'

'I think we would have heard something by now if he had,' said Bale, 'but it should still be as soon as possible, like tonight. If he is suspicious he might be working out his moves before he acts. I'm joining Rohm at his estate in Paarl when he goes down there tomorrow. You can always get me on my mobile.'

Chapter 94

Cape Town

'That was a nice start to your seven days,' said Kirsty, reclining in her seat. It was just after lunch and she and Steiner were in the front lounge of the Mandarin Hotel. They had spent the morning at Hout Bay on the other side Constantiaberg, seven kilometres south of Table Mountain. 'I didn't think it would be so beautiful.'

'There are always surprises in life,' said Steiner. 'I've come to realize that since meeting you.' He smiled. 'Sometimes they are dangerous. What would you like to do this afternoon? I dare not suggest climbing Table Mountain even though you are in such good shape.'

'Thank you,' said Kirsty. 'You are so sweet. I'm quite happy lazing next to the swimming pool with you.'

'We'll do that,' said Steiner. He was about to leave his seat when his phone rang. He took it from the pocket of his jeans. 'Steiner.'

'James, it is Adam Fairley. I hope I'm not disturbing you after such a busy night.'

'You've obviously heard from Weisz,' said Steiner. 'Sitting outside Hamilton's house was the only thing Kirsty and I could think of.'

'Weisz said she was knocked out,' said Fairley. 'I hope she's alright.'

Steiner looked at Kirsty. 'She's strong,' he said. 'How are things going with you?'

'That's why I'm phoning,' said Fairley. 'You said you believe there is an insider in the DSO, someone who is giving information to the people behind these murders. The only people who know what has happened to you and Smith, including your visit to Teichmann and our belief that he was killed because of it, are Weisz and Conran. You met David Strauss when you first arrived but he has never been involved in our discussions concerning the case. I trusted both Weisz and Conran but now I'm not so sure.' He went quiet and Steiner could hear him take a drink. 'On Tuesday evening I was at a bar with Conran and asked him if he had passed anything on to Paul Bale the NDPP concerning you. It was a casual question since Conran sometimes talks to Bale, as does Weisz, and I didn't expect the brief change I saw on Conran's face. He was caught off-balance and it made me think. I haven't said anything to anyone including Weisz but it has not left me.'

Steiner sank back his seat. 'What are you thinking?' he said.

'I think he has said stuff about you to Bale that he shouldn't have and he knows it,' said Fairley. 'The only information we pass on to external parties like the NPA concerns definite progress like making an arrest. I'm not saying Conran is deliberately betraying us. It could simply mean that he is aware he made a slip and regrets it. But it is the uncertainty that gets me.'

'It is that uncertainty that requires investigation,' said Steiner. 'I will have to give it some thought. All we have rests on your interpretation of what you believe you saw in a split second but it is enough for me. If Conran passed on information knowing it would be used against us, he is as guilty of the killings as the people behind them and this might be the break we want. Why don't you come round and see me? We've got some talking to do before we take this further. You could be on to something. What about this evening?'

'It will have to be late,' said Fairley. 'I've got some other things to clear. I can be at your hotel at around ten.'

'That's fine,' said Steiner. 'I'll see you then.' He slipped the phone into his pocket.

'That sounded interesting,' said Kirsty. 'Are you still on the job?'

'What was I saying about surprises?' said Steiner. 'That was Adam Fairley.' He told Kirsty the reason for the call, including Fairley's observations. He added his own thoughts and said that Fairley was coming to the hotel later in the evening at ten.

'One tiny reaction that could open the case wide,' said Kirsty, thoughtfully. 'But Fairley didn't say if Conran suspected he'd been caught off-guard.'

'No,' said Steiner. 'There would have been no way of knowing if he had. That's part of the uncertainty. If Conran had passed on the information we don't know if Bale relayed it to the people behind all this. He might be innocent and if he had heard anything kept it to himself. He is at the top of the tree, reporting only to the minister of justice, Hilton's replacement and a new guy on the block '

Kirsty laughed dryly. 'And the new minister might be in bed with Rohm, if Rohm's behind the killings. We know he was on the list but it might be because he's no threat to an illegal empire he knows about or of which he is a part.'

'I assumed the replacements named on the list were clean politicians but perhaps they are also criminals in their own right,' said Steiner.

'Where are you and Fairley going on this?' asked Kirsty.

'I'm not sure,' said Steiner. 'It means telling Weisz and seeing what he says or going it alone and trying to trap Conran. Maybe it should be a mixture of both. We certainly can't barge in on Conran and accuse him of colluding with the enemy.'

'He would have you arrested,' said Kirsty. 'What about the swimming pool? I'll get the gear from the room.' She got up and left.

Chapter 95

Cape Town

Immediately after the call from Conran, Paul Bale phoned Rohm. Rohm answered.

'Andrew, it is Paul Bale. I've just had another call from Conran.'

'He couldn't have got to Hamilton so quickly,' said Rohm grinning. 'What does he want?'

Bale repeated what Conran had said about the conversation with Fairley. He concluded by saying Conran felt there was a threat of exposure and Fairley had to be killed. 'Conran's going to see it's done. We can't afford to take the risk and Conran's being very honest. I don't hold this against him.'

'I agree,' said Rohm. 'Let him do it.'

'I'll tell him,' said Bale. 'With a bit of luck this will all be completed while we're in Paarl.'

'I can't wait,' said Rohm. 'We'll celebrate together. Make sure you send the letter to the President.'

'I've sent it,' said Bale. He cut the call and phoned Conran.

'John, Paul Bale. I've spoken to Rohm and passed on what you told me about Fairley. He agrees that he should be eliminated.'

'I'll be in contact,' said Conran. 'I hope you enjoy Paarl.'

Chapter 96

Johannesburg

Andrew Rohm was pleased. Things were beginning to move and the end of a plan he had spent hours thinking about was in sight. The final move on his part before he could relax in Paarl and wait for results was to set Kallis loose again. He rang him on his mobile. The phone rang for a while before Kallis answered.

'Marc, Andrew Rohm. I hope you're ready to start moving again.'

'Yes,' said Kallis. 'I want to get paid and get back to my job in Pretoria.'

'Steiner and Callard are still at the Mandarin Hotel in Cape Town,' said Rohm. 'As soon as you finish them you'll be paid.'

'And you're sure you want the girl killed as well?' said Kallis.

'Yes,' said Rohm. 'She was always against what her husband was doing for the group and was the prime mover behind Steiner in getting the files and securing the conviction of our men. I'll regret it later if I don't seize the chance now and remove her.'

'It's not what I like doing but you're paying,' said Kallis. 'Do you know what Steiner has been up to down there?'

'No,' said Rohm. 'He's probably waiting by the pool for you to come for him. I'm going to my estate in Paarl tomorrow morning. I'll be there for a few days, maybe a week.'

'I'll ring you when it's over,' said Kallis.

Chapter 97

Cape Town

Emma Cosgrave wasn't surprised when Hamilton had called off their relationship but she was glad. She was hoping he would because she was fond of him and didn't want to hurt him by doing it herself. For a while the excitement and chemistry that existed between them had died and she was not really interested in rekindling a faltering flame. He had become physically unattractive with a sagging belly and a waist larger than his chest, sadly the affliction of most men over forty-five and mainly the result of stuffing too much food into themselves and insufficient exercise. Perhaps if she and Hamilton had been married she would have tried to persuade him to give their relationship another chance. He had also shown a lack of interest in her, which she had difficulty understanding because she was intelligent and very attractive. After the breakup, Emma and Hamilton still kept in touch with one another and they had met a few times in the city for lunch. She had a flat in the centre and not far from the government buildings where Hamilton worked.

The day before Hamilton was shot, Emma spoke to him on the phone and she was devastated when Weisz phoned her after lunch and told her of the attempt on his life. She calmed down when Weisz assured her that Hamilton was not seriously injured and would be on his feet in a couple of days.

'Do you know who did it?' she asked. 'Who would want to do such a thing?'

'It is certainly the same person who killed his three friends,' said Weisz. 'Unfortunately we don't have a lead.'

'Who found Anthony?' she asked. 'You said it was in the early hours this morning.'

239

'One of our agents James Steiner was the first there,' said Weisz. 'He has been actively engaged in this case and was keeping watch at the house. There were also two guards on duty but the killer came in the back way and killed them. We are dealing with very clever people and Hamilton refused to stay in a safe house. It would have afforded better protection.'

'Anthony mentioned Steiner,' said Emma. 'If I remember correctly, he arrived a week ago and paid a visit to him and Colin Dredge. He comes from London.'

'That's right,' said Weisz. 'He is staying at the Mandarin Hotel near you.' He waited a moment. 'Please contact me if I can be of any help. I'll let you know when we find the people behind this.'

'Thank you,' she said. 'Please keep me informed. They've got a lot to answer for.'

Emma was sitting at her desk and after Weisz had gone she rested her head in her hands, thinking. For a while she sat like that and then she reached for the phone book. She found the listing for the Mandarin Hotel and rang the number. A woman answered. 'Mandarin Hotel; how may I help you?'

'I'd like to speak to James Steiner?' said Emma. 'I believe he is staying there.'

'I can see him seated in the reception,' said the girl. 'I'll call him to the phone.'

Emma waited and then heard the phone being lifted and Steiner's voice. 'James Steiner.'

Emma gave her name and then said: 'I've just had a call from Bruce Weisz of the DSO. He told me someone tried to kill Anthony Hamilton last night and you were first on the scene. Is that correct? Anthony is a friend of mine.'

'Yes,' said Steiner. 'I got there after the man had fired the shots. Unfortunately he escaped.'

'And you don't have a lead?' said Emma. 'Anthony would've been the fourth.'

'I'm aware of that,' said Steiner. 'There's nothing more I can tell you except that we're doing our best to find the people involved.'

'You think it's more than one?' said Emma.

'Yes,' said Steiner. 'At the moment I can't say any more than that.'

'Maybe I can help you,' said Emma. 'I think we should meet. I have a flat near you. Would you like to come there?'

'If you wish,' said Steiner. 'I'm seeing someone later this evening but I'm available earlier.'

'I'm not here then,' said Emma. 'Does eight tomorrow morning suit you?'

'Fine,' said Steiner. 'What's your address?'

Emma gave him the details and added: 'I'll see you at eight.'

After Emma Cosgrave's call, Steiner went back to his table. Kirsty had just returned from collecting their bathing gear. 'I saw you on the phone,' she said. 'Is it a secret admirer?'

'She is hardly that,' said Steiner. 'Her name is Emma Cosgrave, Hamilton's ex-girlfriend. She introduced herself as a friend of his. Weisz told her about Hamilton and that I was the first one there.'

'Fame spreads quickly,' said Kirsty teasingly. 'I assume you told her the guy vanished.'

'Yes,' said Steiner, 'but she said something very interesting. When I said that we think there is more than one person behind the murders she said she may be able to help. She said we should meet and suggested her flat. It's near here.'

'Did you mention me?' said Kirsty.

'No,' said Steiner, 'but you're coming along. We agreed on eight in the morning. She's got another engagement this evening.'

'And she gave you no clue what it's about?' said Kirsty. 'It sounds very mysterious. This might be what you've been waiting for.'

'Fairley, and then this,' said Steiner. He picked up the sports bag containing their gear. 'Let's get changed. I want to see you in that new costume.'

Chapter 98

Cape Town

Adam Fairley worked until eight that night. After speaking to Steiner he had found it difficult to concentrate on the routine jobs he had to clear. He had seen John Conran a few times during the afternoon and they had discussed some of their cases. Conran had been his usual open self and Fairley at one point thought he was completely wrong in his suspicions.

After clearing his desk, Fairley turned out his office lights and made for the exit. The others on his passage had left. In a few minutes he was on the street and heading for his flat, ten minutes' walk from the DSO.

When Fairley reached his flat he turned on the lights and poured a drink. It was a modern, three-bedroom flat, well furnished, and access was by one flight of stairs and a corridor open to the elements. He had just sat down in front of the television set when the doorbell rang. He got up, went to the door and through the peephole saw John Conran.

'John,' he said, opening the door and standing to one side. 'This is a surprise. Come in and have a drink.'

Conran walked a few paces past Fairley into the small reception hall. He was wearing a leather jacket. 'Thanks, but I'm in a hurry. I saw you leave the office. There's something urgent I need to see you about.'

Fairley closed the door. 'What is it? You could have told me at work.'

'I couldn't do it there,' said Conran. He calmly reached inside his jacket, pulled out a silenced Beretta 90two 9mmx19 Luger/Parabellum pistol and fired two shots.

When Fairley saw the gun his mouth opened, a gasping fish, and when the bullets tore into his heart his expression

243

was that of the living dead. He fell to the carpet, his arms swinging uncontrollably away from his sides, flaying the wall with uncontrolled force. He came to rest in a straddled heap, a picture of pathos, his eyes closed. He had never expected the evening to be his last.

For a while Conran stared at stricken man, wondering what had happened to bring him to kill in cold blood a man he liked. He knelt next to the supine form and felt his pulse. Fairley was dead, blood already seeping from the holes in his chest, staining his white shirt. Conran unscrewed the silencer and left the flat for his car, leaving the body where it lay. Thirty minutes later he was at his home in Constantia.

Chapter 99

Cape Town

Steiner and Kirsty left the pool area shortly after six and returned to their room to shower and change. It had been a perfect afternoon for them and at eight-thirty they went downstairs for dinner in one of the hotel's restaurants. The food was Italian and the dishes and service excellent. After dinner they went into the front reception room, found a table and waited for Adam Fairley.

It was ten-thirty when Steiner looked at his watch and said: 'Fairley's late. He must have been held up at work.'

'Give him a ring,' said Kirsty.

Steiner extracted his mobile and rang Fairley's number. After several rings there was no reply and, cancelling the call, he said: 'He's not there. It's unlikely he's sitting at work without his phone but I'll try there.' He rang Fairley's DSO number. The result was the same and he shook his head. 'He's not at his desk.'

'That's very strange,' said Kirsty. 'After what he said to you earlier I don't like it. What do want to do, ring Weisz?'

'No,' said Steiner. 'He'll ask me why I'm concerned and I don't what to refer to Fairley's call. And, if there is something going on, he might be in with Conran.'

'There's only one option,' said Kirsty. 'Go round to Fairley's flat. Do you want me to come with you?'

'I'll go alone,' said Steiner. 'I'll ring you when I get there. If he's not there I might hang on for a while.'

'I'll wait here in the lounge,' she said.

He got up and left the hotel.

Steiner hadn't been to Fairley's flat but he had been given the address. In ten minutes he arrived at the building. The flat was on the second floor and he climbed the stairs to it.

He knocked on the door and waited. When there was no reply he tried Fairley's mobile. There was no answer and he pushed the flap on the letter box. He peered through. He immediately saw Fairley's supine form lying against the passage wall and the blood stain on his chest. For a while he stared at Fairley, the high probability that he was dead slowly sinking in. He had seen this before, the person still, no sign of breathing, blood like a red flower over the heart, and they had been dead. Fairley had been shot. A man with a knife would have gone in low under the ribcage or slit his throat from behind. He released the flap and looked at the lock. He had nothing with him that would allow access to the flat and he rang Kirsty. She answered.

'Fairley's in the flat,' he said, 'and I think he's dead. He's lying in the passage face-up, shot through the heart. I won't be able to get in without bursting the lock.'

'That's no coincidence,' said Kirsty. 'It has to be Conran.'

'Yes,' said Steiner. 'Even if he'd spoken to someone else about it after speaking to me, they wouldn't have acted without Conran's approval. I'll phone Weisz or leave it and let someone find Fairley tomorrow.'

'Are you sure he's dead?' said Kirsty. 'If you leave him and he's not, he might die when he could be saved.'

'Then I'll phone Weisz,' said Steiner, not prepared to take the risk. 'I won't say anything about Conran, just that I'd arranged to meet Fairley for a drink.'

'Do you want me there?' said Kirsty.

'No,' said Steiner. 'I'll phone you when I've contacted Weisz. I think he'll join me.'

Steiner looked again through the flap and then rang Weisz's mobile number. Weisz answered.

'Bruce, Steiner. I'm outside Fairley's flat.' He told Weisz what he'd seen and that he believed Fairley was dead.

'Wait there,' said Weisz. 'I'll be with you in twenty minutes.'

'I'll be here,' said Steiner. He cut the call. He had wanted to tell Weisz not to tell Conran but he couldn't at this stage.

After the call, Weisz phoned Conran at home. He answered.

'John, Weisz. Steiner's just phoned me. He's at Fairley's flat.' He repeated what Steiner had told him.

'What are you doing?' said Conran.

'I'm going there now,' said Weisz. 'I'll be able to get in. Would you like to join us?'

'There's not much I can do,' said Conran. 'Either way it doesn't sound if he's in good shape. He needs a doctor. What was Steiner doing there? I didn't know they saw one another socially.'

'He did not say,' said Weisz. 'I thought I'd keep you informed. I must go.' He cut the call and left his house for Fairley's flat. He'd been there before.

Steiner was leaning on the balcony outside Fairley flat when he saw Weisz appear below and go to the stairs.

'He's still lying there,' said Steiner as Weisz approached him.

Weisz held up a ring of small spike-like tools from his pocket. 'We'll get in with these,' he said, inserting one of the thin tools with a hook on the end into the lock. In seconds the door was open and Weisz went through the space.

Steiner followed, knelt next to Fairley and felt for a pulse at the side of his neck. 'He is dead,' he said. He unbuttoned the top of Fairley's shirt. 'Forensics will confirm the cause but bullet holes don't lie. There are two, very close together.

Using his cellphone, Weisz called a DSO number and gave instructions to the person who answered. 'Someone will be here soon,' he said, after the call. 'What a way to die. He hardly knew anyone and hadn't made any enemies that I knew of.' He looked at Steiner. 'Were you guys meeting for a drink?'

'Yes,' said Steiner. 'He was coming to the hotel but when he neither showed nor answered his phone I came here. The rest you know.'

'It's a pity you didn't come sooner,' said Weisz. 'You might have saved him. He obviously let the person in because he was shot here next to the door. The question is, did he know his killer.'

'We'll only know that when we find him,' said Steiner. 'I take it Adam didn't say anything to you that might have led to this.'

'Absolutely nothing,' said Weisz, 'and he updated me regularly. I'm in the dark.' He walked into the living room and glanced around. 'There's no point in you staying here. I'm glad you came round. You could have waited until the morning before doing anything. I told Conran before I left my house. I'll wait for forensics.'

'Is Conran coming here?' said Steiner.

'No,' said Weisz. 'I'm sure he's as mystified as I am.'

'I'll speak to you tomorrow,' said Steiner. He left the flat for the Mandarin.

When Steiner got back to the hotel he found Kirsty in the lounge. He went to her. 'I thought you might have gone to the room.'

'I said I'd wait down here for you,' she said. 'Did Weisz arrive?'

'Yes,' said Steiner. 'He's waiting for the medics. Fairley was shot. Weisz thinks he must have let in his killer because he was lying near the door but that doesn't mean he knew him. My feeling is that he did.'

248

'Conran?' said Kirsty.

'It's either him or someone connected to him,' said Steiner, 'but speculation doesn't help us. That's another chance gone. We're left with Cosgrave.'

Kirsty got up. 'We'll see what she has to say. Let's go to bed.'

Chapter 100

At the appointed time, Steiner and Kirsty went to Emma Cosgrave's flat. She showed them into the sitting room. 'Thank you for coming,' she said. 'I still can't get over someone wanting to kill Anthony.'

'At least he survived,' said Steiner. 'Did you know him well?'

'I knew him reasonably well,' she said. 'Everyone has secrets but he was fairly open. We had a steady relationship for two years before we split up. We remained good friends. I was going to have lunch with him today.'

'Have you seen him since you spoke to me?' said Kirsty.

'No,' she said. 'I spoke to him on the phone and he'll be out of hospital later today. I'll probably go and see him at his place in Stellenbosch.'

'So he's going there?' said Steiner. 'I've nothing to do with his security but there will be another attempt on his life and his house is not the place to be.'

'I told him that,' said Emma, 'but as before he won't listen.'

'You said you have something to tell me,' said Steiner. He glanced at Kirsty. 'She's in this with me.'

'I gathered that,' said Emma smiling. 'I don't think this is much but it might give you a lead. That's for you to decide.'

'I appreciate that,' said Steiner. 'At the moment we have nothing.'

'This goes back about a month,' said Emma, 'shortly after Hamilton and I had split. I have an older sister Jane who lives in Johannesburg. She is very clever, a lecturer in politics at Wits University. She was the girlfriend of one of South Africa's wealthiest industrialists and one day we were talking on the phone. Her relationship had just finished and like me and Hamilton she had stayed in touch with him.'

'What's the man's name?' said Steiner.

'Andrew Rohm,' said Emma. 'You must have heard of him.'

'I know of him,' said Steiner, expressionless.

'Jane had met several of Rohm's friends,' said Jane, 'and during the discussion she started talking about them and their dealings with Rohm. She mentioned one man and remembered a conversation between him and Rohm because she knew Hamilton was a cabinet minister. At the time I wasn't really interested but now after the killing of Hamilton's friends and the hit on his life I can't help remembering what she said. That's why I phoned you.'

'What did she say?' said Kirsty, her eyes firmly on Emma.

'The two men were in Rohm's study and talking about four cabinet ministers,' said Emma. 'They were Hamilton and his dead friends. Jane was in an adjacent room marking papers and even though the doors between the rooms were closed, she couldn't help hearing some of what was said. She laughed when she said she heard Rohm saying the four men, especially Hilton, had to be removed and asking the other man to arrange it. Jane wondered how it would be done. She called it the usual political manoeuvring that never ends.'

'Is that all?' said Steiner.

'She then spoke about other things,' said Emma, 'and at the time I put what she'd said down to her being a lecturer in politics, hearing that stuff all the time and accepting it as normal political zeal. I'm not so sure now.'

'Who was the other man?' said Steiner.

'Paul Bale, the National Director of Public Prosecutions,' said Emma. 'Apparently he is a close friend of Rohm's.'

Steiner sat forward in his chair, his elbows resting on his knees. 'Why are you not sure?'

'I hate saying this but it is Rohm's use of the word remove,' said Emma. 'That's Mafia-speak for kill. I know Rohm's success is not entirely the result of legitimate business activity and I imagine he protects those interests – how I don't know but it can't always be clean.'

'And you know he's guilty of crime?' said Kirsty, unnerved.

'I have no proof,' said Emma, 'but there were small things I picked up during conversations with Jane. I've never met him.'

'I assume you've spoken to your sister since then?' said Steiner.

'Yes, several times,' said Emma. 'I last spoke to her on Wednesday, the day before Hamilton was shot. I didn't think of raising this then because it hadn't registered. She did say that Rohm is going to his estate near Paarl this morning. I've been through Paarl and the turn-off is marked in the town centre. It simply says Blaukrantz. If anything comes of this and you decide to pay him a visit I also have his Johannesburg address. Apparently he is flying down with another friend, Bryan Jones, and being joined there later today by Bale.'

'I'd like to contact her,' said Steiner. 'Do you mind if I do?'

'Not at all,' said Emma, 'but I think you should be careful in how you approach the subject. She might clam up or accuse you of insinuating that her friend Rohm is responsible for the deaths of the ministers, which is what this is all about.'

'There will be another attempt to kill Hamilton and this time they might succeed,' said Steiner. 'They've been very successful so far. Even if there is not another attempt, the killer has to be arrested for three murders. I'd also like the contact details for Rohm, in Johannesburg and Blaukrantz, and for Paul Bale.'

'Jane has a flat like this in Johannesburg near her work,' said Emma. 'I'll give you her address and phone number. I suggest you phone her first and then depending on how things go arrange to meet her. But I don't think she'll be able to tell you anymore than I have. I haven't told her about the attempt on Anthony's life. I have the details for Rohm in Johannesburg and Blaukrantz, and also for Bale, home and work. Bale is on an internet listing Hamilton gave me for the justice department of which the NPA is a part. It also has his photograph. He lives in Constantia, a few kilometres south of the city.'

'I'll ring Jane first,' said Steiner. 'I don't know what I'll get out of her but there might be something that helps. What you have told us is very interesting but I'm not quite sure how to use it.' He looked at Kirsty. 'What do you think?'

'The break we want is right here,' she said. 'We'll have to work on it and decide what action to take.'

Emma got up and went to a table. She spent five minutes compiling the details on a piece of paper and then gave it and the internet listing showing Bale to Steiner. 'These are what you want,' she said. 'Jane will probably be lecturing now but you can try. Let me know how you get on and I hope it helps find the killer.'

'Thank you,' said Steiner. 'Bale's got a scar on his cheek. Maybe he likes duelling. I'll ring you after I've made contact. If you need me and I'm not at the hotel this is my cellphone number.' He gave her the number. He and Kirsty left.

At the Mandarin Hotel, Steiner and Kirsty went and sat in the lounge. 'Well what do you make of that?' asked Kirsty, when they had found seats near a window overlooking the pool. 'I don't think Jane Cosgrave is going to come up with any more. 'Surely if she thought Rohm was behind the killings she would have gone to the police.'

'I think you're right,' said Steiner, 'but we have to give it try. If what Emma gave us is all we have then it will have to do. It's frustrating hearing something that seems to point somewhere but is not enough to make arrests or finish the case.'

'What about telling Weisz,' said Kirsty. 'He is the guy you want working with you rather than being kept in the dark.'

'I'll see what Emma's sister says when I phone her,' said Steiner. 'I'll try her at lunchtime.'

Chapter 101

The President's office
Cape Town

'I've spoken to Hamilton,' said the President. It was ten o'clock and he and Tyson were in his office. 'He's leaving the hospital this morning and will return to Stellenbosch, determined as ever not to go into hiding in a safe house.'

'He told Weisz the same thing earlier,' said Tyson. 'He's already assigned two guards and they'll be at the hospital when he's ready to leave. He's also going to have one guy on rotation walking the grounds of the house.'

There was a knock at the door and the President's secretary entered. She gave a letter to the President. 'It's special delivery and marked urgent,' she said.

'Aren't they all?' said the President taking the letter. The woman left the office.

The President opened the envelope, extracted a single sheet and read it. When he had finished he slid across his desk to Tyson. 'They're still at it,' he said. 'I didn't expect them to stop. If I don't announce the replacements for Dredge and Hamilton immediately they will publish allegations of corruption against senior black cabinet ministers. They don't say who the ministers are but the message is clear.'

Tyson read the letter. 'What are you going to do?' he asked. 'This time they might have something. If they do and the allegations are substantiated you're definitely finished. You'll be out in days.'

The President stared at him. 'I'm afraid that this time they might have something,' he said without elaborating. 'I'm sure they'll have another go at Hamilton regardless of what I do and I find that unacceptable.'

'I think you should give them what they want,' said Tyson. 'If you don't they will kill Hamilton and you'll be on the street. You have publicly refuted the allegations against the others and these people don't care. They simply want you to stick in their own guys and eliminate Hamilton. Now that they're running out of bodies they're coming up with allegations they can substantiate.'

'I told you I'll name Dredge's replacement tomorrow,' said the President, 'and think about including Hamilton's. I hate being threatened and shuffled around like a pawn. Don't say anything about this to anyone. I'll get back to you later today.'

Chapter 101

Cape Town

When Steiner and Kirsty had gone, Emma Cosgrave sat down in her lounge. It was one thing thinking about something but another telling it to others and she was beginning to regret giving Steiner her sister's contact details. There was no doubting Steiner's sincerity but phoning Jane unannounced and referring to something told to him by her sister did not sound right and she wouldn't blame her for being annoyed. This could damage a relationship Emma valued and as she thought about it she knew she couldn't risk that happening. Jane usually had a ten-minute break on the hour when she was giving lectures. It was now just before nine and she rang Jane's number at work. She was relieved when her sister answered.

'Jane, it is Emma. I'm sorry to disturb you at work. Are you tied up?'

'I have a few minutes,' said Jane. 'What is it?'

'I was going to phone you,' said Emma. 'Someone tried to kill Anthony at his home in Stellenbosch yesterday morning. Fortunately he's not badly hurt and will leave hospital this morning. It's not public knowledge.'

'God, who could do such a thing,' said Jane. 'Who told you about it?'

'The head of the DSO in Cape Town,' said Emma. 'It happened in the early hours of yesterday morning but before the assassin could finish the job he was interrupted and fled.'

'Was that one of the guards?' asked Jane.

'No,' said Emma. 'They had been shot dead. It was a DSO agent James Steiner and he's the reason I'm phoning.'

'I'm all ears,' said Jane. 'What has this to do with me?'

'Do you remember telling me you overheard Andrew asking Paul Bale to remove four cabinet ministers?' asked Emma. 'It was about a month ago.'

'Yes, but I don't understand,' said Jane.

'What do you think he meant?' asked Emma.

'I told you at the time,' said Jane. 'There was talk of a possible cabinet shuffle and Andrew and Bale know some of the people involved. They have preferences and like anyone interested in politics would like people they trust and respect to be in vital positions. I wish you would tell me what this about.'

'Do you think Andrew meant something more sinister?' said Emma.

'What do you think he is,' said Jane, 'some sort of criminal? Surely you're not implying he wanted them killed.' She thought for a moment. 'God, you think Andrew is behind the murder of the cabinet ministers.'

'I don't think that,' said Emma, beginning to wish she had never phoned Steiner. 'I'm only trying to help.'

'Have you said any of this to this guy Steiner?' asked Jane.

'Yes,' said Emma. 'He would like to speak to you.'

'I hope you haven't given him my numbers,' said Jane. 'If you have you can tell him what I've just told you. If he bothers me I'll contact his superiors.'

'He won't phone you,' said Emma. 'After hearing about Anthony my mind was running wild and I was clutching at anything that might help. The DSO think there will be another attempt on his life.'

Jane cooled down. 'I'm sorry,' she said. 'I didn't mean that. I just wanted to clarify things. The DSO would be barking up the wrong tree if they suspect Andrew. I know he does some things that are on the edge but he'd never have anyone murdered.'

'Thank you,' said Emma. 'I'm sure you're right and I'm sorry. I'll let you get back to your lectures.' She terminated the call and reclined in her seat, dispirited. After a moment she phoned Steiner on his mobile. He soon answered.

'James, it is Emma Cosgrave. I have just spoken to my sister. I told her that you'd probably phone her and she wasn't pleased. She is adamant that Andrew Rohm would not resort to anything like murder and I believe her. I think it was a big misunderstanding on my part.'

Steiner thought for a moment. He didn't believe Emma had changed her mind but knew he had to back off. 'If that's what she thinks, I won't contact her,' he said. 'Sometimes the breakthrough in a case comes from the smallest thing and you were right in wanting further explanation. I'm sorry it distressed your sister.'

'I hope you soon get a lead and find the killer,' said Emma. 'Goodbye.' She put down the phone.

'That was Emma Cosgrave,' said Steiner. 'She's bottled out.' He and Kirsty were in their bedroom getting ready before going for a walk round the city. He told her what Emma had said, including her sister's comments on Andrew Rohm.

'It sounds as if Jane is still in bed with him,' said Kirsty. 'I thought they had split up.'

'Habits die hard,' said Steiner. 'I suppose you're going to ask what I plan to do now.'

'I was thinking of it,' she said. 'Perhaps Rohm's not behind it after all and you're not meant to nail him.'

'He's guilty,' said Steiner. 'You heard that he and Bryan Jones, who is one of those on Hilton's list, are flying to his estate in Paarl this morning. He's being joined later by Bale. After what I've heard from Fairley and Emma, Bale, Rohm and Conran are coordinating or linked to these murders and the hit on Hamilton. Fairley mentioned David Strauss who we met last week but said he doesn't know anything. One or more of the three either knows the identity of the killer or knows who does. Rohm might be the top man but he doesn't necessarily know who is at the sharp end.' He looked at Kirsty. 'It is time I made a move. I think Jane Cosgrave will tell Rohm about my visit to her sister and he won't like it. But while I decide what to do let's forget about them and see what the town's got to offer.'

Kirsty had seen the look in his eyes before. 'I want to buy some perfume,' she said. 'You can help me choose it.'

Chapter 102

Johannesburg

Jane Cosgrave couldn't stop thinking about the call from her sister and she was glad when the next break came up and she was alone in her office, even if it was only for ten minutes. She knew from the time spent as Rohm's lover that he sometimes strayed outside the law but he was no different from most other powerful men. She still loved him and thought there was a real chance of them getting together again. They saw one another twice a week for lunch or dinner and knew that he was going to Paarl today in his private plane. There was a landing strip on his estate. Five minutes before her next lecture she rang Rohm at home. She had been upset by the call from Emma and she had to speak to him. He was still there and answered.

'Andrew, I'm glad I caught you. When are you leaving?'

'In thirty minutes,' said Rohm. 'What's wrong? I'm not used to you calling me during the morning.'

'I was hoping to speak to you before you left,' said Jane. 'Earlier this morning I had a call from Emma in Cape Town. It was about you.'

'I'm flattered,' said Rohm. 'I must meet her one day.'

'It was a bit more serious than that,' said Jane. 'I'm in a hurry and must be brief. I once told Emma that I'd heard you ask your friend Paul Bale to arrange for four cabinet ministers to be removed. You might not have heard that an attempt was made yesterday morning on the life of Emma's ex-boyfriend Anthony Hamilton and she remembered what I'd said. She wanted to know what you had meant.'

'What the hell's wrong with her?' said Rohm. 'What did you tell her?'

'I repeated what I had told her at the time. I said there was a cabinet shuffle coming up, which there was, and it was a statement of personal preference regarding very important government positions.'

'Exactly,' said Rohm. 'What did she say to that?'

'She was very embarrassed and apologized,' said Jane. 'She is very upset by the attempt on Hamilton and she admitted grasping at anything that might lead to finding the killer and prevent another attempt. I felt really sorry for her but wanted to tell you.'

'Well, I'd be devastated if you thought there was any truth in the way she interpreted what I'd said to Bale,' said Rohm. 'To be quite honest I'd forgotten it.'

'I think the deaths of the other three ministers and then the attempt on Hamilton's life was too much for her,' said Jane. 'That adds up to four. I'm sorry I ever repeated what I'd heard and it shows how things can be misconstrued.'

'Don't worry about it,' said Rohm. 'I'm glad she spoke to you before going to the police and wasting their time.'

'It wasn't the police who told her about Hamilton,' said Jane. 'It was the DSO. She'd already spoken to someone there about it before phoning me. It was the same man who arrived at Hamilton's house and disturbed the killer. He said he wanted to speak to me.'

'This never ends,' said Rohm, wondering what he would hear next. 'Do you know the man's name? I know a few of them down there.'

'I think it was James Steiner,' said Jane. 'Do you know him? If you do you might want a word with him.'

'James Steiner,' said Rohm softly, the hatred palpable. He went quiet and then said: 'I've heard of him. He and his girlfriend were solely responsible for bringing some very good friends of mine to trial and having them convicted of crimes alleged to have been committed during the apartheid period. They were all innocent and the charges were fabricated because the new government wanted blood to

262

appease the terrorists who had rapidly risen to power. If anyone should be put on trial it is him and his woman.'

'You clearly don't like him,' said Jane. 'I would let it rest. I'm sure they're going after anything however trivial that might bring in the killer. You have a break in one of the loveliest parts of South Africa to look forward to.'

'It's not your problem anyway,' said Rohm enigmatically. 'I'll do as you say and let it pass. My conscience is clear. We must meet when I get back.'

'Enjoy your flight,' said Jane. 'I'll be here when you return.'

As soon as Jane Cosgrave had gone, Rohm phoned Marc Kallis on his mobile. Kallis answered.

'Marc, Andrew Rohm again. I assume you're still up here.'

'Yes,' said Kallis. 'I'm on the ten-thirty flight. Is there a change in plan?'

'When you go after Steiner and Callard I want you to plan it as before but with changes in location.'

'What's brought this on?' said Kallis. 'I hope it's not complicated. I thought all you wanted was to see them dead.'

'The reason is simple and in line with what I've said before,' said Rohm. 'The only difference is that I want to see Steiner and Callard in the flesh and pleading for their lives before you kill them.'

'It sounds as if this has become personal,' said Kallis. 'Something must have got to you.'

'They were directly responsible for the conviction of my friends,' said Rohm, 'and for that they deserve more than a quick death. You hate them for killing your brother and you wanted to see them at your knees, begging for their lives. That's why you abducted Callard and lured Steiner to the farm. The big difference between you and me is that you've got nothing against her. It was only Steiner because you think he killed your brother.'

'Perhaps you should kill the girl so you can get this hatred out of system,' said Kallis. 'A shrink would call it cathartic or liberating. But if I gave her to you I'd expect at least the money you're paying me to kill her. It requires more planning and effort to separate her from Steiner so I can nab her. Last time I had to ask him to meet me in a hotel so she was alone. By the way, Teichmann told me Steiner killed my brother because it was done by a blow to the side of his head.'

'Teichmann didn't know that,' said Rohm. 'He wanted you to believe it. He hated Steiner for betraying him and not returning the files and he needed a killer. When he heard Steiner was in town he decided to use you for personal gratification. All he had to do was rattle your cage, stoke your fire and unchain you. There is a chance that Callard killed both Krige and your brother. She is no angel in white. But we digress. Do you want the job on my terms? If not, I know of someone else who would do it.'

'I still believe Teichmann,' said Kallis, 'but if both are destroyed it doesn't matter which of us does it. Tell me your plan.'

'I knew you would come to your senses,' said Rohm, 'and to satisfy you I will pay more even if I decide to kill them myself. Do the job as required and you'll have a lot more than most in your account.' He went quiet and then said: 'I want you to bring Callard to my estate near Paarl. The name is Dutch for pearl and with its illustrious past and haunting scenic beauty the area is a fitting place for the death of a *femme fatale*.'

'I'm sure Steiner never lets her out of his sight,' said Kallis. Rohm sounded manic, as if the loathing had driven him insane.

'She was out of his sight when he went after you in Durban and when you abducted her the first time,' said Rohm. 'You'll find a way.'

'He guessed I'd gone after Smith,' said Kallis defensively. 'What about Steiner? You must want him to join her?'

'Yes,' said Rohm. 'It's important no one follows him. I don't want to be caught in my house by the DSO with blood on my hands.'

'Will anyone else be there?' said Kallis. 'I don't particularly want an audience.'

'A friend of mine is flying down with me,' said Rohm. 'Paul Bale will also be there.'

'He's the NDPP,' said Kallis, astonished. 'You're planning all this knowing someone in his position is going to be present?'

'He is a close friend,' said Rohm, 'and even though he doesn't know Steiner he has no love for him.'

'So he knows about me and that you are paying me to do your killing?' said Kallis.

'I believe he does,' said Rohm enjoying himself, 'but he's a very useful guy to have on your side. Don't worry, I wouldn't have anyone there I couldn't trust. These guys are highly influential and are very useful contacts.'

Kallis had heard enough. 'I'll phone you when I've got Callard and ready to deliver her to the estate. We can phone Steiner from there. I'm also going to enjoy this. There is something between us that we haven't settled.'

'I can imagine,' said Rohm. 'Don't make any mistakes. He's very dangerous.'

When Kallis had gone, Rohm phoned Bale at his office. Bale answered.

'Paul, Andrew Rohm. There is something to add to what we discussed yesterday.' He told Bale what had happened since last speaking to him and what he had told Kallis to do.

'That suits me,' said Bale. 'I have no time for petty meddlers who take delight in interfering in the affairs of people who want to make a success of their lives. It will be something to look forward to.'

'I think it will,' said Rohm. He liked Bale's uncomplicated view of things. 'I'll see you on the estate later.'

Chapter 103

Cape Town

Steiner returned his phone to his shirt pocket. It was eleven o'clock and he and Kirsty were sitting in a coffee bar after doing some shopping. 'That was Weisz,' he said. 'Hamilton's on his way home. He's just left the hospital.'

'Who's protecting him?' said Kirsty. 'I hope it's better than last time.'

'It'll be as before, two men at the house,' said Steiner. 'Like the others they'll be working on rotation.'

'Weisz should double that,' said Kirsty.

Steiner shrugged his shoulders. 'His hands are tied,' he said. 'It's Hamilton's choice and he doesn't want a platoon in his garden. Those were his words.' He drank some of his coffee. 'Now, back to what I said in the hotel. How do think I should go about it and who should I start with? You're good at this.'

'First you should think about Weisz and whether you want to involve him,' she said.

'I will bring him in later,' said Steiner. 'I feel I can trust him but he would not sanction me going after these people based on what we know. I have to get something concrete to work on but at the start I don't want to take on more than one at a time to get it. Does that make sense?'

'Kirsty looked at him. 'I don't think you should start with Rohm because not only would he be harder to work on but you have nothing with which to threaten him. From what I hear, Bale is in the middle of things and that makes him vulnerable because he doesn't know what you know about the people on either side of him, Rohm and Conran. I would go for him but aren't you forgetting Kallis?'

'Kallis has nothing to do with the ministers,' said Steiner, 'and that is what we are interested in now.

Teichmann might have heard we were in town from Rohm but Teichmann was the driving force behind Kallis. We have nothing that links Kallis to Rohm, Bale or Conran. Kallis is a servant or foot soldier and his master, Teichmann, is dead. The Japanese would call him a *ronin*, or masterless *samurai*, if *samurai* wasn't too good a word for him. They were honourable men who adhered to *bushido*, the way of the *bushi* or feudal warrior. *Budo*, such as *karatedo* and *aikido*, stemmed from that. Kallis will come out in the wash when we deal with him for killing Smith.'

'Thank you for that,' said Kirsty smiling. 'I'd then go for Bale but he might be on the estate with Rohm. How would you separate him?'

'I'll get him wherever he's lurking,' said Steiner. 'He might be there now but I don't know. Emma said it would be later today but I'll find him. Why wouldn't you first go for Conran?'

'Like Kallis he is not high enough in the tree and you might spoil your chances of getting the results you want,' said Kirsty. 'I think Emma's disclosure about Rohm and Bale is a lot more significant than what we know about Conran, and that they are directing the killings. Rohm is the main player but untouchable at the moment.'

Steiner poured some more coffee. 'There is something else. Do we forget about Hamilton? At some stage there is going to be another attempt to kill him. I think it will be sooner rather than later, like tonight. I'm aware that I'm not here to protect Hamilton but in some way I feel responsible for his safety.'

'Weisz would never forgive you if Hamilton is killed and he finds out you were chasing after Rohm on a mere whim,' said Kirsty. 'Neither do I think you'd forgive yourself.'

Steiner thought for a moment. 'Alright, this is how I see it. I agree that Bale should be first on the list and I realize that I can't abandon Hamilton when I believe he is going to be killed. That could be classed as negligence and I've got too much pride to have that stamped on me. But I'd be messing around if I only sat outside Hamilton's place as we did before and ignored the others. This leaves me with only one course of action. I'll deal with Bale and Hamilton simultaneously. What I do after that depends on the results but it has to involve Rohm because he controls everything.'

'Give me a break,' said Kirsty. 'How the hell do you think you're going to do that? I know you have exceptional powers but that's stretching things a bit.'

'I thought that would get you going,' said Steiner, 'but I can arrange what Carl Jung called synchronicity. It is two or more events, causally unrelated, occurring simultaneously in a meaningful manner. Bale, not by choice, is going to be with me at Hamilton's place in Stellenbosch to greet the killer.'

'And how are you going to do that?' said Kirsty. 'Bale's going to Rohm's estate today. You can't just roll up and pull him out of his pond.'

'I hope I don't have to do that,' said Steiner. 'I'll pick him up here in Cape Town. It's a lot more convenient. Naturally, if he's not here I'll have to find him, even if it's at Rohm's estate.'

'It doesn't sound as if I'm involved.' said Kirsty.

'Not at the beginning,' said Steiner. 'It's too uncertain. You'll be here in Cape Town and join me when the time is right.'

'When do you start?' said Kirsty.

'Now, as soon as we get back to the hotel,' said Steiner. 'I'm going to phone him and tell him I want to see him urgently. I won't say who it is because he might contact Rohm but he'll comply. I'll suggest his home but it doesn't matter as long as it's private. You can drop me off and keep the car.'

'Let's go to the hotel and ring Bale,' said Kirsty.

'So Hamilton's on his way back to Stellenbosch,' said Conran. It was eleven-thirty in the morning and he was in Weisz's office. 'I thought you might have persuaded him to stay under guard in Cape Town.'

'He's not having any of that,' said Weisz. 'I could understand his stoicism if he was of Afrikaner stock but he's not. He also rejected the notion of a third guard in the grounds.'

Conran laughed. 'If the killer wants to get in, a third man won't make any difference. Do you think these people will try again soon?'

'Yes,' said Weisz. 'It'll be in the next couple of days. They're not going to hang around. That was how I read the letter the President received.'

'What's Steiner going to do now?' asked Conran. 'He has absolutely sweet nothing to go on.'

'He wants to return to London if he doesn't make a breakthrough in the next seven days,' said Weisz. 'I don't blame him feeling that way and I can't stop him. He's not obliged to stay if he doesn't want to.'

'I still can't get over Adam's death,' said Conran. 'Do you think he was on to something?'

'He didn't say anything to me,' said Weisz. 'We're also in the dark on that one.'

'Please give me a shout if there's anything I can do,' said Conran.

'Thank you,' said Weisz. 'The pressure to come up with something increases daily and I wouldn't be surprised if I'm suddenly relieved of office.'

Chapter 104

Cape Town

Marc Kallis wasn't sure how he was going to get Kirsty Callard alone so he could pick her up without interference from Steiner. It was one o'clock and he was in a bar on the other side of the wide street that ran past the Mandarin Hotel. He hadn't shaved since he'd last seen Kirsty and Steiner, and with the wide-brimmed hat he was wearing felt reasonably confident they wouldn't recognize him unless close up. He had just ordered a drink and was sitting a couple of metres back from the large front window which gave him a good view of the hotel entrance. He wasn't pressed for time and, as much as he didn't want to, he knew he could sit there for the rest of the day without upsetting Rohm. Once he had got hold of Callard he could be at the estate in forty-five minutes using the N1 to the Paarl junction. All he needed, and what he hoped for, was a sighting of Steiner and Kirsty so he could get some idea of their movements. If he saw them and they appeared inseparable, his chance of getting her without disabling Steiner, and delivering her alone to Rohm, was zero. At the moment he had no choice other than to wait.

Chapter 105

Cape Town

'I was really sorry to hear that,' said David Strauss. He was in his office and Weisz had come in and told him about Adam Fairley. 'And you have no idea who killed him?'

Strauss was one of Weisz's top agents and if he had been available, Weisz would not have pulled in Steiner. He was known for his relentless pursuit of dangerous criminals and had a number of prominent convictions under his belt. He had joined the South African Police Service directly after school. He rose to lieutenant and then left for the Scorpions. He was now forty-five, tall and in very good physical condition.

'No,' said Weisz. 'As you know he was investigating the allegations of corruption against the ministers. He hadn't come up with anything, not enough to justify killing him.'

'Where does that leave you?' said Strauss. 'That stuff is attracting a lot of heat from the media and the public. They want an arrest.'

'Steiner's got the hard part,' said Weisz. 'He keeps running up against a brick wall and I think he's frustrated. These people are very clever and the only slip was when they failed in their attempt to kill Hamilton. The thing that bugs me is that the only real way of protecting him is to stick him in isolation and he's having none of it. The two men now guarding him are the best around but I don't think they will stop another cunning, determined attack. Hamilton owes his life to Steiner.'

'I wish you luck,' said Strauss. 'I wouldn't like the hounds baying at my door.'

Chapter 106

Cape Town

'It's time you rang Bale,' said Kirsty. She and Steiner were in their bedroom and had just finished lunch. 'I see you're leaving the gun behind. I thought you would.'

Steiner looked at the piece of paper Emma Cosgrave had given him showing Bale's details. He rang the work number. The call was answered by Bale.

'You don't know me,' said Steiner, 'and I'd like to meet you. It is urgent and there is no time to waste.'

'You expect me to meet someone who hasn't the courtesy to give me his name,' said Bale, surprised but interested. It was not every day he received such a call.

'I'll tell you when we meet,' said Steiner. 'If I tell you now you will only ask questions I don't want to answer on the phone. All will be revealed when we meet. You'll be glad you did.'

'Give me some idea what this is about,' said Bale.

'All I will say is that it concerns your recent dealings with others,' said Steiner, 'and someone you can't trust.'

'Where and when do you suggest we meet?' said Bale. 'I'm at work and will be leaving for the country at six this afternoon.'

'I'll meet you at your house in Constantia at five-thirty,' said Steiner. 'This shouldn't take long and it is in your interest that you don't say anything about this to anyone.'

'I'll be at my house at five-thirty,' said Bale. 'This had better be good.' He cut the call.

'You're on to him,' said Kirsty. 'If he wasn't involved in something he shouldn't be, he would have dismissed you out of hand. What would you have said if he'd wanted to meet now?'

'It's a bit early but I'd have gone,' said Steiner. 'I'll tell you a bit more. I've been vague because I don't know how things are going to play out. If nothing happens I might end up looking very stupid. I'm betting that someone will go for Hamilton tonight and I want Bale with me while I sit outside the house. I'm hoping he cracks.'

'I can see why you call it vague,' said Kirsty. 'You're hoping that with a little bit of persuasion and the fear of someone he knows showing up and incriminating him, Bale will confess and reveal all.'

'Along those lines,' said Steiner. 'But I'm not going to beat him. That's not my method even if I might let them think it. If he is innocent and nothing happens I'll be in shit, starting with Weisz and going to the top. I know I'm taking a chance but I've nothing else to go on and I have to get to the root of all this.'

Kirsty stared into his eyes. 'Steiner, this scares me,' she said. 'I think you're going to get badly hurt. You don't have to do this. It's not your fault that you haven't anything to go on and Weisz recognizes that. Please promise me this. If you are getting nowhere with Bale and don't think things are going your way, back off.'

'That would be difficult because I'd still feel he's involved in this,' said Steiner. 'Don't worry about me. I think the DSO link is Conran, and that Rohm through Bale managed to get him to pass on information to them.'

'So you think Rohm is controlling the killer?' said Kirsty.

'Yes,' said Steiner. 'From what Hilton said in his note to Smith, Rohm is the man who has links with the underworld. He knows who is swimming in the sewer and can pay the money to pull them out when he wants them to do his work.'

'What do we do now?' said Kirsty.

'We leave here at five and drive to Bale's house,' said Steiner. 'You can return here after dropping me off. Either that or I catch a taxi. I don't want Bale to see you.'

'I'll drive you,' said Kirsty. 'He won't see me. Let's go down to the pool.'

Chapter 107

Cape Town

When he had terminated the call from Steiner, Bale sat back in his office chair. He had no idea who it was on the phone. The only thing not part of his usual work and which if revealed would put him away for life was the deal he had got himself involved in with Rohm, the replacement of the ministers. Bale was certain that only Rohm and Conran knew about this. Teichmann knew but he was dead. But it was the way the man spoke that made Bale feel he might be missing something, that there was a leak, and it was this uncertainty that had made him agree to the meeting. Bale had nothing to lose. He had the security of his home and it was inconceivable that someone would go to the trouble of coming to the house to harm him. His two full-time servants were always somewhere in the house and like all people in his position, the place had a security alarm system, wired into a local centre, that could be activated by any number of well-placed buttons. The man would surely know this.

After ten minutes, Bale thought about his visit to Rohm's estate. The caller had said their meeting wouldn't take long and that meant he could still be on the road at six o'clock as planned. Rohm would soon be there, if he wasn't there already, and it would give him a chance to settle in with Bryan Jones who hadn't been there before. Bale turned to the work he wanted to complete before he left. He wanted to be out of the building by five.

Chapter 108

Andrew Rohm's estate near Paarl

'I've often wondered what this place was like,' said Bryan Jones looking out over the valley. He and Rohm had just arrived at Rohm's house on the estate. They had been met at the landing strip two kilometres from the house by Rohm's driver. 'There's not another house in sight. I suppose you are going to tell me you own the valley. It's quite beautiful, mountains, vineyards and forest.'

'Most of it is mine,' said Rohm, seated in one of the large chairs in the reception room. 'There is another farm further down but you can't see it from here. We're about seven kilometres from Paarl. I'll show you around when Bale gets here, if it's still light. I expect him around seven but there is no knowing with him. It will be his first visit.'

'You were going to fill me in on what you've arranged with Kallis,' said Jones. 'When is he going to get rid of James Steiner and his woman?'

Rohm laughed, clearly pleased with himself. 'I've arranged for a little entertainment,' he said. 'I don't know when it will be but I'm hoping for tonight. The key players, those providing the entertainment, will be Steiner and Callard.'

Jones looked at him. 'What the hell have you got going?' he said. 'I thought you were going to get Kallis to kill them in Cape Town. You've got enough going on without dragging this stuff out.'

'They're coming here,' said Rohm. 'Something happened that made me want a bit more than a swift exit for them.' He told Jones about the conversation he'd had with Jane Cosgrave. 'They caused inexcusable damage when our friends were imprisoned, some for a very long time, and they're still at it. Teichmann was directly

277

involved with Steiner at the time and I put his hatred of him down to him handing the files over to the DSO and killing some of his men. But there is more. Steiner never gives up and he is determined to destroy me at all costs.'

'How are you going to get them here?' said Jones. 'It sounds as if you want to do some of the killing.'

'I might,' said Rohm. 'It depends on how I feel when I see them. We've done and seen worse. I've told Kallis to grab Callard in Cape Town and bring her here. We'll then phone Steiner and tell him where she is. He'll be here like a shot and the rest will follow.'

'Yes, and he'll bring the DSO with him,' said Jones, not liking what he was hearing.

'This is what this business with the ministers is all about,' said Rohm. 'There is always a risk and a little bit more won't make any difference. But if you don't like seeing your enemy vanquished in the flesh, you can sit it out. I can arrange for my pilot to take you back to Johannesburg now and there won't be any hard feelings on my part. All I know is that I'm going to finish off Steiner and Callard as I see fit.'

'I'm not going anywhere,' said Jones. 'I'm just playing devil's advocate. Three of the ministers are dead and we've got away with it. I don't want to see you screw up a good job unnecessarily. Hamilton is the only one left and it shouldn't be difficult for Conran's man to finish him off. We'll be left with our operations safe and our men in senior cabinet positions.'

'I appreciate that,' said Rohm, 'but I've set the wheels in motion and I can't stop them. Kallis might even have Callard now. It will be over before you blink.'

'Don't get me wrong,' said Jones. 'I'll also enjoy it. I hate people who go against me as much as you do and I also have some very good friends who are in prison because of Steiner and Callard. Let's have a drink and wait for Kallis to call. I've got an excellent single-malt whisky with me. It's a McCallan.'

Chapter 109

Cape Town

'It's time to go,' said Kirsty. She and Steiner were sitting in the hotel lounge. She picked up his small bag and gave it to him. 'I hope you don't need more than one change of clothing.'

'I won't,' said Steiner. 'If I do I'll ask you to bring it to me.'

They went through the front doors, along the pavement and then down to their car. With Kirsty at the wheel they drove up the ramp and were soon on the way to Constantia.

When Marc Kallis looked at his watch for the fourth time it was five-twenty. He was still in the bar across the street from the Mandarin Hotel and had only left his position at the table to get food and drink and visit the toilet. But he was not dispirited. He knew it might be a long wait but at some point Steiner and Callard had to make an appearance even if it wasn't before most people had gone to bed and the bar was closed. It was then that he would call it a day, find a bed for the rest of the night and resume watch early tomorrow. He'd stick at it until they showed and he could make a move for the woman. Rohm would just have to be patient if he wanted him to do the job.

Kallis had just taken another mouthful of coke when he went still, his hand suspending the bottle above the table. What he wanted to see was happening. Steiner and Callard had appeared in the hotel entrance. They walked slowly along the pavement and as Kallis watched they disappeared down the footway that led to the basement car park.

Four minutes later Kallis saw an Audi saloon leave the car park. He was no more than two hundred metres from it and as it sped off down the street he saw Callard at the wheel and Steiner next to her. She was going to return without Steiner and he would at last get his chance.

Chapter 110

Cape Town

'I will miss you,' said Kirsty when they reached the main route to Constantia. 'Are you sure you've got your phone?'

'Why are you so worried?' said Steiner. 'You were like ice when we went after John Kallis at your farm and then we were up against armed men. This is nothing like that. All I want is a confession from Bale so that we can bring in Rohm and see an end to all this. I'll call Weisz as soon as I've got what I want from Bale.'

'If anything happens tonight it won't be an easy ride,' said Kirsty, unconvinced. 'You won't have time to call Weisz. You are dealing with ruthless people who will stop at nothing. They must be well aware that you are after them. I'm surprised they haven't tried to kill you.'

They drove on in silence and in fifteen minutes reached the outskirts of Constantia. It was not difficult to find Bale's road and when they got to the one end Kirsty stopped. 'There it is,' she said. 'I think you should get out here. He might already be there and watching the road.' She looked at him. 'James, I love you. You're not alone. You've got me.'

Steiner leaned over and kissed her. 'I'll walk from here,' he said. 'Take care of yourself and go back to the hotel.' He grabbed his bag, got out of the car and started walking up the road. She watched until he disappeared round a bend then did a three-point turn and drove back the way they come to the city and the hotel.

When Kirsty reached the hotel it was after six o'clock and she went up the lift into the hotel and to the bedroom. She felt alone and couldn't stop worrying about Steiner. As the minutes ticked by it was getting worse. She lay on the bed and went to sleep.

Chapter 111

The President's office, Cape Town

'I've decided to name Hamilton's replacement this evening along with Dredge's,' said the President. He had just called Tyson into his office. 'By doing that I'll have given those people everything they wanted and there can be no blood on my hands. I'll phone Hamilton beforehand and tell him. He won't be happy but I'll do my best to persuade him that it's for his own good and the people are not going to give up.'

'You've made a wise decision,' said Tyson. 'I don't think they'll hit Hamilton before then and they won't be able to say you didn't comply with their wishes.'

Chapter 112

Stellenbosch

'I think this is going to be a boring job for you two,' said Anthony Hamilton. 'I know these people had a go at me yesterday morning but I think they've been scared off for good.' It was a little after six-thirty and he and his two guards were sitting on the front verandah of his house. They had collected him a few hours earlier at his hospital in Cape Town.

'We can't take any chances,' said one of the guards. 'There are a couple of things here that are difficult to quantify but still pose a risk. One is the desire to satisfy the reason for doing all this and the other is pride. The killer will be proud of his work and he's the sort who can't accept failure.'

'I agree,' said the other guard. 'I think he'll be back but I don't know when. We'll be doing the rounds together and in between one of us will sit outside the room. If anyone can take us by surprise, he is supernatural.'

'I'll leave you guys to it,' said Hamilton, getting up. 'I've got some reading to do before I go to bed.' He left the two men and a little later they returned to their room at the side of the garage.

Chapter 113

Cape Town

Even though Marc Kallis felt sure Kirsty had gone off somewhere to drop Steiner, he could hardly believe it when he saw her return after thirty-five minutes and go down the ramp into the car park. For Kallis that was the signal he needed for undisturbed access to her.

Kallis waited patiently for another ten minutes and when Kirsty did not come out of the car park and onto the pavement he assumed she had used another way to into the hotel. It was time to move and leaving the bar he crossed the street and slowly walked into the hotel foyer. From close to the entrance he ran his eyes over the open-plan lounge. When he didn't see her he went to the reception desk. A young girl looked up. 'I'm meeting a couple here,' said Kallis smiling widely. 'They asked me to come up to the room but I don't have the number.'

The girl studied him briefly, returning his smile. He was very good looking and his expression almost apologetic. 'I'm sure I can help you,' she said. 'What are their names?'

'His name's James Steiner,' said Kallis. 'Her name is Kirsty Callard but I'm not sure if she used that as a surname. You know what it's like today.'

She smiled knowingly, a little embarrassed. 'I'll get the number for you. Do you know when they booked in?'

'I think it was about a week ago,' said Kallis. 'They were at Brown's Hotel.'

She ran her finger down the booking list. 'Here it is,' she said. 'They're under their own names. The room is 154 on the first floor. The lift is over there.' She pointed.

'Thank you,' said Kallis. 'They'll be surprised.'

Kallis went to the stairs and climbed to the first floor. He went along the passage to room 154, pressed the bell and soon heard someone walking to the door. They stopped and said: 'Who is it?'

Kallis knew it was Kirsty and he felt a surge of excitement. 'This is room service,' he said. 'I have your order.'

'It's not for here,' said Kirsty. She opened the door and gasped when she saw Kallis. She tried to close it but he was too quick and easily pushed her aside as he entered. She went back a few steps and he closed the door.

'We meet again,' said Kallis. 'We'll have to stop meeting like this.' He grinned, patently enjoying himself.

She went back further, still facing him. 'What do you want?' she whispered. 'I've nothing to give you.'

'You have as much as you had last time,' said Kallis. 'Steiner can't do without you.'

She quickly understood. 'You're not going to go through that again?' she said quietly.

'I am but this time it's for someone else,' said Kallis. 'They want to be involved in the action.'

'Who are you talking about?' said Kirsty regaining some of her composure. 'Your master is dead.'

'I'll introduce you when I take you to his estate,' said Kallis. 'He's really looking forward to seeing you. I'm not quite sure what he'll do to you but I know he will enjoy himself. He's that type. He always gets his way.'

Kirsty went quiet, infused by a feeling of dread. She knew who he was referring to. 'You're talking about Andrew Rohm,' she said. 'So he has taken the place of Teichmann. You really like switching sides. I'm surprised they trust you.'

Kallis took two steps forward and before she could move struck her viciously on the side of the face.

She reeled backwards, falling onto the bed, her black skirt riding high up her legs, her hand going to where she'd been hit. The embossed skull on the silver ring he was wearing had drawn blood.

He went to her, his right hand grabbing the front of her white shirt, tearing it open. 'If you're not careful and I had more time I'd screw you before handing you over.' He stared at her full, heaving breasts. 'Steiner won't be getting any more of that.'

She was scared, tears welling in her eyes, trying hard to show a brave face and silently calling Steiner to return. She saw hate in Kallis's eyes, the hate of a born killer who was used to getting what he wanted. She knew she was again going to be bait to lure Steiner to his death. The only difference was that she was also on the list. When they were at the farm she had felt Kallis intended to spare her and that he had only wanted Steiner dead. Someone or something had changed his mind. 'Where is this place?' she asked, depleted; knowing wouldn't make any difference. She was powerless. They would have their way and there was no one to stop them.

'You will soon find out,' said Kallis. 'He took her by the arm and dragged her to her feet. Change your shirt and let's go. We'll go out the way you came in. Any squeal out of you or resistance and I'll finish you off with this.' He put his hand under his jacket and pulled out a silenced pistol. He pointed it to the cupboard. 'Change, my patience is running out. Do it where I can see you.'

Kirsty obeyed and in a few minutes had replaced her torn shirt with one from the cupboard. She stood still, facing him.

Kallis checked she had nothing on her and then saw her mobile on a table. It could stay there. He waved her towards the door. They left the room and she led the way to the lifts, walking slightly ahead of him. They took the first lift to the car park, went up the ramp to the pavement and with his discreet guidance moved along to where he had parked his black Chevrolet. After guiding her to the co-driver's seat through the driver's door, he got in, started the engine and drove off towards the main street. He turned left into it and a few minutes later entered the N1 freeway. It was fifty-five kilometres to the Paarl junction and another ten to Rohm's estate.

Chapter 114

Constantia

When Steiner came to Bale's house he walked up the drive to the main door and rang the bell. Like all the houses he had seen it was an impressive two-story building, a well-developed garden and trees at the front. A maid answered the door.

'I'm here to see Paul Bale,' said Steiner.

The maid made way for him and after closing the door led him to a room at the far end of the hall. She opened the door, revealing a beautifully furnished study.

Paul Bale was seated at an oak desk in front of a wall of books on built-in shelves and he came to his feet as Steiner entered. He showed no recognition. 'Paul Bale, please sit down.' He indicated a chair on the other side of his desk. 'Perhaps you'll tell me your name and the reason for wanting to see me. I must admit I'm a little intrigued.'

Steiner went to the chair but before sitting down said: 'You've heard of me. James Steiner.'

Bale's blank expression didn't change. 'The DSO is an independent agency but it comes under the NPA,' he said. 'As head of the NPA I know what they do and who they hire. I thought you were chasing the person who killed the cabinet ministers and who a couple of days ago had a go at Hamilton.'

'That's why I'm here,' said Steiner. 'I think you're one of the men behind it.'

Bale laughed harshly, a brief inflection. 'You've really got a nerve,' he said. 'You come round here and accuse me, the NDPP, of being behind those murders. Which loony bin did Weisz find you in?'

'I like your sense of humour,' said Steiner. 'Let me see if you find this humorous. I have evidence that Andrew

Rohm ordered you to dispose of Hilton, Delaware, Dredge and Hamilton. I also know that John Conran of the DSO is feeding you information that you pass on to Rohm. Even if you didn't kill the men you conspired to kill them and the sentence is the same. You as a lawyer should know that.'

'You're playing some strange game,' said Bale, 'and you're wasting my time. You have absolutely no evidence. I know both men but only in a business capacity.'

'And that's why you're going to Rohm's estate in Paarl after this meeting,' said Steiner. 'Has Conran been invited?'

'I've had enough of this,' said Bale. His hand went for the drawer of his desk but before he could open it Steiner had closed the distance between them.

'Whatever you're going for, don't,' said Steiner. 'You're coming for a ride with me.'

'Where are you taking me?' said Bale impassively, lowering his hand to his side. He was unnerved but had been trained not to show it. 'You're making a big mistake. You'll pay the price.'

'Move this side of the desk,' said Steiner, stepping to the side. 'I've a bit more to say before we go.'

Bale walked past Steiner and stood in the open area of the study. He had to play along until an opportunity to reverse his position arose. 'Get on with it,' he said. 'Whatever it is I'm going to prosecute you for this. You will never return to London. How you escaped after murdering Andrew Cartwright the Durban lawyer and those men in Pretoria, including Jan Krige, the husband of your lover, is one of the biggest miscarriages of justice this country has seen.'

'Is that why you told Johan Teichmann that I and Kirsty Callard were in Cape Town?' said Steiner. 'Only the DSO knew I was here and either you or Rohm told Teichmann. I suspect it was Rohm because he knew Teichmann. That information was grist to the mill for Teichmann. It fuelled his sick desire to see me and Peter Smith of the Durban DSO dead. You must know that Fairley, the DSO agent who suspected Conran, is now dead. I think Conran told you that Fairley presented a risk of exposure and Rohm had him killed.'

'You've really missed your vocation,' said Bale, shaking his head. 'You should have been writing scripts.'

'There is more,' said Steiner. 'Teichmann hired someone I think you know or have heard of to kill me and Smith. His name is Marc Kallis.' Steiner walked a little closer to Bale. 'You're the one who should be on stage. That blank expression wouldn't fool a saint. Now I'll get to the present. You know as well as I do that Hamilton is still alive. The killer failed in his attempt to kill him. I know the identity of the killer.'

'You're lying,' said Bale. 'If you know him why don't you pull him in before he can kill again?'

'I am going to stop him,' said Steiner, 'but all in good time. The killer knows all about you and I want you with me when he makes his second attempt on Hamilton's life. I can't wait to see the look on your face when I introduce you to him.'

'You're out of your skull,' hissed Bale. 'How do you intend to do that? If I knew him he'd be locked up.'

'I believe the killer will make his second attempt on Hamilton tonight,' said Steiner, 'and we'll be there to greet him. If he doesn't show we'll there tomorrow night.'

'And where will we be during the day?' said Bale.

'I'll look after you,' said Steiner. 'I might become impatient and turn a little nasty but you'll have to put up with that. You could of course end all this now by admitting your involvement in all this crap. I'll then hand you over to the DSO. I don't think they're any different from other security forces in how they extract exactly what they want.'

'You're really trying,' said Bale, 'and you're all bluff. You don't have anything to go on. I'll call your bluff.'

Steiner stepped up to Bale and searched him, starting inside his jacket. He found a wallet, keys and a mobile phone. 'I'll take these with me,' he said. 'If someone phones and I let you answer I'll tell you what to say.' He stepped back. 'Lead the way to your car. If we see your maid tell her you'll be back. I'll drive.' He pointed to the door.

Bale glared at Steiner and then slowly went to the door. They left the house through the front entrance and went round to the garage at the side. Bale had a black Mercedes Benz saloon. Steiner led him round to the driver's door, told him to get in and move across and then got in himself. He started the engine, reversed out through the gates and drove off down the street to the main road that joined the N1 to Stellenbosch.

Chapter 115

N1 freeway to Paarl

'When will we be there?' said Kirsty, preparing herself for what she thought lay ahead. She and Kallis were thirty kilometres from Cape Town on the N1 freeway. 'Why won't you tell me where we're going?'

'You'll soon find out,' said Kallis, 'but there's no harm in telling you now. We're going to Andrew Rohm's estate outside Paarl.'

'And then you're going to phone Steiner and hope he comes for me,' she said. 'Why are you doing this? You let us go at the farm when you had your chance. What sort of hold has Rohm got on you?'

'What happened at the farm was unfinished business,' said Kallis. 'Steiner was lucky. I had to be somewhere else and was running out of time.'

'Putting a bullet into someone unarmed and in front of you only takes a second,' said Kirsty. 'Surely Teichmann would have understood that.'

'I never said anything about Teichmann,' said Kallis.

'So Rohm was behind you from the start,' said Kirsty, 'and it was pure coincidence that Teichmann, a friend of your brother's, was shot dead two days later. That means Rohm was the one who knew Steiner and I were in Cape Town and primed you to kill us. We all know you weren't working alone as you claimed. It surprises me that a man of Rohm's stature and wealth would stoop so low.'

'I was working alone,' growled Kallis. 'This job is totally unrelated. I wanted revenge for the cold-blooded murder of my brother.'

'So what is this all about?' said Kirsty. 'Didn't Rohm tell you? I'm disappointed. I thought you had more intelligence. From what I hear, Rohm suddenly appeared and asked you to use me as bait to pull in Steiner so he can kill him. That bears an uncanny resemblance to what you planned before. Why haven't you tried to complete your unfinished business on your own? Where has the passion for revenge gone?' She looked at him. 'I think you know the real reason Rohm wants us dead or you are a complete idiot. Rohm doesn't want us killed only because Steiner pinched the group files. I'm sure he knew about the business at the farm so why pay you to have another go when you would probably do it anyway. Rohm has another reason for wanting us dead.'

'You don't give up do you,' said Kallis. 'Rohm wants you dead because he believes you and Steiner killed my brother and Krige, and you and Steiner were responsible for stealing the files. Rohm supported the group. He is paying me to bring the two of you to him.'

'We believe the reason you backed off at the farm was to kill Peter Smith,' said Kirsty. 'I also think you killed Teichmann. But, life sentences usually run concurrently.'

Kallis had heard enough. Keeping his right hand on the wheel, he swung his left hand in a vicious arc, striking Kirsty with full force on her right eye, driving her head hard against the door pillar. She lost consciousness immediately, her head and chest falling forward, restrained only by the seat belt, her eye already swollen and bruised.

'You deserved that,' he whispered, returning his hand to the wheel and letting Kirsty hang in the seat belt. 'And you're going to get more. I'll see to that.' He glanced at his watch. In fifteen minutes he would be at the estate.

Chapter 116

Stellenbosch

Forty-five minutes after leaving Cape Town, Steiner and Bale reached the Stellenbosch turn-off and a little later took the road to Sleepy Hollow. When they reached the village Steiner took the left fork and they soon came to Hamilton's house and the car park a short distance past it. He switched off the engine.

'What now?' said Bale. 'We're just going to sit here until your phantom appears?'

'Yes,' said Steiner. 'Hamilton is clearly there and I'm sure the guards are in position. It will be interesting to see how the killer gets in this time. I hope you are nice to him when I introduce you.'

Bale looked at him. 'You really are something else,' he said. 'Everything I've heard about you is true. Where the hell did Smith find you?'

'That sounds as if you've heard a lot about me,' said Steiner. 'Smith was the only one in the DSO who really knew anything about me. Weisz only knows that I successfully retrieved the group files. I can only conclude you heard it from Rohm and I'm sure you can tell me why he was so interested in me. I said earlier that Rohm asked you to eliminate the four ministers. Rohm felt Hilton was getting too close to his illegal operations and for that reason wanted him dead. But because the other three were Hilton's friends, Rohm feared they had learned too much and wanted them killed as well. When Rohm heard I was on the case he remembered from the group trials that I was responsible for retrieving the files and because some of those convicted were his mates he wanted me killed. Teichmann heard about this and because he'd had dealings with me, wanted to do the job himself. Teichmann hired Kallis. I'm right, am I not?'

'Your imagination never dries up,' said Bale. 'If this guy turns up I'll take great pleasure in exposing you.' He reclined his seat and closed his eyes.

Steiner knew that he wasn't going to get anything out of Bale. Something had to happen before he got what he wanted.

Chapter 117

Andrew Rohm's estate, Paarl

'That's a very good malt,' said Andrew Rohm. 'It's deceptively smooth and has a strong tendency to take you by surprise.' He and Bryan Jones were on the verandah overlooking the valley.

'I only drink the single malts and this is regarded by many as the best,' said Jones. 'If Bale doesn't hurry up we'll have to go into Paarl to get more. I'm looking forward to meeting him.'

'I thought he would've been here by now,' said Rohm. He's very clever and I first met him when he was moving up in political circles. He and I have very similar ideas on life.' He was about to take another sip of the golden liquid when a car came through the iron gates and came up to the house. 'That must be him now. It looks as if he's got someone with him.'

Rohm got up and was about to go to the steps when he stopped. 'It's Marc Kallis,' he said softly. 'He's got the girl with him.' He watched as Kallis went round the front of the Cheverolet, opened the co-driver's door and pulled Kirsty out onto her feet.

'I didn't expect you until much later,' said Rohm.

Kallis led Kirsty up to the steps. 'I was waiting and seized my chance,' he said. He liked seeing the look of satisfaction on Rohm's face. 'I'm afraid she got a bit cheeky on the way. I had to shut her up.'

'Bring her up here,' said Rohm. 'This is my close friend Bryan Jones.'

Kallis nodded to Jones and came up the steps with Kirsty. She had regained consciousness shortly after being struck and had been silent for the rest of the trip, trying to regain her senses, the pain around her eye intense. He sat her down in a chair and looked at Rohm. 'It's now in your hands.'

Rohm cackled, pleased with what he saw. 'You have done well,' he said. 'It's time to phone Steiner.' He looked at Kirsty. 'I've always wanted to meet you. I assume Marc Kallis has told why you've been brought here?'

Kirsty lifted her head and stared at Rohm, the disgust she felt for him evident. 'How you as a prominent businessman can lower yourself to this makes me want to throw up. You're scum and to condone what this thug has done to me is a crime. If South Africa still had the death penalty you would hang for murdering the three cabinet ministers.' She spat on the floor in front of him.

'You bitch,' screeched Rohm, stepping closer. In a fluid movement he whipped his hand across her face, her head twisting to the side as if caught in the blast from a hose, her hands only half-raised, ineffectively trying to protect her. 'You and your lover have dared to think you can bring me down. First you destroy the lives of my closest friends and then accuse me of murder.'

Kirsty, her lips bleeding, hung her head. She knew she was going to die, that Steiner, the man she loved, would not now be able to help her. They would kill him too. How had life come to this?

Rohm stepped away from her and looked at Kallis. 'Take her inside,' he said. 'We'll join you in a minute and then I'll ring Steiner. I'm also going to phone Bale and find out when he's going to arrive. I don't want him to miss the action.' He waited while Kallis dragged Kirsty out of the chair and led her inside. 'Things are going to plan,' he said. 'All I need now is Steiner.'

'Kallis is a good man,' said Jones. 'Teichmann did well to come up with him. I'm sure you'll have further use for him when all this is over.'

'Yes,' said Rohm. 'If the President doesn't comply with my letter and name the replacements for Dredge and

Hamilton I might even target some of the black ministers rather than just accuse them in the press of corruption.'

Jones laughed. 'If you start that you'll end up owning the entire cabinet.'

Rohm picked up his glass. 'Let's go in inside. You can listen when I speak to Steiner.'

Chapter 118

Stellenbosch

It was nearly seven-thirty and Paul Bale was still lying in his seat with his eyes closed when Steiner's phone rang. He took it out of his shirt pocket, saw it was a private call and answered. 'Steiner.' He saw Bale's eyes open.

'Steiner, Andrew Rohm. I have your woman, Kirsty Callard. I'm sure you'd like to see her.'

Steiner was stunned by what he'd heard. 'Rohm? Where is she?'

'She's on my estate near Paarl,' said Rohm. 'She was delivered to me forty-five minutes ago. I told her I'd phone you.'

'What are you doing with her?' said Steiner softly, his mind racing. 'I want to speak to her.'

'You'll have a few seconds,' said Rohm. 'Here she is.'

'James,' said Kirsty, her voice a near whisper. He knew immediately she'd been hurt. 'Don't come....' The phone was taken from her.

'She's safe,' said Rohm. 'Are you coming?'

'You've hurt her,' said Steiner. 'Why do you want her?'

'You know the answer to that,' said Rohm. 'I want both of you and it's easier this way.'

Steiner knew he had to go to the estate. Rohm held all the cards and nothing could be resolved over the phone. 'What's the address and your phone number?'

'You're being sensible,' said Rohm. 'I like that. You'll see a sign pointing to the estate when you get to Paarl. It says Blaukrantz.' He gave Steiner the phone number. 'I'm ten kilometres from the town. If you contact anyone else about this you'll never see the girl again. When can I expect you?'

'As long as it takes from now,' said Steiner. 'If I'm delayed I'll ring you.'

'Remember, she loves you,' said Rohm. He cut the call.

Steiner looked at Bale. 'You heard that,' he said, replacing the phone in his pocket. 'Rohm's got Kirsty Callard on his estate. I'm sure you're not surprised. You were looking forward to this.'

'This has nothing to do with me,' said Bale. 'What does he want?'

'The same thing Kallis wanted when he abducted her and took her to the farm,' said Steiner. 'The only difference this time is that Rohm is involved and he wants to kill both of us.'

'And he wants you to go to the estate?' said Bale. 'I didn't hear you tell him that you're busy sitting outside Hamilton's house with me. He would have loved that.'

Steiner looked at Bale. 'You are probably thinking now that you're saved,' he said, 'but I wouldn't count on it. I have to go to Rohm's estate but you don't. I could truss you up like a turkey and leave you here in the bush to be picked up later, hand you over to Hamilton and his guards and tell them what I know, or take you with me. I could of course phone Bruce Weisz and tell him that Rohm's holding Kirsty on his estate and wants me as ransom to go and collect her.' Steiner laughed briefly. 'He'd love that but this is between me and Rohm.'

'Hamilton would never believe you,' said Bale. He wanted to go with Steiner. Kallis and Jones would be at Rohm's and Steiner had no chance against four. Neither did he think Steiner would walk in armed. Bale had heard how John Kallis had been killed. 'Do you think he'd side with you against me, head of the NPA?'

'I've met Hamilton and I think he would,' said Steiner, 'but I'm not going to let you off so easily. For the same reason I'm not going to truss you up and leave you in the bush. I want you with me when I face Rohm.' He thought for a moment. 'Rohm didn't say how Kirsty had got there and I didn't ask but this smells of Marc Kallis. I'm sure you know of him but have you met him?'

'I've never heard of Marc Kallis,' said Bale emphatically.

'You'll meet him tonight,' said Steiner. He started the engine and drove out of the car park. 'I was really looking forward to introducing you to the assassin but Kirsty is far more important to me than anyone or anything. If any harm has come to her I'm going to hold Rohm, his mates and you equally responsible.'

Chapter 119

Sleepy Hollow

The man was annoyed when he missed his chance to kill Hamilton. Callard had not even appeared when Hamilton showed himself at the top of the stairs and she was not to blame. How he could have missed at that range, even though the target was raised and at an angle, was inexcusable for someone with his ability in the use of pistols. But the fact that Hamilton had survived remained and he now had to have another go. Hamilton's death was a condition of the job and there was no payment for anything less. It was also annoying that he had carefully planned how he would come in through Hamilton's back-garden, catch the guards by surprise and then after nullifying their threat enter the house and kill Hamilton. The plan had gone like clockwork until the woman had appeared, he had bungled the two shots and the woman and Steiner had appeared. But now for the second attempt the same plan could not be used. The previous guards had been caught short not only because they were surprised but because that hadn't expected someone to come in through the back. The back entrance could not be used again.

It was seven-forty, ten minutes after Steiner and Bale had left for Rohm's estate, when the man reached the village of Sleepy Hollow and took the left fork for Hamilton's house. It was pure chance that he had missed Steiner and Bale and he didn't know his good fortune. If he had shown up when they were waiting outside in the car park, things could have been difficult and if anyone had asked him the whereabouts of the two men he would have said Cape Town. Now, as he came to the house he stopped the car in front of the gates. His lights on and the engine running, he opened the gates, drove through, closed them and took the car up to the side of the house near the guards' room. One of the guards had already seen the car and he was waiting as it approached.

As the man got out of his car, the guard walked forward, his pistol hanging at his side. 'Good evening sir,' he said. 'This is private property.'

'I know that,' said the man, standing next his car, a faint smile on his face. 'You haven't been informed but I'm carrying out a routine security check for the DSO.'

'May I see identification?' said the guard. 'It'll have to be from the agency.'

The man unclipped a plastic wallet from his belt and handed it to him. He took it and held it to the light, comparing the photograph. 'That's fine,' he said, returning the wallet. 'Please come inside. My partner's in there.' He walked towards the room door, the man following.

Inside the room, the man was introduced to the other guard. 'I'm glad to see the DSO is on the job,' he said. 'I take it this is a routine check. I can show you around. Do you want to see Hamilton?'

'No,' said the man. 'You guys have keys to the house?'

'They're in the desk,' said the first guard. 'But if you wanted to see him I think he's still up. He turns off the lights downstairs when he hits the sack.'

'No,' repeated the man. 'I hope you've got the back way covered. Who would've thought the killer would come in there. I've looked at it on the map. There're tens of acres of vineyards between the fence and the other road.'

'He obviously caught our two friends with their trousers down,' said the second guard. 'It was a smart move. Do you have other stuff out here that you're looking at tonight? It's a long way to come if it's just us.'

'Hamilton's a high-profile case,' said the man casually. 'The DSO doesn't want him pumped if they help it. Three dead cabinet ministers is bad news and if Hamilton goes heads will start to role. I wouldn't be surprised if the President is one of them.'

'We know he's under a lot of pressure to find the people behind it but they don't leave any tracks,' said the first guard. 'Is the DSO getting any closer?'

'No,' said the man. 'They'll never catch him.' He walked to the door and then turned, pulling a Beretta 90two semi-automatic from under his jacket. Before the two guards, both sitting on opposite sides of the desk, could absorb what they saw and react, the man fired one bullet into each before adding a second. The first guard, front on, was hit in the head, and the second, his head slightly turned, took the lead through his temple into his brain. Both men were dead before they slumped forward onto the table.

The man went to the drawer in the desk, removed the bunch of keys and left the room. He went to the verandah, walked slowly to the door and, recognizing the key he'd used the night before, unlocked it. As he entered the hall he heard Hamilton call out from the reception room on his right. 'Hullo. Who is that?' He was sure it was one of the guards.

The man walked to the room and saw Hamilton seated in front of a large television set, a book open on his lap. His eyes were on the door, a faint smile on his lips.

'Sorry to disturb you,' said the man. He entered and before Hamilton could say anything, revealed the Beretta, pointing it at Hamilton's head and firing twice. Like a plant wilting under the intensity of the sun, Hamilton closed into a ball, dying in the chair he loved, only the bottom of his legs and one hand dangling over the front edge.

For a moment the man stared at the body. This time he had made sure. He walked from the room, calmly left through the front door and went to his car. In seconds he had gone from the scene of his crime, leaving three dead men. Hamilton was the last of the four and the man could expect payment.

Chapter 120

Rohm's estate

Steiner and Bale reached Paarl twenty minutes after leaving Hamilton's house. They came into the main street and Steiner soon saw the sign to Rohm's estate. It simply said Blaukratz and pointed to the right. Steiner took the road and after two kilometres entered the wine country, vineyards, valleys and forest. He kept on and when his milometer showed a little over ten kilometres he came to a narrow road that led to the estate.

'You'll soon see your master,' said Steiner, turning into the road. 'He won't expect to see his right-hand man roll up in the company of the man he so desperately wants to kill.'

Bale chose to keep quiet. He wanted Rohm to take control and was very pleased with the way things were turning out. If the killer had appeared at Hamilton's and Steiner had nailed him he didn't know what he would have done. Kallis deserved double the money for moving so quickly in bringing in Callard. It might have saved his life.

A kilometre down the road Steiner came to iron gates and after passing through continued. A little later after going round a bend they saw the sprawling house and he drove up to the front of the verandah. His prime aim was to get Kirsty but he knew it would not be simple. Rohm had been clear what he wanted and anything could happen. He got out and without a glance at Bale went up the steps to the open doors.

Across the room next to a large fire place, his hands in his pocket and a leer on his face, was Rohm. Steiner knew it was him. Near Rohm and slumped in a chair, her eye swollen and bruised, was Kirsty, and standing behind her, a metre separating them, Kallis and Jones. Like Rohm, Steiner had never met Jones but knew it was him.

Steiner walked a few paces into the room. Kirsty was staring at him, abject despair written on her face. 'Someone's hit her,' he said, glancing at Rohm. 'I'm holding you and your thugs, Kallis and Bale, responsible.'

'I didn't expect you so soon,' said Rohm, removing his hands from his pockets. 'You must have been in the area.'

'I'm here to get Kirsty,' said Steiner. He started to go towards her but before he could move a pace, Kallis came forward, his pistol hanging in his hand.

'Leave her,' said Kallis acidly. 'She's mine. She never wanted you. You're the only thug here, a born killer.'

At that moment Bale appeared in the doorway and ambled into the room. 'We were in the area,' he said to Rohm. 'He came to my home and forced me to accompany him to Hamilton's house. He thinks we're behind the deaths of Hilton and his friends.'

'What Bale said is right,' said Steiner to Rohm. 'I think you killed Hilton, Delaware and Dredge, and had a go at Hamilton yesterday morning. I believe your assassin will have another go and I wanted to introduce him to Bale. The game's up Rohm. The DSO knows everything about you and they agreed that I should be at Hamilton's house with Bale tonight. They are also in the area near the house.'

Rohm didn't know if what he was hearing was the truth. But he had seen men lie their way out of a difficult position before and the rule he followed was to weigh it up and if there was no perceived threat dismiss it and carry on. In this case he could not see the DSO suddenly appearing at the estate. The only ones working anywhere close to Steiner or aware of his movements were Weisz, Conran and Fairley. Fairley was dead and Conran would have immediately contacted Bale if Steiner had revealed what he intended to do tonight. That left Weisz and he would never act on a whim. That was how Steiner worked. And, no one else could possibly know what had happened in the last hour but a check could easily be made.

Rohm looked at Bale. 'Paul, you were in the car when Steiner received my call?'

'Yes,' said Bale. He guessed what was coming.

'Did Steiner phone anyone after getting the call?' said Rohm. 'Did he speak to Weisz.'

'No,' said Bale. 'After some more of his bullshit we came straight here. He's dancing on air and working alone.'

Rohm looked at Steiner. 'You're exposed like a lion alone up a tree, no retractable claws, unknown territory, no one to help you and outnumbered. You're going to die.'

'And you are you prepared to take a risk that what I say is a lie?' said Steiner. He had to play things out. 'Do you think that Weisz is the only one who knows my plans and movements? The DSO in Durban and Johannesburg has been on to you ever since Hilton gave evidence to Peter Smith that you were heavily involved in serious organized crime and asked him to initiate a complete investigation in preparation for your prosecution and conviction.' Steiner was prepared to use anything to cast doubt in Rohm's mind and give him time. He had also not forgotten that Kallis was present. He glanced at him and then again looked at Rohm. 'It is interesting to see Marc Kallis here and I don't need a high IQ to know that he abducted Kirsty in Cape Town at your behest and brought her here. You knew that as soon as I was told, I'd come here and you'd be able to kill both of us together. You're too sure of yourself Rohm. The DSO knows that it could only have been Kallis who murdered Smith and he did that straight after he tried to kill me on the farm. Kallis's presence here confirms his direct link with you and while we believed Teichmann was behind Kallis I now think it was you. Neither is it a coincidence that Teichmann was murdered the day after Kallis and I met on the farm. I'm beginning to think you asked Kallis to kill Teichmann because you feared a link being made to you.'

Kirsty watched, wishing she could hold Steiner in her arms, fervently hoping he wouldn't do anything that would get him killed. She knew he would be waiting for his chance to overpower Rohm and the others, the men she had come to hate.

'You really are stretching things out and playing for time,' said Rohm. 'Kallis and I are going to kill you and Callard, and I asked him to get you here because he was able to identify you and he also wants the two of you dead for killing his brother. Kallis calls it unfinished business. You are an avowed enemy of the people who built this country, many of whom are now rotting and serving long sentences because of you and Callard, and I want you dead for that reason. As I told her before you came, I had nothing to do with the murders of the cabinet ministers and the fact you are here proves nothing except that you are trespassing and making false accusations. Kallis is not guilty of anything and neither is Bale. He is a personal friend and like Bryan Jones was coming here for a break. The DSO has nothing on us and never will even after you are dead.'

Steiner looked at Jones. 'And what do think of all this?' he said. 'Maybe I shouldn't ask because you're also on the list Hilton gave Peter Smith. Aside from corruption, you will go down for conspiring with Rohm when he is indicted on charges of murder. You, Bale and Rohm will make quite a little threesome when you stand in the dock.' He looked at Rohm. 'I mustn't forget Conran, your man in the DSO and one of their top agents who directs everything he hears to Bale. I don't know what kind of hold you've got on him or what you're paying him but it must be considerable. He will also be in the dock.' He glanced at Kirsty, her bruised face, the cut on her cheek. 'You're going to answer to me for that Rohm. No court will give you what you deserve for what you've done to her.'

There was silence in the room. Rohm moved away from the fire place and was about to speak when the distinct ring of a mobile phone was heard. It came from Steiner's pocket and he knew it was Bale's. As he reached for it Bale moved across. 'I'll get that,' he said. 'It's my phone.'

Steiner wanted to see who was calling but Kallis had already levelled his gun and he knew he wouldn't hesitate to fire. He took his hand away from his pocket and stood still.

Bale removed the phone, glanced at the display and walked over to the doors where he was furthest from the others. He lifted the phone to his ear. 'Yes?' He listened to the call and then said: 'Thank you. I'll be in touch.' He cut the call, stuck the phone into his jacket pocket and went over to Rohm. 'We need to speak alone.'

Rohm glanced at Kallis. 'Keep the gun on Steiner,' he said. 'I'll be a minute.' He and Bale left the room.

Steiner looked at Kirsty. 'I love you,' he said.

Kirsty stared at him, forcing a smile. 'I'm so glad you're here. I love you too.' She looked away, tears in her eyes.

After a short while, Rohm and Bale appeared. Rohm walked over and stopped a couple of metres from Steiner. 'I've just had news,' he said. 'It's too good for me not to tell you. Hamilton is dead. He was killed shortly after his and Dredge's replacements were named.'

'So you finally got all four,' said Steiner. 'It must be very satisfying to know you have the money to hire an assassin to kill government ministers. That must have been him on the phone. I know you wanted to silence them but there must be something more.'

Rohm laughed, enjoying every moment. He glanced at the others and then said: 'After that news there is no reason why I shouldn't really enjoy myself before you die. I was being too cautious when I needn't have been. I directed the killing of Hilton, Delaware, Dredge and now Hamilton.

They were getting too close to my business interests and I had to eliminate the risk.'

'I assume that includes Bale and Conran,' said Steiner, a little surprised at the confession but recognizing some people had the innate desire to boast of their conquests when things were going well. Rohm must have been burning inside to get it out.

'They are friends,' said Rohm. 'I only learned of your arrival in Cape Town through them. That's all there is to know.'

'The fact that Bale hears your admission and does nothing about it makes him equally guilty,' said Steiner. 'That also applies to your silent friend Jones.'

Bale stepped forward. 'You've had it Steiner,' he said. He knew Steiner was right and there was no point in denying it. He was also proud of the part he had played. 'Rohm is taking all the credit. I was also involved.'

'And Conran?' said Steiner.

'He is a senior agent in the DSO and obliged to pass on information to the NPA,' said Bale. 'I'm the head of the NPA.'

Steiner thought back to the conversation with Fairley. Perhaps Fairley was wrong in his suspicion and Conran was only doing his job. But he persisted. 'Why are you protecting him? I can only think you like keeping things close to your chest even when you hold the advantage. I find that admirable.' When he could see he was not going to get a response he changed tack. 'If what you say is true, one or both of you knows the identity of the assassin.'

Rohm hooted. 'Whether or not you believe that is your problem but we don't know his identity. In some ways it makes this more exciting.'

'Who killed Peter Smith?' said Steiner. 'Surely you must know that.'

'I did,' said Kallis. 'You and Smith were part of the same package. If you'd been quicker you might have stopped me. If you want to talk about complicity you should start with him. He was as guilty as you for killing my brother and having his friends convicted.'

'That leaves Teichmann,' said Steiner. He was not going to achieve anything by raising the murder of Adam Fairley. There was enough on the table.

'Teichmann became a risk,' said Rohm, 'and was expendable. Kallis removed him for me.'

'So Kallis went to the man who trusted him and put two bullets in him,' said Steiner.

'Yes,' said Kallis. 'I didn't particularly like doing it but it was necessary.'

'What sick minds you've got,' said Steiner, 'but you won't get away with it.' He knew he was going nowhere with talk and out of nowhere he leapt forward, landing behind Rohm, encircling his neck with his right arm and taking hold of his left bicep to form a lock. 'Drop the gun Kallis,' he said, bending Rohm back against his chest. 'If you don't I'll break his neck.'

Rohm, trying in vain to relieve the pain, rasped: 'Do as he says. I can't breathe.'

Bale and Jones were immobile, both staring at what had unfolded in front of them, daring not to offer assistance and take on Steiner. Kirsty was quiet, still, taken aback by the speed and suddenness of Steiner's move, the way he had so adroitly spun behind Rohm, rendering him impotent.

For a moment, Kallis was chiselled from stone, and then in a blur he jumped behind Kirsty, taking the muzzle of his Beretta to her neck. 'Back off Steiner,' he said, 'or the girl dies. Let Rohm go.'

Steiner did not show the anger he felt for not anticipating Kallis's move. For some reason he had not thought Kallis would hold his nerve and go for Kirsty. But he couldn't trust Kallis or the others and if he released Rohm, he and Kirsty would be killed. 'I don't trust you Kallis. If I release Rohm there is nothing in it for Kirsty or me. You'll kill us both. You and your master won't change your mind.' He lessened the pressure on Rohm's neck slightly. 'What does your boss think?'

Rohm knew that Steiner would not release him unless he at least had assurance and believed he and Callard could leave without being harmed. It was a stalemate. Kallis had the woman and Steiner had Rohm. Steiner would not risk her life by killing Rohm if he thought there was a possibility of her being freed. Rohm also knew that Steiner had nothing that could be used against him as evidence. If Steiner and Callard went and revealed what he'd said, it would be their word against his, the leading industrialist in the country, Jones, an eminent businessman, and Paul Bale, the NDPP. He twisted his neck. 'Release me and you and the woman go free,' he said. 'Kallis will not let her go while you hold me and he might kill both of you. If you kill me you will be charged with premeditated murder and there are witnesses. You can't slaughter all of us.'

Steiner knew Rohm was right but couldn't trust them. 'That's not good enough. It would mean me accepting your word and that's not on.'

Rohm thought for a moment. 'This is the deal Steiner. Kallis will leave with Callard. You and he can have this out at a place of your choosing. I've heard about you, your ability as a killer and I also know Kallis, his training in the street and his prowess in the ring in Thailand. It will be as it was at the farm and a simple case of who is best.' He looked across at Kallis. 'Marc, you will not get what you want from this position. You can arrange the time and place. Take the girl with you.'

'I can have it out with him now,' said Kallis. 'There is no difference between here and some other place. I'll kill him and you will also have the girl.'

Rohm didn't like it. If Steiner killed Kallis in his own house there was no way of knowing what he would do next. It was too complicated and not how he had planned things. 'No,' he said. 'I want a clean break. You have no choice and it's the only way you'll get your money.'

Kallis knew Rohm had made his decision and would stick to it. In the end he wanted Steiner dead and the place was not important. He could see Rohm was scared of the risks and that he was backing off. Whatever Rohm had said about the involvement of Callard in the killing of his brother, Kallis believed Steiner was essentially to blame and without his death all this would have been a wasted exercise. Rohm was clever and as long as he paid up, reducing everything to a play-off between him and Steiner was what it was all about. 'Steiner's still got you by the neck,' he said.

Steiner released the hold on Rohm but remained immediately behind him. He didn't like Kallis walking off with Kirsty. He had come here to take her away with him. But he knew Kallis would not kill her as long as there was a chance of a one-to-one contest and he would have a say in where it would be. If he exposed himself and got embroiled now with Kallis, Rohm and the others would be free to do what they liked and whatever the outcome they would be in control. He had to take a risk and let Kallis go. 'I agree with Rohm but if you harm Kirsty I'll never rest until I find you. You can phone me to arrange the place.' He looked at Kirsty. 'Go with Kallis. I'll see you soon.'

Kallis lowered the Beretta. 'I'll be in contact,' he said to Rohm. 'I'm letting you and Bale off the hook.' He took Kirsty by the arm and together they walked from the room to the car outside.

When the car had gone, Rohm faced Steiner. 'I won't see you again. This is the last time you'll interfere in my affairs. I already have people in very high places.' He looked at Bale. 'Whose car did you use?'

'We came in mine,' said Bale. 'He'll have to take it. He's got the keys. I'll collect them from the desk at the Mandarin hotel.' Bale knew that Steiner had no other way of getting out and was only too glad to see the end of him. He was confident Steiner had nothing against them that would stand up in court.

'I'm sure you have men in high places,' said Steiner to Rohm. 'All four are now in their jobs.' He turned, left the room and went to the Mercedes parked outside. The others soon heard the car leave the yard.

'I'm glad to see him go,' said Jones. 'I'd have liked to see the two of them fight it out.'

'If their past exploits are anything to go by they are two of the most dangerous men alive. I was glad to see them both go. We can now get on with more important business.'

'And you're confident Steiner has nothing against you?' said Bale.

'He has nothing against any of us,' said Rohm calmly.

'What about Conran?' said Bale. 'Before we got here he was going on about the DSO agent Fairley suspecting Conran was passing on information to me. From what Conran told me, Fairley's suspicion, which he'd obviously conveyed to Steiner, was based on a change in facial expression and mere interpretation. He heard nothing that meant anything.'

'That sums it up,' said Rohm. 'Steiner was trying anything and has absolutely no evidence of any kind against Conran. That's why he stopped referring to him. Anyway, I think Kallis will put an end to him and that includes Callard. When are you going back to Cape Town? There's a lot here to show you.'

'I'm going back on Sunday,' said Bale. 'I'll need a car.'

'I'll have one sent out from Paarl,' said Rohm. He looked at Jones. 'Where's that malt?'

'Where are you taking me?' said Kirsty, speaking for the first time since leaving the estate. She and Kallis had just joined the N1 freeway to Cape Town.

'You'll soon find out,' said Kallis. 'I half-expected Rohm to back off but that doesn't stop me from completing what I started when I took you to the farm.'

'Does that mean you're taking me back there?' said Kirsty.

'No,' said Kallis. 'I must admit that the farm is a perfect setting but it's a long drive and I want to finish this.'

Chapter 121

Sleepy Hollow

Steiner knew when he left the estate that Kallis and Kirsty had too good a start on him for there to be any chance of catching them. But he also knew that he wouldn't achieve anything if he did. Kallis had control because he had Kirsty and if pressure was put on him he there was the danger he would use her as he had done before. The only way forward was to wait for him to make contact and meet him on his own terms, and that meant returning to the hotel.

Now as he met up with the N1 to Cape Town, Steiner went over what he had heard in the room. Rohm and Bale were guilty of the murder of the ministers, enough to put them away for life even though they hadn't pulled the trigger. Kallis would also get life for killing Smith and Teichmann. Steiner wasn't sure about Jones but his presence and that he didn't deny involvement would put him under a lot of heat. Steiner thought again about Conran and whether Fairley's suspicion had any substance. He had to admit that it was slim but it still bothered him. Fairley was a very experienced operator and had had considerable experience interrogating people when he was with New Scotland Yard in London. He relied on his powers of interpretation and was fairly certain that his observation concerning Conran meant something other than the passing on of routine information. Steiner thought about the assassin. His identity was still unknown, as was that of Fairley's killer. If Rohm and Bale had known they would surely have said so when happily boasting about their crimes. He didn't like having to wait for Kallis to contact him and he worried about Kirsty. Kallis was unpredictable and there was no knowing what he might do to her. Steiner thought about phoning Weisz but he didn't want to get him involved until he had cleared things up with Kallis and got Kirsty back.

Steiner had been on the N1 for five kilometres when he thought about the phone call Bale had received on the estate, the call that had told him of Hamilton's death. There was no way now of knowing who had made the call but it had to be either the assassin or someone close to him who was reporting to Bale. The call had been made just over an hour ago and the fact that Steiner hadn't heard anything from the DSO meant that the guards had also been killed and that there was a possibility that no one other than Bale and the killer knew about the killing. The DSO, possibly through the police, would have been the first to be told. Steiner was annoyed he hadn't thought about this before. He hadn't yet come to the Stellenbosch turn-off but it was close and two kilometres further on he saw it and left the N1.

After passing through Sleepy Hollow, Steiner soon neared Hamilton's house and went slowly up to the gates. There was no sign of any activity, no cars in sight, and the place was as quiet as Steiner would have expected it to be at this time. Only the lights in the front room of the house were on and he could see the reflection of light from the guard's room. He opened the gates, drove through and up to house. There was still no sign of anyone and, leaving the car, went to the guard's room.

Even Steiner, from what he had seen in the past, was chilled by the sight of the two dead men, one, thrown back into the seat, his arms dangling pathetically, the other, his head lying on the table, a rivulet of blood from his temple reaching and covering his eye. Both men had clearly been taken by surprise and Steiner found that difficult to understand after what had happened the morning before when the attempt was made on Hamilton's life. There was now supposed to be one guard outside the room at all times and these two were sitting together as if they had been

318

talking to someone they knew or whose appearance they accepted.

Steiner switched off the light and left the room. He went onto the verandah of the house and along to the door. It was half-open and he entered. He went to the nearest room, the one with lights on, looked inside and saw Hamilton slumped in his chair. He crossed to him and saw the killer's trademark, two bullet holes half-a-centimetre apart, this time in the head.

Steiner turned off the lights and after closing the front door left the house and went to his car. One person again came to mind. It was Conran, and Steiner now knew that he wouldn't be able to rest until he had spoken to him.

Conran's contact details were on the list given to him by Weisz and it was at the hotel. After leaving the house he soon joined the N1 freeway and thirty minutes later arrived at the Mandarin Hotel. He went to his room, noting Kirsty's discarded and torn shirt, and collected the list. He found the car keys on the table but left them there.

Chapter 122

Constantia

A short while later Steiner was in Bale's car and heading for Constantia. He knew the route from his earlier meeting with Bale and when he was in the area he stopped and checked his street map.

Steiner quickly located the street in which Conran lived and noticed that it was a few streets away from Bale. The area was particularly exclusive and the properties reminded Steiner of Bishop's Avenue in Highgate, London, commonly known as billionaires' row.

When Steiner came to Conran's street he drove down it. He was looking for number 42 and when he saw it went past and pulled up against the grass verge. He looked back through the rear window. There were very few cars in the street, not surprising when there were adequate facilities inside the grounds, and only one car outside Conran's house. At first Steiner didn't pay any attention to it but then his mind went back to Rohm's house on the estate. When he had arrived with Bale there was only one car parked in front of the house, a black Chevrolet, and he remembered the first three digits on the number plate. They were 371, the same as the car now outside Conran's house and the car was a black Chevrolet.

Steiner slowly digested what he was seeing. The car outside Rohm's had to be the one used by Kallis and that meant Kallis was paying Conran a visit, probably with Kirsty.

Steiner got out of the car, crossed the street and walked slowly to Conran's gates. He let himself into the grounds and using trees and shrubs as cover moved quickly towards the house. He stopped when he first saw it, situated in all its splendour on the other side of a manicured lawn. It was a symmetrical two-storey building with the main door positioned in the centre. The only light in the house was a dull glow in the downstairs hall and strong luminescence emanating from the window of a room on the first floor, directly above and a little to the right of the door. Whoever was in the house, had to be in the room.

Steiner went swiftly over the lawn and halted on the verandah. There was no sound inside the house and he tried the door. As expected it didn't yield and he went along the front wall to the nearest window. It was of the sash design and opened smoothly, sliding upwards in its grooves and providing easy access. He climbed through the space, finding himself in a reception room, and went swiftly to the door. He opened it and a couple of metres from him a wide stairway went up to the first floor. The only light was from a skylight but it was perfect and he began his ascent.

When Steiner reached the first floor he went along the passage to where he expected to find the room. It was unmistakeable, a sliver of light coming from the bottom of a closed door, and he went to it. A metre from the door he heard a man speaking and he halted, listening. It was Kallis but Steiner could not make out what he was saying. Then Kallis went quiet and Steiner heard the voice of Conran. Steiner moved closer. It was still not clear what was being said and there was nothing to be gained by delaying entry.

Steiner opened the door and entered the room. It was large, fifteen metres by ten. Kirsty was seated in a chair near the window and over to the left, seated round a table in the middle of the room and on the near side of an oak desk, were Conran and Kallis. All three turned and stared at him, his sudden appearance completely unexpected.

'What the hell is this,' said Conran making to rise.

'Sit down,' said Steiner, advancing further into the room. He looked at Kallis. 'Your time's up Kallis. I'm taking you in for abducting and assaulting Kirsty and for the murder of Peter Smith.' He faced Conran. 'Your

321

explanation had better be good. I believe you killed Adam Fairley because he got too close. He was sure you were in bed with Bale.' He glanced at Kirsty, keeping an eye on the two men. 'Are you alright?'

She nodded, without saying anything, and stayed in her seat. She had never been so glad to see anyone. She could feel Steiner's strength, the strength she had felt before. His presence sent a strange shiver of excitement through her.

'This is rich,' said Kallis, grinning and getting to his feet. 'You're out of touch Steiner. Conran and I are friends. We first met in Durban when my brother worked for the DSO. This is between you and me. You were supposed to wait for my call but now I'm pleased you came.'

'And you've got nothing to say?' said Steiner to Conran, wanting him to speak. 'You know that Kallis murdered Smith and here he is in your house with Kirsty. You were quite happy to pretend you'd never heard of him. You must also be one of Rohm's mates.'

Conran knew he'd been caught and he cursed himself. He should have known that Steiner would not give up and that at some point he'd pay him a visit, either with Weisz or alone. Steiner had not got anywhere with Bale and Kallis at the estate and, except for Conran, had run out of people on his list. He got out of his seat. 'You're going nowhere fast Steiner. You've shot your wad. I'm not really surprised you came to see me and in some ways I'm glad you did. You've been making a real fool of yourself, jumping around aimlessly like a monkey in the trees. This time you came up against professionals and your lack of class shows. I always wondered where Smith found you and how Weisz fell for it. He should have put me on the job.'

'What's Rohm paying you?' said Steiner. 'You must know how he's been killing the ministers, Hilton, Delaware, Dredge and now Hamilton. You were the one who phoned Bale at the estate.'

Kallis howled with laughter. 'Don't keep him in suspense,' he said to Conran. 'After all the effort he's put in running round the country after his lover he deserves something.'

Conran also laughed. He was beginning to enjoy himself and was sure from what Kallis had told him about events at the estate that Steiner was working alone, that he had not confided in anyone except Callard. When the two were removed there would be no one to expose him. 'You really have no idea who killed the ministers?' he said. 'I'll almost feel sorry for Weisz when he calls me in and says you've hit another blank. Fairley was the only one who got close. I thought he might interpret something from a conversation we had and tell you. I couldn't afford to take the risk and killed him. He should have stayed with Scotland Yard's Specialist Crime Directorate. It would've been safer.'

'You're dragging it out,' said Kallis grinning. 'He and I have something to settle and I want to get on with it before I enjoy myself with his woman.'

Steiner was patient. It had been ingrained in him by the Japanese. 'Go on,' he said to Conran. 'I'm listening. It sounds as if Kallis knows as much as you do. That doesn't surprise me. You of course know he killed Johan Teichmann and Peter Smith.'

'Yes,' said Conran. 'I guessed it was him before he told me.' He took a step back and rested his rear on the edge of the desk. He wanted to reveal his involvement with Bale and Rohm. 'Ten days ago, Bale approached me with an offer I couldn't refuse. He told me a friend of his who he didn't name at the time wanted four allegedly corrupt cabinet ministers to be replaced with people of his choice. A letter was to be sent to the President saying that if the four were not replaced immediately they would be killed.'

'And you knew they would be killed regardless?' said Steiner, shaking his head.

'No,' said Conran, 'but I soon suspected that killing them was paramount.'

'I think everyone knew that,' said Steiner. 'Smith was a personal friend of Hilton's and the suggestion he was corrupt was risible. And Bale's friend, Rohm, didn't give the President much chance to replace them before they were being killed. What was the offer?'

Conran ignored the comment. It was the first thing that had come to mind when approached by Bale and he could have refused then to collaborate. 'Bale asked me to arrange the killing of the four men,' he said. 'I accepted and Hilton was the first to go on the Wednesday, two days later.'

'Tell him who did it,' said Kallis. 'The suspense must be driving him crazy.'

'I killed Hilton,' said Conran unambiguously. 'Unfortunately his wife was also there and I was forced to take her out as well.'

Steiner looked at Kirsty. She had visibly brightened up since his arrival. 'That's a surprise,' he said to her. 'We never put him in the frame.' He faced Conran. 'Are you saying you carried on and killed the others?'

Kallis quickly interrupted. 'No,' he said. 'He's not saying that and can't steal all the thunder. After he'd spoken to Bale he asked me to do the full job for a fee. I couldn't fit in Hilton and we agreed I'd have the others. Delaware and Dredge were easy but Conran then said he'd go for Hamilton. I believe your bitch over there poked her nose in when Conran was about to kill him.' He took out a cigarette, lit it and casually blew two smoke rings into the dry air. 'She alerted Hamilton with her scream and Conran had to silence her. Hamilton appeared but Conran only wounded him. You know the rest.'

Steiner turned to Conran. 'I finally get it,' he said. 'You returned and killed Hamilton. How did you surprise the guards?'

'After the first attempt I couldn't use the quiet approach again and come in through the back,' said Conran. 'I decided to drive in through the gates and show them my DSO pass. It was easy.'

'You then phoned Bale, not knowing I was with him at Rohm's.' said Steiner.

'I didn't know where he was,' said Conran. 'Neither did I know Kallis had been asked by Rohm to pick up your woman and lure you to his estate. Kallis told me earlier that Hamilton would have to wait and because I didn't want to wait I said I'd do it.' Conran smiled, his handsome features glowing mockingly. 'There you have it. I'm sorry it's of no value.'

Steiner knew that he and Kirsty were not going to be allowed to leave without interference from Kallis and Conran, and the talking was over. He faced Kallis. 'The stage is yours Kallis. This is what you wanted.'

Kirsty watched quietly. She knew what was coming and that the result was inevitable. She had seen Steiner at work before and this time he wouldn't make a mistake.

It was exactly what Kallis wanted. He was armed but didn't need it. He was sure Steiner wasn't carrying anything. There were three metres separating them, too far for either man to strike without taking a step, and he had to close it. Like a predator stalking its prey he started to advance and was surprised when Steiner remained still, revealing nothing. He could feel Steiner's energy and it was strong, unlike he had felt before. He couldn't let it get to him. When he had covered one metre he lunged, his left foot taking a giant step, sweeping through with his right, his hand ready for the killing strike.

Before the strike came Steiner knew it was coming. He had read Kallis's intent perfectly and as his right foot was about to touch the floor and form a base, he swept it away in a precise execution of *ashi barai*. Unable to control himself, Kallis spun into the air, his body assuming the horizontal a metre above the floor. With a cry and complete expulsion of breath, summoning all the power at his command, Steiner blended with Kallis, lifting his hand and striking him on the side of his head with the bottom of his fist. He was dead before he hit the floor, a figure of consummate depletion.

Leaving the body like a streak of light, his lungs instantly filled with air, Steiner rose, springing towards Conran, pivoting on the ball of his foot and delivering a reverse kick that hit him in the middle of his chest, driving him in a disconnection of arms and legs over the desk, his head hitting the wall as he fell to the floor. He was out cold.

Kirsty left the chair in a burst, running to him and throwing her arms around his neck, kissing him and weeping like a child. 'I knew you could do it,' she cried. 'They were never in your class.'

He held her to him, kissing her and passing his hand through her hair, exalted by once again having the woman he loved in his arms. 'The sight of what they'd done to you gave me strength,' he said. 'But now it's over.' He smiled and squeezed her. 'Kallis won't hurt you again. When we leave here I'm taking you to a doctor. You need a cover for your eye and treatment for the cuts on your cheek and lips.'

'You killed him,' said Kirsty, glancing at the man who had beaten her. 'Look at his expression, a mixture of surprise and the realization he'd screwed up and made a mistake. What about Conran? I never imagined it was him. How well he concealed it.'

'His head hit the wall and he hasn't moved,' said Steiner. 'He's unconscious but will soon come to life. I must phone Weisz. It is time to pull in Rohm and Bale, and I'll need his help.'

'But you've no evidence,' said Kirsty, dejectedly. 'They're aware of that and were quite happy to let you go and leave you to Kallis.'

'You were there when Weisz gave me this,' said Steiner. He extracted the pen recorder from his jacket pocket. 'I nearly didn't take it but now it's my little friend.'

'Are you saying you picked up what was said at the farm?' she said. 'Oh, I love you.' She looked at him. 'Did you get anything here?'

'Yes,' said Steiner. 'There're still a few hours left before it's full. I'll give it to Weisz. Conran might still have something to say.' He went to the phone on the desk and dialled Weisz's cell phone number. He answered. 'Weisz.'

'Bruce, James Steiner. I'm at Conran's house. I found him entertaining Marc Kallis. I think you should come round.'

'This doesn't sound good,' said Weisz.

'Depends on how you look at it,' said Steiner. 'Kirsty's with me.'

'I'll leave now,' said Weisz, not knowing what to expect. 'It'll take me twenty minutes.' He cut the call.

'We'll see him in twenty minutes,' said Steiner to Kirsty. He was about to go over to her when he heard Conran move. He went round the desk and looked at him. 'He's stopped dreaming.'

Conran lifted his head and stared at Steiner. 'You've called Weisz,' he said. 'I wondered when you'd invite him to the party.'

'I had to do it alone,' said Steiner. 'I wanted to bring him good news.'

'Where's Kallis?' said Conran. 'He's gone pretty quiet.'

'So would you be,' said Steiner. 'He didn't make it. He made the mistake of being too sure of himself. I expected more from him.'

Conran slowly got to his feet, his eyes never leaving Steiner. 'Do you mind if I sit down?' he said.

'Over here where I can see you,' said Steiner making way. He waited while Conran came round the desk and sat down. 'Weisz is on his way.'

Chapter 123

Rohm's estate

'I wonder how Kallis is getting on?' said Jones. 'I'll be happy when he's killed Steiner. He can't be underestimated.' Jones and the other two were on the verandah having a drink. They'd just finished a superb meal.

'Kallis will never underestimate him,' said Rohm. 'He's had too much experience against people who would have slit his throat given half a chance. He's only been gone a couple of hours.'

'I don't think you you'll hear from him before tomorrow,' said Bale. 'He'll want to make sure he gets it right.'

'Did Conran have anything else to say?' said Jones. 'We don't know how his man managed to pull it off. Surely the guards would have been a lot more careful after the earlier fiasco.'

'I was thinking about that,' said Bale. 'Perhaps they knew him.'

'That's hardly likely,' said Rohm. 'The only people who know the identity of a class assassin are those who are employing him. I think he was using a very clever disguise like the killer in Forsyth's *Day of the Jackal*.' He lifted his glass. 'Who's for another malt? I feel in a very good mood.'

Chapter 124

Cape Town

Twenty-five minutes after receiving the call from Steiner, Bruce Weisz arrived at Conran's house. He rang the doorbell.

Kirsty opened it after checking it was Weisz. 'Hullo,' she said, stepping aside for him to enter.

'What happened to your eye?' said Weisz.

'I'll tell you later,' she said. 'Steiner's upstairs.'

'This had better be good,' said Weisz, entering the hall. 'I was in the middle of a dinner party for eight. My wife is not pleased.'

'She'll understand when you tell her what it's about,' said Kirsty. 'You might even be received by the President. I'll lead the way.' They went up the stairs and to the room.

When they entered Weisz halted and stared. It was not what he had expected. 'What's going on?'

Steiner got up and came forward. 'I'm glad you could make it,' he said. 'You've met Conran and that's Marc Kallis on the floor.'

Weisz sat in the nearest chair, his eyes on Conran. 'It looks as if you've got some explaining to do.'

'Steiner's dying to tell you,' said Conran. 'Let him do the talking.'

Weisz looked at Steiner. 'I'm listening.'

Steiner briefly described the events that had taken place since getting Bale to go with him to Hamilton's house. 'You don't seem surprised,' he said when he'd finished.

Weisz was quiet and then he said: 'It's all so perfect. I didn't know about Hamilton otherwise you'd have heard from me. No one on the outside could have found out what was going on.' He glanced at Steiner. 'Without your intervention and Rohm using Kallis to lure you to the estate

329

they would have achieved their objective and we'd still be in the dark. But we have no evidence and you killed Kallis.'

'I wanted to hear what he'd say,' said Conran, 'before I said anything. I admit that I knew Kallis but there was nothing that linked him to the earlier abduction of Callard. We didn't know what went on at the farm. It was Steiner's account and we still don't know Kallis killed Smith and Teichmann. I was as surprised as Steiner when Kallis turned up here with Callard. And the accusation that I killed Adam Fairley is fantasy. He was a close friend of mine.'

'Tell him about modern science,' said Kirsty. 'I'm sure he knows what's admissible in court.'

Steiner reached inside his jacket and extracted the recorder. 'Do you remember giving me this,' he said to Weisz, holding it up. 'The Beretta you gave me is still in the hotel but this came in useful. It contains a recording of what was said at Rohm's estate and the verbal exchanges in this room.' He looked at Conran. 'You are in deep shit and in some ways I'm sorry Kallis is not going to be next to you in court.'

Weisz reached out and took the pen, a thin smile on his lips. 'If this has got on it what you say it has we can go now and pull in Rohm, Bale and Jones. With them, the three other guys named by Hilton will follow.'

'That's not all,' said Steiner. 'We don't have the forensic evidence we'd like, DNA and fingerprints, but we've got the bullets that killed the first three ministers, Smith, Teichmann and Fairley. There must be some at Hamilton's. I think you'll find Conran's pistol in this room and Kallis is wearing his.' He indicated the Beretta held in a holster behind Kallis' hip. 'There'll be a match if the slugs are in good condition.'

'Excellent,' said Weisz, rubbing his hands together. 'Who else besides Bale and Jones is at the estate?'

'I didn't see anyone but there must be servants,' said Steiner. 'He wouldn't be there alone.'

Weisz went to the phone on Conran's desk. 'I'm going to get some people to pick up Conran and Kallis. I'll also ask Strauss and Mellor to join us when we head for Rohm's estate. I don't want there to be any mistakes.'

'I want to take Kirsty to the hotel and get someone to look at her,' said Steiner. 'Strauss and Mellor should be enough.'

'No,' said Weisz. 'I'll come to the hotel with you and get one of our doctors. You're coming with me to Rohm's.' He glanced at Kallis. 'Besides your obvious ability I want to see Rohm's face when you show up.' He picked up the phone and made his calls.

When Weisz had finished he turned to Steiner and Kirsty. 'A doctor will be at the hotel,' he said. 'Steiner and I will meet Strauss and Mellor at the DSO and head out to the estate. We'll take Bale's car with us and leave it at the DSO. He won't need it again.'

Thirty minutes later three men from the DSO arrived at the house. Kallis was carried to a van and driven off by one of them and Conran taken away by the others.

'I've found Conran's gun,' said Weisz, coming away from the desk. 'Let's go. There's nothing more we can do here.'

Steiner and Kirsty went to the hotel in Bale's car and met Weisz there. A doctor arrived and treated Kisty's eye.

'Don't underestimate Rohm,' said Kirsty when she was alone with Steiner and Weisz. 'I'd like to be going with you.'

'Not this time,' said Weisz, smiling. 'You shouldn't have been at Hamilton's house yesterday morning. You've got to learn that we can look after ourselves.'

'We won't underestimate Rohm,' said Steiner, softly. 'He is the most dangerous type. I'll phone you when it's finished and we're on our way back.' He kissed her and with Weisz left the hotel to meet Strauss and Mellor.

Chapter 125

Rohm's estate

'I'll recognize Rohm's voice anywhere,' said Weisz. 'I've seen and heard him a few times on television.' He was with Steiner, Strauss and Mellor in his office and they had just heard Steiner's recording. 'It is a superb instrument and a very clear recording. I don't think Conran will like hearing his voice on it.'

'I still find it hard to believe,' said Strauss. 'He was sitting under our noses and together with Kallis casually eliminating members of the cabinet. The people will have to be content with Conran now that Kallis is dead. They might feel Steiner cheated them.'

'Rohm is the prize,' said Weisz. 'He is so fat I'll be able to live on his conviction for a long time. But we still have to bring him in.'

'What's the plan?' said Mellor.

'We'll go in two cars,' said Weisz. 'That will be enough to bring in the three of them. Whatever Jones says, we'll grab him as well. He was present, heard everything and did nothing. I've also told a couple of other guys where we're going and the recording is on my machine. I'll also take Steiner's pen recorder. The more we get the better.'

The four men left the DSO, Steiner and Weisz in the front car. 'Rohm's arrest will not only satisfy us,' said Weisz, when they were on the N1. 'I've friends in Interpol and in the Specialist Crime Directorate at New Scotland Yard. If we can get Rohm to talk it could lead to arrests in the UK and Europe. There might be work for you over there rounding up some of his pals.'

'I'm sure the Met has enough competent officers who can pick up them up,' said Steiner. 'This work is too dangerous and Kirsty doesn't like me being involved. She would have stopped me coming if I hadn't agreed to her presence. If Kallis had decided to use his gun we might not be on this road. He could see I wasn't armed and I have to give him some credit for being fair.'

Weisz snorted derisively. 'He wasn't being fair,' he said. 'He thought he could lick you. He obviously hadn't been told of your past.'

'He knew enough,' said Steiner, 'and I presented a challenge. He had been trained somewhere, and to a very high standard. What will you do with him? I accept that there will be an inquest. Conran will play on that.'

'Conran won't play on anything,' said Weisz. 'There were no witnesses and he's lucky you didn't kill him. There will be no inquest. You were unarmed and acted in self-defence.'

'So you like me being unarmed,' said Steiner.

'Yes, in this case,' said Weisz. 'I wouldn't exactly call you unarmed but that's our secret.'

A few kilometres further on, they left the freeway. They soon reached Paarl and took the road to Rohm's estate. When they saw the gates, Weisz drew up off the road and stopped, flagging the second car to do the same. 'We'll leave the cars here,' he said, getting out. 'You told me the house is close to the gates.'

'It's a few hundred metres past that bend,' said Steiner. 'You'll be impressed.'

They were joined by Strauss and Mellor and the four men moved along the road towards the house. When they rounded the bend they saw it, the only lights on those in the front lounge, where Steiner had been before. They slowed and when they were still in shadow, with a clear view through the open doors, Weisz halted. 'I can see Rohm and another guy,' he said. 'He must be Jones. Bale is not there from what I can tell.' He thought for a moment. 'Steiner and I will go in now and get Rohm.' He looked at Strauss and Mellor. 'You two can take the back.'

'We'll see you inside,' said Strauss. He and Mellor left and started off in a circle that took them down the side of the building.

Paul Bale had just left the lounge in Rohm's house when Weisz, Steiner and the other two were approaching the building. He wanted to stretch his legs and get some papers he had meant to show Rohm concerning a court case that interested him. He got a glass of water in the kitchen and was about to go to his room at the rear of the house when he saw two men through the back window. Bale knew the servants had all been released for the night and there was no one else around. Something was not right and he slipped into the pantry adjacent to the kitchen, drawing a silenced semi-automatic Glock 17 9mmx19 Luger/Parabellum pistol from the holster on his belt.

Bale waited and then through a small hatch saw the two men come through the back door into the kitchen. He didn't know one of the men but recognized Strauss and was certain their visit was linked to Steiner. He and Rohm did not believe that Steiner would go to the DSO without evidence but for some reason he must have contacted them on his departure from the estate. If these men were on the estate then so were Steiner and Weisz, and without evidence they must have decided to take the law into their own hands. They were dangerous and out for the kill. They could not be allowed to live.

Strauss and Mellor did not wait in the kitchen and as they moved to the passage which led to the front of the house, Bale stepped out behind them, his pistol levelled. 'Get your hands up,' he said, his voice low. 'Face me.'

Both men stopped, lifted their hands and turned slowly. When he saw Bale, Strauss said: 'Bale, you really are in with them.'

Bale waved his pistol towards the scullery. 'Get in there,' he said. 'I'll decide what to do with you later.'

'Give in quietly,' said Strauss. 'There's too much evidence against you.'

'What evidence?' said Bale. 'There's nothing on us.'

'You'll find out,' said Mellor. 'Make things easier for yourself and give up.'

'Get in the room,' said Bale, waving the pistol.

The scullery was a large room, used for all household washing. First Strauss then Mellor entered, Bale close behind. Inside, the two men turned and looked at Bale. 'What now?' said Strauss. 'I suppose you're going to run off and report to your boss.'

'After this,' said Bale. Without a flicker of emotion he pulled the trigger of his gun, firing two bullets into each man's heart, alternating between them after each shot. They died where they stood, a look of shock and disbelief on their tanned features, and quietly dropped to the floor.

Turning quickly, Bale left the room and made his way down the passage to the lounge.

When Strauss and Mellor had disappeared, Weisz said: 'Now's the moment I've been waiting for. Let's go.' He and Steiner went swiftly to the verandah and up the steps to the doors. Rohm and Jones, clearly enjoying one another's company, looked round when the two men appeared in the doorway.

'What do you want?' said Rohm, perfectly calm. He eyed Steiner. 'I told you to get out a couple of hours ago. Who's your friend?'

'Bruce Weisz,' said Steiner, mildly amused. 'He's head of the DSO in Cape Town and here to pull you in.'

'What's the meaning of this, Weisz?' said Rohm. 'I hope for your sake you know who I am.

'I know exactly who you are,' said Weisz, advancing into the room, 'and that you are responsible for the murders of four cabinet ministers, David Hilton, John Delaware,

Colin Dredge and Anthony Hamilton. We've already picked up John Conran, and Marc Kallis is dead.'

'Who killed him?' said Rohm. He didn't believe Weisz had anything on him. 'He was here when Steiner burst in and accused him of abducting his girlfriend.'

'Kallis abducted her before and lured Steiner to her farm so he could kill him,' said Weisz, not altogether surprised by the fabrication he was hearing and a little intrigued. Rohm was not where he was for nothing but this time he had no cards left to play. 'He did the same here and at your behest. This time he went too far and made a fatal mistake.' He faced Bryan Jones. 'I believe you are Bryan Jones.'

'Yes,' said Jones, 'and you're in serious trouble, coming in here like a flat-foot and making wild accusations.'

'You were here earlier,' said Weisz, 'and I'm taking you in for conspiracy in the murders.' He turned on Rohm. 'Where's Bale? He was also here earlier and I want him for murder.'

At that moment, the passage door was flung open and Paul Bale entered the room, holding the pistol at shoulder height, stretched out in front of him. 'Good evening Weisz,' he said, pointing the gun at him. 'You're taking nobody in. Strauss and his friend are dead.' He faced Rohm. 'They were sure they've got evidence against us and that can only mean Steiner was recording his earlier visit. They'll have to disappear.'

Weisz and Steiner could only listen and wait for a chance, if it came. In killing Strauss and Mellor, Bale was no novice with a gun and he had now turned things around.

'If that is true it explains why Weisz's so sure of himself,' said Rohm. 'It's a good thing you were out the back.' He moved further to the side to give Bale all the space he needed and stared at Weisz. 'You really blew it. Did you really think you could get the better of me? The best you could do was to bring in one of Peter Smith's also-rans, a pretentious killer who has had more luck than he deserves.'

'Bale's right about the recording,' said Steiner, not bothering to respond to the description of him. He'd heard it before. 'The DSO has it in their possession.' As he spoke he was judging the distance to Bale and probing for the intent that would precede and motivate Bale's physical action. Knowing the opponent's mind was vital when they had the advantage.

Weisz half-lifted his hands. 'Steiner works for me,' he said. 'I'm responsible. This is between you and me.'

Rohm laughed dismissively and glanced at Bale. 'Give it to him.'

As Rohm gutted the last word, Steiner moved, leaping forward and reaching out with his hands to deflect Bale's aim. In a flourish, Bale swung the muzzle off Weisz and squeezed the trigger. With full impact, the slug hit Steiner on the right side of his chest, spinning him over like a tumble weed on a desert dune. He landed on his back but before Bale could react, stretched out his legs, grabbing him between them in a scissor movement and bringing him heavily to floor. He sprang up, kicking the gun across to Weisz and went for Rohm, pirouetting in a sweep and delivering a side-kick that drove him brutally back into Bryan Jones, both men falling in concert to the carpet. Blood staining his white shirt, Steiner went to Rohm's side, dragging him to his feet. 'You're a lucky man, Rohm,' he said. 'When Kirsty told me you hit her I wanted to kill you.' He pushed him towards Weisz. 'He's all yours.'

Weisz took a pair of cuffs from his back pocket. 'It'll be a pleasure. You saved my life. Thank you. You're bleeding and need a doctor.' He clamped the cuffs on Rohm.

'It's not serious,' said Steiner, walking to the passage door. 'I'll go and find the others. We'll need an ambulance for them.'

'I'll phone the hospital in Paarl,' said Weisz. 'I'll look after these guys.'

Steiner left the room and soon found Strauss and Mellor. He confirmed they were dead and draped two sheets from the ironing basket over them. He removed the cuffs they were carrying and returned to the lounge. 'They're dead,' he said to Weisz. He went over to Rohm, cuffed him, and did the same to Jones.

'They were two of my best men,' said Weisz. 'I'm sorry they died at the hands of someone like Bale. 'The ambulance is on its way. You should call Kirsty. Don't tell her you were shot until you see her.'

'I'll ring her,' said Steiner, taking the cell phone from his pocket. 'I'm glad this is over.'

Chapter 126

Saturday 15 August
Cape Town

'You were nearly killed,' said Kirsty. 'I think you like this sort of thing.' She and Steiner had just finished breakfast and were sitting in the hotel lounge.

'The only thing I like is seeing people like Rohm and Bale not getting away with it,' said Steiner. 'Weisz told them he was responsible for the visit. In other words he was prepared to carry the can. I could never have lived with myself if I'd not tried to stop him being killed in cold blood.'

'He's a nice man,' said Kirsty, 'and lucky you were there. You don't think of yourself and that's one of things I love about you.'

'What are the others?' said Steiner. 'Don't tell me, I can guess.'

'You're a fantastic lover,' she said, 'and you love me.'

'What time is the plane?' said Steiner smiling. 'I'm looking forward to meeting your sons. You never told them you killed their father. If you intend to you should do it sooner rather than later.'

'If I tell them I'll have to reveal what he'd done,' said Kirsty. 'I think it's better to leave it as it is. They have happy memories of him and he was a good father. They'll finish school this year and I'd like them come to London to see where we live.' She drank some coffee. 'The plane is at eleven-thirty and on Tuesday we're flying home.'

John Conran was sentenced to life imprisonment for the murders of Hilton, Hamilton and Fairley. Andrew Rohm, Paul Bale and Bryan Jones received life sentences for complicity in these murders and those of Delaware, Dredge and Peter Smith. Bale also received life sentences for the murders of Mellor and Strauss. These were to run concurrently.

Although not officially confirmed, the Scorpions was believed to be investigating allegations of involvement in serious organized crime against Rohm, Jones and the other three business men named by David Hilton.

www.ingramcontent.com/pod-product-compliance
Lightning Source LLC
Chambersburg PA
CBHW030920050726
47498CB00003BA/837